Arvuria: The Ethereal Children

Luke Morgan

To my parents who have always supported me

&

To my friends with whom I have shared many fantasy worlds with.

Arvuria: The Ethereal Children

Resnia: The Resnian Kingdom was founded by King Herreken and King Theo—partners, brothers, and allies from distant lands lost to time. Together, they led the survivors of humanity's previous collapse to the shores of Ideneor, eventually reaching the land of Resnia, where the native Rhenn people lived. Through trust and cooperation, humanity was granted land by the Rhenn, but with that gift came ambition and greed. As King Herreken began to succumb to darker impulses, the Kingdom fractured into civil war. The Theothen Empire and the Resnian Kingdom were born from this conflict, and the Resnians, now emboldened, forcibly displaced the Rhenn from their homeland to solidify their control. Now, centuries later, Resnia stands resolute, defending itself from the warmongering Theo bloodline that once left for a hopeful future.

Theothen: Ruled by the Theo bloodline, the Empire's origins trace back to King Theo's rebellion against the Resnian Kingdom, spurred by ideological differences with King Herreken and his allegiance to The Pale Dragon. Seeking a new path, King Theo forged an alliance with the Golden Dragon, laying the foundation for a nation that would be renowned for its righteousness, justice, and unwavering respect for all its people. At the heart of this empire stands the White City of Arvur, a fortress of humanity and the symbol of their strength and valour. Yet, the power once upheld by noble ideals has slowly decayed, tainted by the very bloodline that built it.

Ideneor: Ideneor and its native people are one—resilient, spiritual, and born from the ashes of catastrophe. Legend speaks of Zergrath, The Red Dragon, whose wrathful destruction of Ideneor's vast expanse occurred centuries before humanity's arrival, leaving the land scarred and the people struggling to recover. The desert is nearly uninhabitable, with only the eastern reaches offering a fragile hope for a comfortable life. Since humanity's arrival, many Ideneorians have left their homeland, blending into the larger world and mingling with human societies.

Everria: Everria is a land shrouded in mystery, where its inhabitants rarely leave its shores. The country permits only traders and political envoys to enter, while smugglers exchange tales of the Everrians alongside their stolen goods. The Everrians themselves are an ancient, almost amphibious people, believed to spend their tranquil days riding the fierce waves and gliding across snowy shores on wooden boards. Masters of The Arcane, they have long used their magical prowess to protect their land—an effort aided by Mitrand, the Blue Dragon, who has stood as their guardian for centuries.

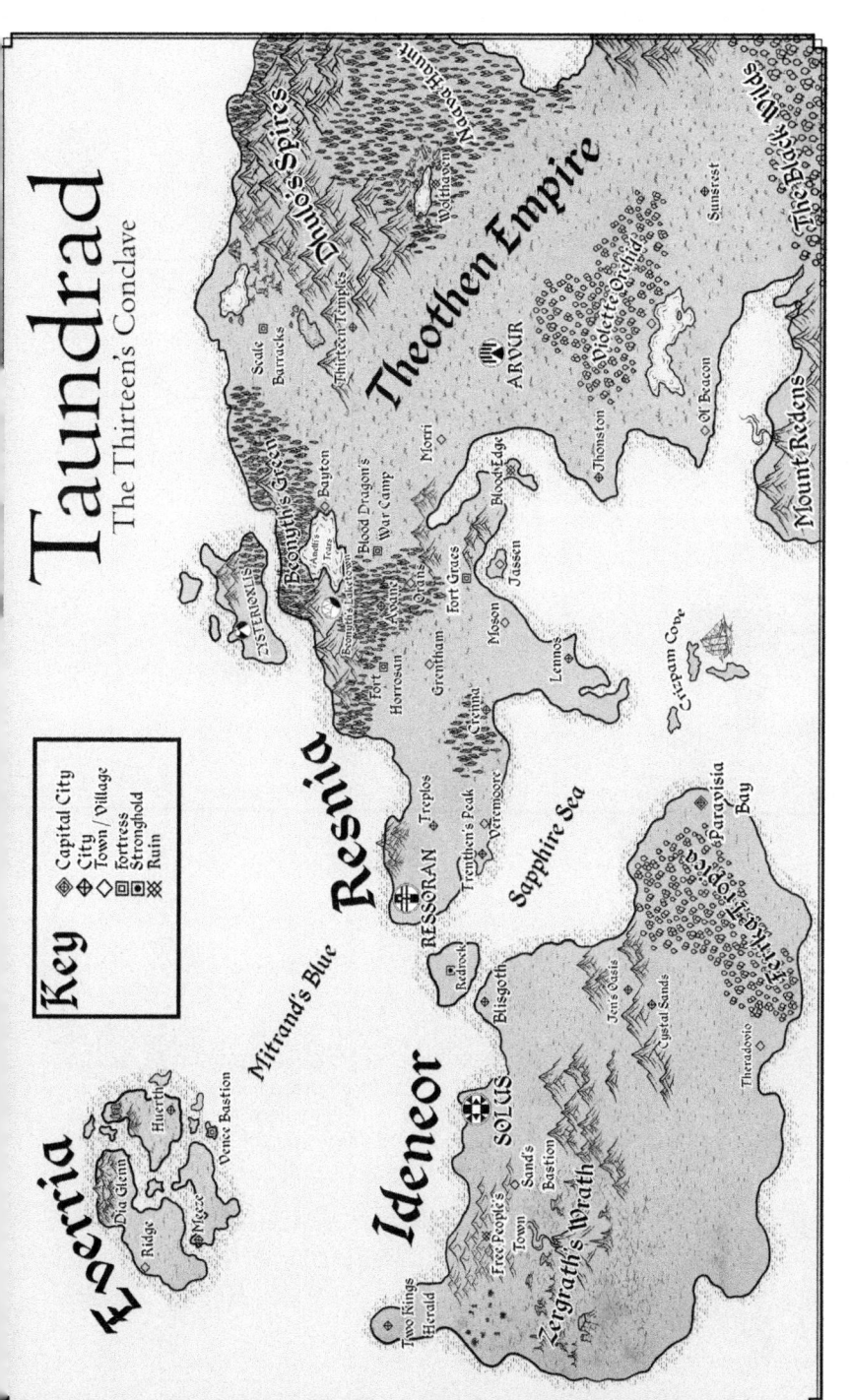

Arvuria: The Ethereal Children

Luke Morgan

THE WAR OF WHITE AND GOLD

*FIRE IN THE CLOUDS..
THE CITY BURNS.
THE PALE BLIGHT BEGINS.*

THE SOLDIER AND his Enemy lowered their swords as the screech of The Pale Dragon pierced the skies. The night sky cascaded a luminescent blue as his shadow cast over them, Brigir The Pale Dragon looked down onto the humans below as the city burned. Destroyed. There was no hope for any of them anymore. What started as a battle of two leaders had become something so much more. Humanity had failed itself. It had divided itself under The Ethereals. Humanity had not relied on itself for generations… maybe this was the night it finally realised that they were *all* human. They arrived on these shores together, from The Broken World that they had all but forgotten. There never needed to be a divide.

The Soldier pulled the arm of his enemy, at the sight of the unleashed might of Brigir, an apocalypse for all - no matter their allegiance. The lines of their war ended as the blue fire and acid mutilated their shared land - as The Pale swarm of humanoid monsters ravaged the inner walls of the city.

"Come! We can't beat this!" The Soldier shouted amongst the deafening sounds of The Pale Dragon as he began to hurry through the town of Garren that his army had used to stage their assault. They had been beaten back this far. Their assault was failing. They were losing, and with The Pale entering the battlefield they all knew now that they had truly lost.

"A tide of Pale. Creatures as monstrous as the beast! How are we meant to survive?!" The Loyalist shouted behind The Soldier as they both ran through the main road of the town - their footsteps flowed into the fleeing ranks of both armies where the yellow and blue colours met the red and black. What would have been a clash of sworn enemies was beginning to form into one defensive block of men willing to fight; with but a few running past the wall of humanity hoping to live another day.

"Hold the line!" A grizzled veteran in yellow and blue colours roared as he held the banner of The Golden Dragon, "If we falter here thousands of innocents will die! Our differences do not matter! *Hold the line!*"

The Soldier heard the older man's voice touch the Wisp in his chest. He was right. The Soldier remembered his young daughter waving goodbye to him as he left Orans - Sunflower was her name. Sunflower was his Wisp. His heart and soul. On the day he parted she called his name to him after her mother had shouted goodbye to copy her. *Berren*. He cried that day. He cried knowing that he may not come home to her to be the father she needed. Yet he did not cry today. For today he knew that he had the chance to give his daughter the opportunity to live. He had the opportunity to be the father Sunflower *needed* - the father who was willing to stop a tide of death from sweeping across Taundrad.

"Hold the line!" Berren roared as he joined the line of defence forming. He took his place next to the Veteran and white-knuckled his chipped sword with hundreds of men and women behind and beside him. He saw his Enemy catching up to him, he could see the decision being made in his own mind. For a moment Berren saw The Enemy begin to turn to run past the mounting resistance but something in him made him stop for the briefest of moments. The Ally then turned to join him. The two stood side by side amongst the shield of humanity.

"Hold the line," The New Ally whispered to him.

Berren looked to his left, towards the man he was trying to kill moments ago. "For you?" he asked.

"My Wife... She was behind those walls. I have nothing to live for, but I can save others," The Man in Red spoke calmly as anger began to rise on his face. A grimace of violence. A hunger for blood. The Pale will have consumed his wife by now. They will have turned her into one of them. He was going to get his vengeance.

"For you?" he asked Berren through his fury.

"My daughter," The Soldier smiled.

The Pale were at the edge of the town now. The Defence of Humanity had one last burst of defiance.

"**Hold the line!**" Each and every single soldier roared in unison. One defiant scream against the darkness. One last act of heroism from the common man who each fought for their people. Who each fought for something more. Who each fought for each other.

Arvuria: The Ethereal Children

Luke Morgan

- Chapter I -
VANN ERENDON
The First Strand To Unravel.

IT' IS EASIER to hunt for your food than it was to pay for it. The hum of war on the horizon meant starvation for them, but they wanted to get ahead of it, at least for today.

Vann crouched behind Tristan who was wielding their caretaker's old bow - it was their turn to bring home some food, to bring home anything that could feed the six of them back home. The two teenage boys crouched from tree to tree as they followed the trails in the mud, with any luck they would find their quarry with ease. Luck would have been on their side of course if heavy drops of rain didn't begin to pitter and patter onto the trees above and shower onto their muddied linen capes. The cold bite of the wind and the vision of rain blurring the search for their quarry.

Vann rested a hand onto the handle of his father's sheathed sword and tapped Tristan's shoulder with his other, "Left side, behind the tree," he whispered delicately to his hunting partner who nodded to Vann in return. Tristan wiped some of the new rain from his brows and moved his softly curled black hair from his eyes. Vann watched his friend correct his posture as he knocked an arrow to the bow. He breathed in as he pulled the bowstring and exhaled as the arrow released, missing the intended target and hitting the tree beside it. The Deer's eyes met the two of them, taunting them, before it bolted farther into the woods.

The Archer looked behind himself to Vann and shook his head with an annoyed smile, one which Vann met, "Next time, right?" he laughed, but Vann knew the starvation in Tristan's stomach told a different story. Vann exhaled his disappointment and patted his friend on the back, "I won't tell anyone you wasted an arrow."

The two hunters stood up from the mud and leaves to begin to walk the opposite direction that the deer had fled, both knowing it would be a miracle to find the animal again in the dense woods - with their honest lack of hunting skills playing a part. It had seemed that all the soldiers assigned to Avane and all those who resided nearby the city had all but killed every animal in the forest - or maybe the animals had fled the danger that the human's posed during wartime, Vann didn't know. To him, it just seemed that The Ethereals above were trying to make his life more difficult each day.

But at the end of every day that Vann survived, the same sun would always begin to set while the two moons would ready to rise. This moment was always the time that the group as a whole had scheduled the daily hunters to return home. An agreement so that should the hunters not return, the rest of them would come looking, the reliability of the idea was questioned quite often by Vann as he'd like to mention it would cause more of them to be lost but their small group ran as a democracy. The view of all was to keep everyone safe and to keep them all together.

"Do you think Emerie managed to get anything from the market?" Vann asked Tristan who tucked the bow over his shoulder and counted that they had three arrows left from what Owain and Leon had found on a Resnian Scouts corpse the other day.

"Emerie could steal the crown from the Emperor if she had the chance," Tristan answered.

"I don't reckon it would sit well on her tiny head," Vann laughed. The two boys and Emerie had fled their village that sat at the border of the Resnia and Theothen. Neither of the three had wanted to, but Vann's father had forced them to leave as soon as the war had begun - an old soldier, scared of what his son and the twins would experience. It was a common story this many miles away from the battlefield, a similar situation had happened to Owain too, except his story is one that he kept to himself, only having shared glimpses of what his family had lost, even before the war. On the opposite side of Owain and the rest of the small group there was Leon, who left the desert land of Ideneor to set out on a pilgrimage to Zaer's grand temple. He willingly left the homeland after tiring of living through The Red Dragon's tyranny. Vann and the rest of them had been following Tristan for the last few months, he was the one who banded all of them together and found them a home at a farmstead where an old retired monster hunter and his wife had offered them a place to stay.

That's where they were headed: home. A luxury that most didn't have.

They walked through their old tracks, mostly now in silence as they pondered today's defeat by the deer and by the weather - The freezing arrows of the rain was beginning to get to them, souring their mood as their journey back to a small amount of warmth continued on. Vann considered how the meat would have tasted, how Leon would have seared it on the ancient grill that the old man Firven had given to them. His mouth began to water at the thought of it. Meat. Something that they hadn't tasted properly in nearly two weeks - their only blessing of food other than what they found was what Firven and his wife Clarissa could spare, which wasn't much, and usually just gristle and old scraps. They offered them work in return for a place to stay, it would have been wrong of him and his friends to expect anything more than that from the couple, so when they were given food by the kind folks, no matter what it was, it felt like a day of celebration.

Near half an hour passed before they walked through the treeline to see the farmstead sitting on the small hill before them. The rotten fences defended the array of colourful flowers that were beginning to bloom as Spring had begun, and behind the land of flowers sat two buildings, a cosy thatched home sitting at the top of the hill and just below it was a barn where Firven and Clarissa's animals used to reside - but now it was where their workers lived. All six of them.

Tristan continued to lead Vann on the journey home but for a moment he looked over his shoulder with a meek smile, "We shouldn't tell them that we saw a deer. It would just upset them."

Van nodded in agreement as his stomach rumbled at the thought of meat once more. "The usual excuse of nothing in the woods?" Vann asked, "but what about the missing arrow?"

He saw Tristan look into the sky before pinching his nose in stress. "Let's just say an Arachnex was nearby and we used the arrow as a distraction to slip past," Tristan thought aloud. Vann, again, nodded in agreement. He then looked over his own shoulder, back towards the woods, as Tristan continued towards the farmstead. Were there Arachnex's this far from Beonyth's Green?

His worried thoughts disappeared as he heard a soft voice bellow from the top of the hill as the youngest of their group, Martell, ran down the lengthy incline waving his arms, "Hurry up! Emerie brought something!" he shouted. Vann considered that if there were Arachnex nearby then they certainly would have been warded away after hearing such a piercing of sound.

Vann and Tristan lifted their hoods as the cover of the trees disappeared, causing the rain that hit them to become heavier. "Go back inside Martell you'll become sick," Tristan called back towards the excited young boy who ignored his words and continued to run underneath the terrible weather, "We will be there in a moment!" Tristan added, hoping to stop the boy from running.

Martell eventually met the two teenagers halfway and Vann witnessed Tristan almost fall back down the incline as the six year old jumped into his arms.

"Did you bring anything too?" he asked innocently and with hope. Vann's gaze met Martell's who had smiled to him as his cheeks rested into Tristan's shoulders - Vann shook his head but gave a soft smile while Tristan patted Martell's blonde hair, "Maybe tomorrow we will be as successful as my sister."

"That would be a surprise," Martell laughed. Tristan feigned offence and lifted Martell in the air, turning to pass him towards Vann who took the young boy off of him. He watched as Tristan ran up the incline to finish his journey towards the barn where Vann looked at the boy in his arms and the two of them laughed to each other over Tristan's terrible acting.

"How has work been today, Squire?" Vann asked Martell as he wrapped his deep green cloak around him with his spare arm. The young boy pondered for a moment, tapping a finger on his cheek in imitation of Owain. "I helped Owain repair some of the fences," Martell revealed, "I hammered some nails... Owain said don't tell Emerie."

Vann knew the reason not to tell her. Owain would be in trouble over handing a six year old sharp objects and a hammer, naturally. Owain's idea of raising Martell to be strong was to give him the option to experience danger every chance he gets - of course the rest of the group disagreed with this idea. Vann however tended to keep his opinions regarding Martell to himself, he knew that a group of teenagers shouldn't be raising a child but at the end of the day it was the situation they were stuck with. He was however thankful that Leon had taken the lead in the protection of Martell, an obvious thing of course since the group found the two of them together.

Vann carried the young Squire and himself up the few final muddied steps that sat up the top of the hill and moved into the barn, opening the creaking doors to see Owain twisting a piece of wood into tinder to try and light the fire for the night. His cheeks began to match his red hair as he blew on the sparks hoping to ignite them. Watching over him on the log of a tree they had carried in a few weeks ago to use as a bench was Leon in his red and yellow robes - Leon was advising him to blow more delicately, and in return was repeatedly told by Owain "I know what I'm doing."

"Try blowing harder," Vann offered in assistance as he placed Martell on the floor to then try to dry Martell's hair with the inside of his cape. Owain looked towards Vann and gave him a tired look, "Don't you start as well, I've heard enough from him," he pointed towards Leon.

Martell hurried over towards Owain and asked to have a go at lighting the fire, and in his frustration Owain agreed. Within ten seconds of the young boy rubbing the stick into the tinder the fire ignited to which Leon began to point and laugh - a rare sight of the young priest. Vann watched as Martell began to giggle at Leon's contagious snicker, causing him to hide his own humour at the situation so as not to annoy the fiery red-head further.

"Typical," Owain huffed as he began to sulk. It was obvious to the rest of the boys that Owain wanted to throw all the wood they had on the fire in frustration so seeing him managing to control his temper by placing the wood delicately made at least Vann proud of him. The first few weeks that Vann had known Owain, they had been at odds fairly often, but as the weeks went by, they had become close friends - The growth occurred during their days of travel during their turns for hunting.

"Where's Emerie?" Vann asked Leon. The Priest pointed a thumb over his shoulder towards her makeshift room which was just simply two worn blankets that covered the windows of an old singular horse stable within the barn. "She's telling Tristan about our adventure today. We had luck, Zaer willed it so."

Vann gave Leon a small thumbs up as he walked past him, carrying his wet cape over his shoulders where the rain began to drip onto the hard sanded floor. It was common knowledge that if Tristan and Emerie needed to debrief their respected days, that something had gone wrong for one of them - the twins were the caretakers of the rest of them, so it was understood that whatever they talk about will trickle down to the boys eventually. Vann never felt like Emerie really treated the rest of them with as much friendship as she had the ability to give, sure, he and Emerie had known each other since they were young but she was never really close before they left their village of Orans, he was closer to Tristan in their youth, with Emerie spending more time with Vann's mother. Vann did always try to involve her though. He always made the effort. Even still, the last few months of travelling, he was trying to get her to open up a little bit more because he wasn't a fan of how she would sometimes act nervous and brash around him.

Vann met one of the blankets that she was using as a door and tapped his fist against the wood beside it where he heard an abrupt invitation from Emerie. He walked into the room to see Tristan sitting on a stool and Emerie standing before him pulling items out of a brown rucksack. On the table was rope, a small hand-axe, some biscuits and a pile of clothes - she looked excited as she reached her hands further into the still half-filled bag. "And look at this," She said with the rare happy tone in her voice as she pulled three purple balls from the bag, "I'm pretty sure these are smokes."

Tristan stood up from the stool and took one of the smoke bombs from her hands, "Who did you steal this from?" he asked with a hint of worry.

Vann took one of the other smokes from her and analysed it in his hand, "Judging by the size of them, just one of these could cover the entirety of the barn."

"Right?" Emerie smiled, "We could use them to steal from the stock house in town," she spoke as she took the smoke bombs from their hands and placed them back into the rucksack. Vann looked worriedly between the two twins, he felt it in the air before their voices spoke once more. An argument between the twins, usually one of the scariest things the boys would experience living in the barn.

"Absolutely not," Tristan ordered.

"Why not? Avane's people don't give a damn about us," Emerie replied, "Why should we care for them?"

Vann took hold of the hand-axe and began to look it over as the twins bickered about the ifs, buts, and maybes of whether or not stealing food from city-folk was a good idea. The axe had a newly polished handle, and the metal of the weapon had also been recently cleaned and sharpened as far as Vann knew. He absent-mindedly tapped the edge of the blade a little too hard onto the table just away from where the rucksack sat - the bickering between the two twins paused. They looked at him with tilted heads after noticing the axe was now embedded onto the table.

"Why did you do that?" Emerie asked with confusion.

Vann shrugged, "I don't know, I just wanted to see how sharp it was and then I guess I just..."

There was a pause. "It is sharp by the way," he added.

Emerie pulled the axe from the table and placed it away from Vann and side-eyed him. Well done Vann he thought to himself, as he realised he had once again given Emerie a reason to see him as irresponsible. He did however have an idea that could solve the bickering.

"Tristan, what if I go with Emerie to Avane and we look over the storehouse? Scouting only, no stealing," Vann offered, "We'll leave the smoke bombs and everything else here of course. I just think that we need to start taking all options into account because we can't keep living on scraps forever. We need a meal."

Tristan pondered for a moment before nodding towards him. Vann knew that he always had Tristan's trust, but he could see the small annoyance on Emerie's face while her eyes avoided him entirely.

"Fine," Tristan relented, "But Owain comes with you both, and I will be instructing him to not let either of you do anything stupid. I know what you're like when you're together."

Luke Morgan

Arvuria: The Ethereal Children

- Chapter 2 -
VANN ERENDON
A Father's Sword.

OWAIN LED AHEAD of both Emerie and Vann as they turned the final corner to see the large fortress city. The ancient bastion of Avane still remained unharmed by the war that was now just a few miles away. It was an ancient Rhenn built city created to withstand a siege from the Humans after they had taken much of their land. Nowadays it was maintained to be the first point of contact between the two countries of Resnia and Theothen, or at least that would be the case if politics hadn't caused another pointless war. The woods around the city contrasted against the cold grey walls that protected the inhabitants from the wilds outside, inside the walls were restored buildings in all kinds of styles - the city had become a beacon for all manner of strange.

Arvuria: The Ethereal Children

There were of course the standard modern Theothen buildings with the white walls and black beams, but they were mixed in alongside some Everrian's flowing white architecture, and also the Rhenn's hunter themed stone houses. Sitting at the back of the walled bastion was a large keep built by one of the Paragons of The Rhenn whose name had been forgotten with the passage of time, but their passion for architecture remained to this day. The Keep's bland and boring design compared to modern day strongholds is what gives it its notoriety, entirely built and constructed with the intent of defence instead of The Empire's common theme of over-designing with the aim of looking better than what the Resnian's could build. Atop the keep is one of the largest Ressorance Crystals ever seen known as the Eye of Valen after The Ethereal of Destiny. The Rhenn's name for it was lost due to the passage of time, and the intent to change it to something more *human*. and it is used as a guiding light to those lost in the forests around the city, and to help wanderers find shelter.

Vann looked to Emerie who hurried to walk beside Owain, he couldn't help but notice that she had an aura of mischief surrounding her as she saw the town once again. It had only been a day since she had entered the walls last but he knew she was always excited to see Avane - he and Tristan always joked that Emerie would end up a princess with how obsessed she is with castles. Emerie turned around and smiled towards Vann, a rare gift from her, "Come on Vann, at least try to be excited."

He was excited, he just had a hard time expressing it on the outside. When his turn came to visit Avane he'd veto the chance half the time in favour of one of his friends going instead, especially if it was Emerie who had mentioned wanting to visit the city in passing. He wasn't a fan of crowds, they always made him feel claustrophobic - That was what he would tell them, but the truth was that he loved being surrounded by all kinds of people, it was in a weird way that amongst hundreds of souls, it was always easier to feel lost than to be in the woods alone. He found comfort in that.

Emerie stepped forward and grabbed his hand to pull him along quicker, "You're taking too long" she muttered with frustration. Vann gently tightened his grip around her hand but when she looked down to their connection with a faintly nervous look he removed his grasp from hers so as not to worry her.

"I haven't been here in so long, and you know how I am in crowds," he lied.

Owain nudged him as they queued up to enter the fortress town, "Don't worry sweetheart, I'll protect you from the evil market stalls trying to take your coin," he goaded.

Emerie laughed, "Vann Erendon, Defender of Coin," she motioned with her hands as if she was reading from a wanted poster. Vann lightly smacked the both of them around the backs of their hands, scolding them as if he was a teacher.

The three teens eventually found themselves at the gate where one of the guardsmen looked them over after he had halted them with outstretched hands, "Location?" he asked the three of them. "Firvan's Flowers Farmstead," Owain rattled the tongue twister. The guard paused for a moment, his expression being unreadable underneath the face guard of his helmet. The three teens waited for an awkward few seconds before being waved on into the city.

"What was that?" Owain asked as they walked towards the second gate, "I swear each day they get more and more weird."

Arvuria: The Ethereal Children

"It's not surprising if the battlefield has become just a few miles away, they're probably scared," Vann answered as if the idea of an army marching through their current home didn't terrify him too. The group had been ignoring the threat of the approaching army for weeks now, nobody wanted to bring it up because nobody wanted to leave the security of their barn home. Nobody wanted to be the one to take it from the rest.

Emerie hurried a few steps in front of Vann and Owain, "Let's not ruin today with talk like that," she spoke aloud. "Is there anywhere you want to go, Vann?" she asked him curiously.

Vann thought for a moment as he looked at the rows of buildings before him, it had been weeks since he had seen the inner workings of the large trade town but each time he had been to the walls of Avane it had astounded him.

"Let's just go to the storehouse and scout it," Vann asked, hiding his tone of excitement. He knew that he didn't succeed very well when he saw his two friends give each other a knowing smile.

"Whatever you say," Owain answered in a sarcastic tone.

Vann was led by the other two down the market road in an attempt to get him to open up a little bit more than he had done recently. He had been so focused on trying to keep everyone happy that everyone had begun to notice his mask had been slipping, even if it was just a little bit. Owain pointed him towards a market stall that had paintings of castles where the both of them compared their ideas of how they would build their own.

They peaked through the windows of a bakery and steamed up the glass as their hunger radiated out of them. After they had been told to get lost by the owner of the establishment, Emerie and Owain then led Vann towards a blacksmith who was repairing what seemed to be a noble's golden-coloured sword.

The black-haired noble was an incredibly handsome young man who was dressed in black leathers with golden accents. Vann looked at him and he knew right away the noble was a military leader by birth. He had the emblem of the Court of Dragons imprinted onto his left shoulder pad, it was delicately hidden by the deep black of the leather pads but the etching appeared next to the Blacksmiths forge as the fire lit its surroundings. The noble looked at him peculiarly. His eyes were squinted as he eyed Vann up and down, his eyes pierced directly onto the sword that hung sheathed from Vann's Waist.

"Your sword. How have you managed to afford that?" The Noble questioned.

Vann's eyes widened and his heart pinged nervously as the man of higher birth spoke to him. It was a rarity that even a lesser noble would speak to a street kid such as him, and if they did it usually meant you wouldn't be leaving with much dignity, or even both hands.

"It was my fathers my lord, he gave it to me before he forced me to flee the border," Vann answered as he nervously placed his hand onto the hilt of the sheathed weapon, "But I intend to fight. I am to enlist when the booth opens," Vann lied. The Noble stood up from the wooden bench he had been relaxing on and extended both of his hands outwards as he silently asked Vann to place the sword in his hands. Vann unsheathed his fathers blade as his two friends watched closely, "It's not much but it reminds me of him," Vann spoke to the Nobleman of his own age.

"The sword of a father is no small thing. Have you used it yet?" The Noble asked him as he looked over the blade that was now placed into his hands by Vann.

"No my lord. Not against another person anyway. I have struck a wolf in defence, that is as much as I have used it," Vann answered, refraining from saying how he hated harming the creature.

The memory of fighting a small pack of beasts played in his head, it was the day that he, Tristan, Emerie, and Owain found Leon and Martell. The only person who fell one of the beasts that night was Tristan who impaled a wolf that pounced on him with his own sword. The noble inspected the weapon with an experienced gaze before returning it to Vann, "You would rather keep the sword than sell it to feed you and your friends?"

Vann looked to his two friends beside him, before looking back at his interrogator. "A sword can protect you where coin cannot." Vann answered with honesty in his voice. "A rich man only stays that way when the tip of a blade isn't pointing in his direction."

"By sword or by hunger," The Noble spoke as he corrected his posture upon noticing Emerie beside Vann. He reached to his belt and passed Vann a pouch which contents clanked as he dropped it into the street kid's open hand. "Some rich men do willingly share their purse. I'm sure I'll be seeing you volunteer for the Vanguard when they arrive this evening. I'll be watching over the city," The Noble warned, almost hinting at Vann and the others to leave the area, "If I do not, I would sleep with a less heavy heart."

Vann stood astounded at the weight of the coins in his hands. Emerie spoke up to give the thanks that the noble clearly expected. "You are the kindest of all the lords we have met, we will never forget the patronage you have bestowed on us this day," she thanked with a bow, which Owain and Vann both copied. The Noble surprisingly returned the gesture and waved them off with a hand, "Go. Enjoy what time in Avane you have left."

Luke Morgan

The three survivors walked away from the blacksmiths in stunned silence. A Noble just handed them a small weighted bag of coins simply because he felt like it? Vann felt as though Zaer, the great father above, had come along himself and blessed him and his friends. He considered that maybe Leon was right in being a priest for the mighty Ethereal.

"Is anyone else really confused by what just happened?" Owain asked in bewilderment, "There must be enough coins for us to get to Beonyth's Laketown at least."

Vann pulled the string from the pouch and looked inside it to see golden coloured sovereigns gleam under the afternoon sun. "And we could afford enough supplies to comfortably get there," he muttered quietly before putting the pouch into the front pocket of his tunic. Emerie stopped in front of the two boys and turned to face them both, "We should still take a look at the stock house, we could still use the food there."

Vann furrowed his brow. They had just been blessed with a gift of charity, with an incredibly lucky encounter and Emerie wanted to push their luck even further? It didn't make sense to him, and it didn't to Owain either.

"If we so much as bring any attention to ourselves now, that guy knows who we are," Vann warned, "And then there is the guard at the gate who knows where we live."

"And also," Owain began, "he certainly took a liking to you Em."

"What?" Emerie snapped back, "He looked at me once, that's all."

Owain laughed, "Come on Emerie, you didn't see him puff his chest out when he saw you? He even went a little bashful when you said, and I quote, 'You are the most handsome of all the lords we have met, we will never forget the handsome patronage you have bestowed on us this day my truest most handsome Noble in all the la-"

"Say handsome one more time and I'll shave that dumb haircut of yours in your sleep," Emerie warned with a stare that promised violence.

Vann's chest felt a sharp ping inside of it at the thought of Emerie saying such words towards the Noble, he was very protective of everyone in the group, that had to be why. "So what should we do now?" Vann asked to distract himself, leaving the responsibility of the decision to his two friends. He knew that whatever they decide to do with the sovereigns would be judged by Tristan and Leon, and whatever they buy will be all they have for weeks.

Owain tapped a finger on his cheek as he thought, "What if..."

Vann exhaled because he knew exactly what was about to come out of Owain's mouth; he then looked towards Emerie who rolled her eyes to him and then shrugged.

"One Sovereign each," Emerie interjected, "no more than that and it has to be something small."

Vann was surprised to see that Emerie agreed to Owain's coming plan of buying themselves something. It was a big lie to the rest of the group and a very dishonest move for them to do - but he couldn't pretend like he didn't want to purchase something from a stall himself. He reached into the pouch and gave Owain a golden piece and then one towards Emerie, then finally putting one more into his own pocket. He counted that they had twenty-four Sovereign's left which was still more than enough to get them to Beonyth's Laketown. The three of the group paused for a moment before smiling at each other and hurrying off to their intended destinations. Vann saw Owain head towards the bakery that the three of them were drooling over earlier in the afternoon, and Emerie headed off towards the busiest part of the market street. Vann himself hadn't had much idea as to what to purchase for himself. There was no point in buying much food because that would be on the to-buy list for the group anyway, and he didn't need any weapons or clothing, he already had his sword and just barely enough shirts to get by, so he decided to see where his eyes would take him as he window-shopped each stall that he walked past.

Despite his excuses and hesitance in buying clothing or weapons, those were the two items that caught his eyes the most. He spent the first quarter of his gold piece on a deep blue coat that was a little too large on him but he could hear his mothers voice in his head telling him that he would grow into it. The coat was quilted and promised a little bit more protection from the cold as it also sat just below his waistline, on the inside of it was two pockets on each side and a row of bronze buttons running down the centre to secure it together should he want to. He whipped the coat around his arms after his purchase and continued along his shopping spree.

As he carried on he noticed Emerie in the distance behind a crowd full of people. He saw her hold what seemed to be a silver piece of metal in her hand as she stood in front of a stand that sold jewellery. She ended up returning whatever she was holding to the seller after counting the coins that she had left from her pocket. Vann waited a little bit by browsing at the stand before him which sold cutlery that was of the quality that his parents would use - cheap and sturdy. He brushed off the seller trying to get his attention as he saw Emerie leave the stand where he then stealthed towards it as he watched his friend disappear further down the market street.

Arvuria: The Ethereal Children

"Good day," Vann greeted the seller before him. She was an older lady who was laden with gold and silver of her own, items that she must have held dear to her. "Oh there's plenty of young ones today," The old lady greeted Vann with a wide smile as she met her second young customer of the afternoon. She waved her hands over the silver and gold jewellery before her that sat behind a glass wall, "What are you looking for today dear boy."

Vann scratched his hair as he looked at the items before him, trying to figure out which one Emerie had picked up a few minutes ago - but he eventually gave up and enquired the assistance of the seller. "The girl who was here a few moments ago, the one with curly black hair, what was she looking at?"

The old lady smiled and reached underneath the counter before pulling out a box and opening it. She then handed Vann a dainty silver necklace that housed a ruby gem pendant underneath. His eyes widened for a moment as the image of Emerie's mother wearing something similar appeared in his mind - the wedding gift that Emerie's father had given to her mother at their Ceremony.

"Seven Silver Sovereigns," the old lady spoke upon seeing the interest of Vann. The teenage boy, now almost a man, smiled softly to the old woman before him, "Would you be able to do six?" he asked with a tender tone in hopes just that would persuade the seller. The Jeweller sniffed and hogged as she considered it. "I have other similar items if you can't afford it," she tested, once again hovering a hand over the items before her.

"Please," Vann sighed, "I only have six left and it's so close to what her mother wore," he begged as he took the hand that hovered before him delicately. The older woman's eyes squinted as she looked at him, "Young love is it?" she asked him. Vann closed his eyes in defeat and nodded. If he had to lie he would.

"We're arguing right now, I really love her so much and I know this would be the best apology. She has me sleeping away from the fire these days," he pretended as he imagined what his dad would have complained about. The Old Lady relented and agreed to six silver sovereigns - she even went to package the ruby necklace into a nice box but Vann declined. He didn't want it to be obvious that he bought it for her; he wanted to give it to her at the right moment. He didn't know why he wanted to do this however, he just knew he wanted to do something nice for Emerie.

Arvuria: The Ethereal Children

- Chapter 3 -
THURIAN THEO
One Last Night of Peace.

THURIAN'S LEGS DANGLED from the battlements above the Keep that watched over Avane with it's guiding light dimmed to not hinder the sleep of those it protected. He overlooked the warm lights that covered the market in the centre of the ancient bastion where the sellers of the day were packing up their goods and beginning to cart them back into their homes. Some were quicker than others but it always felt like none of them were hurrying, he knew their lives would never move as fast as his did. Thurian was used to the competing nobles in the court, who all vied for his and his sister's attention - every day would be a new task and a new backstabber to befriend, so on one of his last nights he wanted to take time to himself to watch how the peasants lived their lives.

Arvuria: The Ethereal Children

He pitied them for the most part. They were dirty, short-lived, and the loudest were always the least-educated.

However, he was always inspired by how they banded together when times were hardest, especially in Avane, a city which had lived through many wars and hundreds of battles. It took a certain type of person to set up their home near the only easily-accessible land between the Theothen Empire, and the Kingdom of Resnia. His mind wandered to the peasants he met at the blacksmith.

He thought of the man he met who was of his own age, how their lives couldn't be more different but for a brief moment Thurian managed to relate to him - both trying to honour their fathers in their own way. Although his father was not the man that he used to be since the rot had taken over his mind, he would still honour the man he used to be nonetheless.

Thurian had journeyed alone, ahead of the army, he didn't want the watchful eyes of Commander Markarth on him as he scouted the city, thinking of ways that he could sneak out to the battlefield for his last fight. He watched as the first of the two moons began to rise over the valley's edge, reminding him again of the young man from earlier who had a strong looking friend beside him who was just a few inches taller and carried a wider frame. The loyalty inside of the friend radiated and that was the most threatening thing about him - Thurian had felt the intense stare of the redhead as soon as he touched the peasants sword. It was half the reason why Thurian had decided to give it back.

The Noble watched the market street still. A man had brought a box towards another store and pulled some flowers from it before giving it to another gentleman. They both laughed and embraced afterwards and Thurian wondered if they were just friends or something more. He smiled to himself. That would be a nice thing to experience. To have a friend. Or something more.

His mind wandered to the girl he had briefly encountered in that group of three. She was taller than most girls, and surely of Tropica heritage, he could tell by the deeper shade in her skin and how her ears pointed just a little bit more than a Theothen's would. He hadn't seen hair as curly and wild as hers in many seasons, especially with the fashion of the court always being so precise. Not that he could judge of course, as he sat in his pristine and manoeuvrable leather armour.

Thurian smiled to himself, if he had met her during a Court Masquerade he would surely have asked her to dance.

The final merchant lowered his lamplight and thus the street market was finally closed for the day, a sign for Thurian to turn into the Tavern room he had rented for his last night. His final evening of being as normal as he could be before he planned to leave for the battlefront. He breathed in deeply the crisp evening air and exhaled his life back into the world that felt as tense as it always did. Like it could snap at any moment.

The night was silent now as he aimed to stand atop the highest peak of Avane. He slapped his hands onto his thighs before reaching to the cold stone beside him to prop himself up. But as he stood away from viewing the open sprawl of homes beneath him, he felt a light heat on his body as if the summer sun had suddenly risen - following it was a dim flash of light that vanished as soon as it appeared. He turned back to the sprawling view as he stood atop the wall and looked upwards into the night sky.

A golden inferno was barrelling downwards. Curving its yellow trail down from The Ethereals towards the outskirts of Avane.

Arvuria: The Ethereal Children

It wasn't thrown from a trebuchet, there was no attack from the Resnians; It was as if it was falling from The First Layer itself. The inferno grew bigger and brighter for a few moments until pieces of it began to detach and fall into the lands of Theothen - The inferno split apart continuously as it headed towards the ground until there was just a single speck of fire left. The ember rock that remained soared over his head and barrelled deep into the nearby woods causing a rumble in the ground as the impact sounded.

It had landed…

A Golden Meteor.

Luke Morgan

Arvuria: The Ethereal Children

- Chapter 4 -
VANN ERENDON
The Golden Meteor.

VANN'S LEGS CARRIED him quickly towards the landing of the blazing star. It hadn't fallen far from their home, and he couldn't tell if any of its remnants had fallen onto the farmstead itself. He barrelled through the trees to meet the site of the farmstead that remained unharmed in the far distance. He saw that the large yellow fire that had appeared around the impact quickly died down amongst the trees as if nothing had fallen from The First Layer at all.

"Slow down you fool!" Owain called behind him as he lugged his new mace over his shoulder. He stopped beside Vann and placed a hand on his shoulder, "See? I told you it didn't land there," Owain spoke, catching his breath as he tried to calm Vann's worry of losing their home. Emerie caught up besides the two men and took a few deep breaths of her own. Vann looked at her and sighed to himself, "I'm sorry - I was scared."

"We all were," Emerie answered. She stood in front of her two boys and looked over towards the impact that remained hidden behind an army of green "We should avoid whatever that was. If that noble was right, it might be the Resnian army. Maybe an Arcanist sent a warning shot."

Vann looked away from Emerie and waved the idea off. He knew that he wouldn't be able to sleep that night if he hadn't checked to see if anyone had been harmed. "You two can go home, I'm going to see what it was," Vann ordered, a rarity for the group to experience.

Owain and Emerie looked at each other before they both silently agreed to follow Vann and his foolish idea. Vann, not wanting to argue as always, hurried towards the impact with his left hand ready on the hilt of his father's sword, keeping it from bouncing as he sprinted through the woods. He purposefully left Owain and Emerie in the dust behind him, he didn't want them to go headfirst into danger if there was any, especially on his account - He heard Emerie's voice echo from behind him telling him to slow down but he didn't listen.

After a few minutes more Emerie's and Owain's voices turned to muffled sounds in the distance, and after a few more minutes of running the crater sat before him.

A ring-wall of white fire surrounded the edges of the impact and smoke covered the indented ground - the fire that only blazed a few inches from the earth disappeared and allowed him in as he attempted to walk over and through it. It made him hesitate. Was he being welcomed in? The cold fire tickled his body as he stepped over it and slid down the steep ramp of the crater where he began to cough as the smoke filled his lungs. He knew that he should be frightened, but somehow and some way, he knew that someone was in need of help here.

"Hello?" he called out, "Is anyone hurt?" he called again. There was no reply. If anyone was under this inferno before it landed, there would be no remnants of them, so he wondered instead if someone had climbed into the crater as he did - maybe he could help them. Vann heard a small murmur and that was enough persuasion for him to continue onward. A little groan sounded again as if it was coming from just a few feet before him, he hurried forward through the thick smoke until a faint silhouette of a person stood moving towards him.

"Are you okay?" he asked towards the shadowy figure. His right hand reached towards the handle of his sword, it hovered over it remembering his fathers words. Never hold this weapon in fear. Vann's hand slowly moved away from his weapon, and instead it reached out in front of him with a tender invitation - an invitation that was accepted delicately by a pale hand, which was quickly followed with a girl falling towards him and collapsing into his arms.

The girl's long golden hair flowed around Vann's body, almost forming a protective shield around him from the smoke. Where their skin touched he felt as if frost was eating away at him - her breath however was warm and comforting as it ever so faintly made its way across his neck while he held her up from the ground.

"You're okay. I have you," Vann whispered before scooping her legs up to carry her from the smokey fog. He whispered a thank you to the Ethereals that he had managed to find this girl within the thick smoke, and he thanked them once more that his friends had followed behind him.

"Vann!" Emerie called out to him in worry.

"Where the pale are you?" Owain beckoned. Vann turned around to face their voices and followed what he assumed was his pathway where he hurried back to his entrance of the impact. He caught the attention of Owain by calling his name, causing the larger teen to hurry over and reach an arm out to him and the girl as he tried to give Vann some leverage. Vann moved the girl over one of his shoulders and tried to run up the steep incline to reach Owain but each time he attempted his escape he was just a few inches away from Owain's help.

"You don't need to rush buddy, you've got this," Owain encouraged. Vann took a deep breath, the next attempt would be his success, he had this.

"Hurry up," Emerie called out with worry in her tone as her eyes carried past Vann. Owain brushed her off but his eyes quickly widened when he saw a large shadow creeping up behind Vann. "Okay this time I've got this," Vann hyped himself up.

"Vann, hurry!" Owain screamed to his friend, now reaching out his arm just that little bit further in hopes of helping his friend from the crater. Vann, panicked over his friend's sudden change in attitude, took a step back and ran up the slope with the dead weight of the girl remaining over his shoulder.

He clasped his hand with Owain's, but he felt something wrap around his left leg - almost on instinct he let go of Owain's hand and threw the girl towards his friend who just barely grabbed hold of her. The grip around his leg yanked him away from the edge of the crater and pulled him further and further into the thick smoke.

He felt his coat and tunic ride up to his shoulders where his now open skin was being scratched apart as he was dragged through the burnt ground beneath him.

Clanking around him as they escaped his coat were the golden sovereigns that the Noble had gifted him.

When he came to a stop he saw the shadow that had pulled him from safety was beginning to move around him. The times he saw it as he stood up to his feet it seemed that it was almost three times the size of him on all accounts. His hand, yet again, hovered over the hilt of his weapon but in fear of his enemy he was still hesitant to draw his weapon from its scabbard.

'Come on Vann, just find a moment and run out of here' he thought to himself. If he could just avoid whatever the shadow had used to grab him the last time then he could use that as his opening. That was his plan, but his plan quickly vanished when he heard a deafening screech - one that he had heard described in many stories that his father had told him growing up. The screech of an Arachnex

His legs moved before his brain could even register what was happening. His terror carried him forward and it was his fear that was helping him duck and dodge the black haired lashes that tried to whip him. "Owain!" Vann screamed as he followed the long trail on the ground that his body had created.

Vann exited the smoke that had enveloped him; he saw his friend running towards the edge of the top of the crater and leaping with his mace over his head, both hands white knuckled as they gripped onto the leather wraps that held the fierce metal. Vann looked over his shoulder to see the eight legs of the Arachnex clicker and the humanoid torso tower from the abdomen as it too exited the smoke in chase of him. The Arachnex's long lashes that draped from the side of its torso went to wrap around Vann once more but its many eyes looked up to see the brunt end of Owain's mace smack down onto the top of the armour of its head. Owain's weight and damage knocked the arachnid monster back as he rolled into the Smoke along with it - but he quickly returned out of the grey cascade - not before, however, the violence prone Ginger decided to clank it's armoured head once more on the way out.

Vann ran towards Owain as he noticed one of the Arachnex's whips wrapping around Owain's ankles exactly as it had done to him just a few moments before. He witnessed Owain stumble and plant his face into the ground as he was tripped by the injured Arachnex, his mace fell ahead of him out of his grip as he attempted to take the damage of gravity. Vann bolted forward and hurried to his friend's aid, he took hold of the mace and jumped upwards, swinging it towards the already damaged armour on the Arachnex's thick mandibles. The monster rocked backwards onto the hind of its abdomen and screeched once more where the sound pierced the ears of the two boys.

Emerie moved away from the girl she was tending to and now too ran towards the edge of the crater, "Vann, get him out of there!" she screamed as she outstretched an arm, calling them both towards her. Vann lifted Owain up from the ground and returned his mace to him.

"Thanks," Owain huffed, trying to get air back into his lungs. The two boys then ran away from the creature once more but were quickly stopped a collective third time by the creature.

"Vann!" Emerie feared.

Vann was lifted into the air where his face was met by the hungry look of the monster before him. The Arachnex's jaws opened and slowly moved towards his Vann's battered face. In a desperate attempt, Vann gripped the damaged mandible of the monster and roared as he ripped it from the face of the creature which reeled in pain and dropped him to his head. In his hand he held onto the mandible, a look of disgust appeared on Vann's face as the sickly green meat melted onto his skin. He tossed the mandible towards the monster as he attempted to scurry away on his back.

The Arachnex collected itself and began another assault as it scurried towards the two boys in anger - but a bright white light stopped it in its tracks. Vann watched the monster's eyes grow afraid as white fire roared towards it from the edge of the crater. He tucked his head down as the blinding white beam scorched the creature that had tried with all of its might to feast on him - and when his foe had been vanquished, he saw the mysterious blonde girl look towards him with a smile of relief on her face, before falling back into Emerie's arms.

Vann hurried his way out of the crater as Owain began to kick the burnt remnants of the Arachnex's torso, hammering the limbs of it with his mace. He belted the head of the monster from its body with his mace and then it sailed into the smoke behind the two boys as the mace-wielding warrior booted it away with a swift and powerful kick.

"Try and eat us now you freaky bitch!" Owain shouted with his broad accent.

Emerie delicately held the body of the new girl in her lap, caressing her face trying to wake her up once more but the blonde was out of energy - unconscious. Vann lifted her up into his arms once more and shouted towards Owain to hurry out of the crater, should more Arachnex's appear.

"She'll be okay, won't she?" Emerie croaked as she lifted herself to her feet. Vann looked over the girl in his arms. Her long golden hair reached his waist as it fell towards the floor.

Contrasting her hair were dark coloured eyebrows and rosy cheeks much like Owain's, though less fierce and prominent. Her skin was pale and fair to look at, but it was as tough as iron as Vann noticed the grip of his fingers that held her did not dent her skin. The charred ground and smoke had sullied what looked like newly cleaned white garments, but the golden patterned accents that ran over her shoulders and down her chest still gleamed as if they had been recently polished. "If we get her to Leon, he might be able to help," Vann answered Emerie as he began to hurry away from his friends yet again.

"Go, I'll help Owain," Emerie encouraged as she reached her arm into the crater once more, gripping the handle of the bloodied mace that Owain extended towards her.

VANN'S STAMINA DIDN'T relent as he hurried back to the farmstead. The girl had saved him and Owain from an Arachnex, he had to return the favour and get Leon's help; There would be no forgiveness to himself otherwise. He hoped that the young Priest of Zaer would be able to tend to whatever ailed the woman in his arms, Leon had always been the one to go to when it came to medical issues within the group. The tutelage of his temple was an incredible boon.

Vann reached the pathway to the farm and forced his legs to carry him forwards just a little bit further - he wanted to call out to Leon and Tristan inside the barn but he knew if he awoke Firvan or Clarissa they would not be content with harbouring another runaway. He barged his body against the two large doors of the barn and collapsed forward to the ground, but managed to remain on his knees with the girl in his arms.

Tristan was the first to hurry over to him as his worried hands hovered over him and the girl, "Help her first," Vann spoke with a breathless voice. Leon cleared the contents that sat on the table by the fire quickly and motioned for Tristan to place the mysterious girl onto it, the priest then opened a trunk and rubbed liquid onto his hands.

"What happened to her?" Leon questioned the exhausted Vann - who fell to the floor willingly as Martell passed him a cup of water.

"Did you see that fireball that fell from the sky? I found her in that," Vann answered, then sipping the water before pouring its contents over his tired and sweaty face as he led on his back.

Leon pondered for a moment as he examined what should have been an injured girl, but he could see no signs of harm or distress physically. He placed his hands a few centimetres from her face and uttered a prayer to Zaer, the great father of the world. The priest pressed his palms together and ripped them sideways in the air where his hands began to faintly glow the colour of white and the mist that escaped his palms began to seep into the girl's skin. Vann's eyes widened, it was the same colour of Arcane that the girl had used to save him.

"Leon, keep doing whatever that is," Vann encouraged, forcing a moment of distraction from the Priest's face. Vann then scurried from the floor towards the table and stood opposite the healer where his eyes dashed between the girl and his friend.

"Is it working?" Vann asked, to which he was quickly silenced with a shush by Leon.

Vann's gaze then turned to Tristan as the leader opened the barn doors fully and looked out into the distance.

"Emerie and Owain should be on their way, Em told me to get this girl here," Vann called over. Leon shushed him once more, causing Vann to now press his own lips together to keep him from distracting Leon again. The Priest's hands began to glow even brighter - they began to shake as he concentrated with all of his might to heal the girl before him. The Arcane that he was able to tether continued to seep into the skin of the girl until the last bit of mist from his hands vanished completely.

"That was all the power Zaer willed of me," Leon announced, "If she is to awaken then it shall be of her own volition."

Luke Morgan

Arvuria: The Ethereal Children

- Chapter 5 -
THURIAN THEO
The Giant-Kin.

THE VANGUARD COLLECTED Thurian from the tavern he had slept in overnight, and when they did so Thurian made sure to have them help him don his regal golden armour before he left to meet Commander Markarth. He wanted to remind the eager giant-kin that he was in charge, to show that although he wasn't as dominant in the court as his sister was - he was still an imposing figure. Well, as imposing as a nineteen year old could be to a forty-something year old veteran soldier.

The Elite Vanguard of Markarth's forces had warned Thurian that the Commander was in no good of a mood upon hearing that he had left to scout ahead. That in doing so he had put the entire reinforcement legion at risk, though Thurian did not see how he endangered anyone as he had sent a squire to inform the Commander of his intentions. Thurian assumed the Commander was probably blowing smoke for the sake of it - naturally. He followed the Vanguard to the gates of the city where he could see the black and red tents of the reinforcements being put up so as not to busy the defensive buildings of Avane, and of course to not fill the city up with thousands of soldiers trying to get a roof over their heads.

Thurian saw the Commander standing by himself watching over the spread of the Legion while he was awaiting Thurian at the edge of the stone bridge to Avane. . Commander Markarth looked as you would imagine a grizzled veteran to be. He was adorned with plate armour with a blood red half-cape flowing down the left side of his body, and in his right arm he held his helmet which was silver with the face plate reminiscent of a dragon's face. Rigged and damaged, its teeth bearing sharp notches where it had been used as a weapon. His armour was chipped and scuffed, purposefully not replaced or repaired. Thurian noticed, as the Giant Commander turned to him, that he was holding an opened scroll in his left hand.

"Did you witness the comet in the sky?" Markarth questioned with the usual sour expression on his face, "...or were you sleeping comfortably inside the tavern?"

Thurian rolled his eyes and extended a hand towards the Commander, silently motioning him to pass him the open scroll with a flick of his fingers. "What's this?" he took the scroll, "A new order from The Emperor?"

The Commander soured. "The letter is from your cousin, it is regarding the golden comet last night."

Thurian hadn't seen his cousin since they both left Arvur weeks ago, he bid him a fond farewell and asked for Thurian to visit him should he ever head to the expanse to the south-east. Thurian unravelled the scroll and began to read it's contents:

Luke Morgan

Dearest Thurian,

I awoke during my slumber this evening due to the feel of an immense Arcane power that drilled through the barrier that sits between The First Layer and Taundrad. If I felt the surge of The Arcane, then so too did other Arcanists of my calibre. I consulted with Princess Dira and The Empress, they accepted my request to pass this order to you: Secure the comet and its contents. Once you have done so bring it to Sunsrest, to me, so that I may study the power it holds in a safe space. Do not let the Resnian's or anyone else get their hands on it.

The First Arcanist of the Second Expedition, Theradon Theo.

"Commander?" Thurian spoke, then awaiting Markarths eyes to meet him. "Why was this scroll opened before it met my hands? You forget your place."

Commander Markarth stepped forward, towards the noble, and towered over him, taking the scroll from his hands and breathed into his face as he spoke his next words. "When scrolls of the court arrive into the premises of my legion, and there is no higher rank to read it to me; do you not think it is a responsibility of mine to ensure its contents are read? Should my men fall prey to potential danger because you decided to run ahead for an extra day of comfort?"

Thurian grimaced, and made a display of himself holding his breath before turning his head away from Markarth, exhaling and then inhaling away from him.

Arvuria: The Ethereal Children

"I think it is your responsibility, Commander, to remember who you are speaking to. I understand the pressures you face, and the stress you must so clearly feel to earn the promotion that, if I may remind you, I will be judging your worth for. So watch your tone and treat me with the same respect that you would my sister. Unless you want to move down the ranks instead? Being closer to the dirt from which you rose might humble you," Thurian threatened with venom in his tongue.

He knew that he was assigned the mission with Markarth purposefully by his older sister, Dira, who was The Crown's and the Court's golden child. At the age of eighteen she had already dismantled rebellions, invaded islands of Ideneor, and defended the city he resides in now from Resnia's advances years ago. 'The Blood Dragon.' That was what the people of Theothen called her, she had already become a legend in her own right. And she used every single chance she could find to torment Thurian with her success - a chance such as having him in charge of her die-hard loyalist that was Markarth.

The Commander's gaze pierced through Thurian, the noble could see one of many veins pop out from the brow of the man towering before him. He managed to stifle a laugh at the sight.

Thurian took the erupted veins as a challenge. He wondered if he could burst one. He barged past Commander Markarth and began to walk towards the reinforcements stationed before him, "I will be taking two of your Elite and a Sensor Mage too, I will want one of your men to confirm my findings, just to keep that head of yours from exploding - were you worry over the truth of my words. You, meanwhile, can do what you have been tasked to do: Secure Avane and prepare the Vanguard to head to the border. I will remind you one more time that the dealings of the Court are of none of your concern."

Arvuria: The Ethereal Children

- Chapter 6 -
VANN ERENDON
Petrichor and Flowers.

THERE WAS A smell of petrichor as Vann swung the axe down onto the wood in front of him, splitting it cleanly down the centre. He picked up the two pieces with his left hand and threw them to the pile beside him. In front of him, in the field of flowers was Tristan who was sparring with the young boy Martell, attempting to teach him what swordplay he could. Tristan had fashioned Martell two wooden swords weeks ago so that everyone could keep their practice up so that if danger ever prevented itself on the road, the group would be able to protect themselves, or at the very least feel some level of confidence in doing so.

Vann leaned side-to-side to crack his back and stretched his body after splitting some more firewood. He heard the rare sound of the door from the house creak open and slam back shut - where he was then surprised to see that Firvan, the old man who owned the farmstead, was out in his overalls with an axe over his shoulder - he was looking towards the ground as he walked but seemed pleasantly surprised to see that Vann had already started on the task he was prepared for. Firvan smiled at him and it gave Vann a small bump of happiness to know that after all these weeks of being at the Farm, Firvan was still glad to see them.

"Always working I see," Firvan spoke with a relieved tone towards Vann, then turning to Martell and Tristan, "And I see the young boy is giving you bruises once more." he laughed. The old man's hearty chuckle was contagious, it had a slight crackle to it that would always cause the boys to crack up along with him. As if he was a grandfather telling a terrible joke that you couldn't quite keep yourself from laughing at.

"How are you feeling sir?" Tristan asked Firvan before he surrendered to Martell with his hands raised, but the young boy struck the teenager behind his knees causing him to wince and hop away. The old man sat on the pile of broken wood that Vann had created and caught the breath that he had lost during the journey from his house. Vann looked to the old man, and could see in his eyes that he was irritated to no longer be in his youthful years.

"I just felt like getting out of that stuffy house," Firvan breathed and nodded towards Vann who loaded another stump of wood onto the larger log and cracked straight down the centre once more. "I'm telling you boys, getting old is for the weak," Firven laughed to himself, "I shoulda died to a Levia when I was young, had a story written about me to sing in Taverns. That would've been great."

Vann could see that the old man had noticed the bandages around his lower torso as he spoke, and the dried red that sat underneath them. Firvan lifted the back of Vann's half-open buttoned shirt up and squinted his eyes to the young man in worry, "What in Anelli's name caused such a wound?" he questioned.

"I fell," Vann answered with honesty, "I slipped down the hill last night and some twigs caught me," he added a shrug to make it seem that he didn't care, but he knew that he wasn't fooling Firvan; to Vann's surprise the old man didn't press him, but instead accepted his answer.

"How is the girl?" Firvan asked as he looked over the flowers in his farm. Most of the array of colours were ready to be picked and sold at the market in Avane but they would all miss the colours they would bring to the stead.

Vann's chest pinged upon hearing the question, "Girl?" he quickly replied, much to the confusion of the farm owner. He was sure that Firven and Clarissa hadn't seen him bring the meteor girl to the barn. He prayed that they didn't, they had already been warned of the consequences of dishonesty by the couple that had taken them in. Tristan straightened himself and pushed Martell away for a moment as the young boy attempted to clamber onto him.

"Emerie? She's fine sir, she just didn't sleep much last night so she is getting a few extra hours," Tristan saved Vann.

"Good, make sure you look after her. The world is cruel to kind hearts, you must steel her as you are the boy," Firvan replied with a firm tone as he looked at Martell, who stood with his wooden sword digging into the ground, his attention fixed onto Firven.

Firvan's dark eyes lit back into their cheery mood as the air grew thick.

"Did you fellas see that light show in the sky last night? There must have been one of those festivals in Avane,

Arvuria: The Ethereal Children

Clarissa has been wanting to go to another one for months now. Had I known we'd have gone with you three last night. Was it any good?" Firven droned excitedly as he looked towards Vann near the end.

Vann wished it had been a light show, it would have felt less heavy to lie to the old guardian beside him. How was he supposed to tell him what happened? That he rushed towards an inferno, saved a helpless girl, was attacked by an Arachnex with Owain, and then almost died to said Arachnex, only to be saved by the 'helpless girl'... well, he could say it like that but he knew that would open up a whole new conversation and would risk them all losing their place at the farm.

"It was a surprise welcome to the soldiers that are apparently arriving soon," Vann lied. A surprise for soldiers who hadn't arrived yet. What a brilliant lie he had told. He knew it wasn't one of his best - he made a mental note to think of a better one next time.

Firven thought about what Vann said with a moment of great intensity before looking towards Martell, and telling him to go into the barn. The young boy contested the idea but relented when the old man repeated his request. Vann and Tristan looked to each other with worry before Tristan vaulted over the wooden fence to stand with Vann and Firvan. The two young men turned their attention completely to the old man who motioned them to come a step forward.

"Each time soldiers have come to Avane, a few always come here. They always check our licence and take some flowers for themselves of course to woo the people of the night. The flowers I do not care about; the issue is that my licence and ownership of my land does not cover seven youths living in a second building." Firven lectured. Vann was picking at a splinter in his hand absentmindedly as he heard the old man's words slowly escape him, "So you want us to hide? Or is it easier for us to leave?" Vann asked curiously, "We have no intention of causing you trouble after all you have done for us."

"Vann's right, you've housed us for nearly three months, we cannot ask more of you," Tristan added softly.

Firvan simply raised his hand in the air and silenced them with a wave and a huff of his voice. "Come on lads, it's no trouble for me. I just need you all to behave when the soldiers come to cause trouble over us housing you. Clarissa and I have our Sovereigns saved for issues such as this," Firvan admitted.

Vann's brows met each other in confusion as he wondered if he had heard Firvan correctly. "You mean to tell us that you're going to bribe them? On our account?" Vann interrogated. "No. We won't allow it."

"Boy, you have no cause to disagree with me on my own land," Firvan looked up to the young man with a frown, "This was Clarissa's idea; but it is the both of us who have grown fond of you all. And we look forward to meeting the girl you brought home last night... I am old but I am far from stupid. My body is addled but my mind is sharp."

The same fearful ping shot through Vann's heart once more, and his usual guilty face appeared. He was almost sure that Firvan and Clarissa would have removed them from their land if they were causing trouble, and if they brought anyone else to the farmstead - they had even said as much. Vann then remembered how his parents would tell him one thing and then expect the opposite from him anyway. They would prepare for his mistakes. He smiled at the thought of Firvan and Clarissa treating the group as their own children - ones who never listened.

Vann watched as Tristan stepped forward and placed a hand delicately onto the withered but rough hand of

Firvan who was still sitting on the pile of firewood that Vann had created. "I want you to know that every single one of us deeply appreciates your generosity," he thanked the old monster hunter who began to laugh and place his other hand onto Tristan's.

"You boys love to treat me as you would your Grandfather," Firven laughed. His chuckle died down as the spring rain began to pitter patter down onto their home, giving him the hint to head back indoors. Vann helped Firvan stand up from his makeshift stool and the old man cracked his bones as his knees lifted him. He then smiled to himself and pointed to the firewood that sat beside Vann, "Don't suppose one of you fellas could bring some of that to the house? If this rain keeps up we'll need the heat."

Tristan stepped forward and began to stack some wood into his arms and followed Firvan to his house.

Vann in the meantime placed another log onto the large stump and split it in two with a fierce swing. And then another. And then another. He was angry with himself that he expected the worst from two of the sweetest people in Theothen; he was so used to people being bastards with the way he, Tristan, and Emerie were treated during their journey to Avane that he had come to expect everyone to serve themselves.

The rain began to fall harder now. And so did Vann's single strikes towards the firewood.

He wished for a moment that he had decided to wear his blue wax coat, but he was so ashamed that he had selfishly purchased it and then lost what gold remained during his battle with the Arachnex. A safe trip to Beonyth's Laketown was ruined because of him. He volunteered to head back to the crater to find the gold but everyone else deemed it too dangerous with the soldiers of Avane nearby. Tristan told him that him buying the coat didn't matter because the three of them had made it home safely and saved the life of the girl, but Vann knew he messed up. - that was enough to get under his skin.

"Did these logs piss you off or something?," Emerie's voice sounded behind him.

He turned to see her wearing his long blue coat that was just oversized on her enough for it to cover most of her legs as well as her torso - she was shielded well from the small shower of rain. Vann gave her a meek smile before loading another piece of wood. The protected girl moved to sit where Firvan was previously, and looked to Vann with her soft brown eyes.

Vann became nervous.

"So are you preparing the firewood to get us through the entirety of Spring? Or are you getting ahead of next Winter too?" Emerie goaded, trying to get a reaction from the obviously frustrated man in front of her.

"We should sell that coat," Vann muttered to himself as he ignored her jab. He placed another log onto the stump and prepared his axe.

Emerie sniffled and brushed her hand against her nose. "I like it. it's warm."

The girl watched him place more wood. Vann felt her irritation grow for just a moment.

"Stop it. You are being a fool. Losing the Sovereigns is not your fault, we can still make it to Beonyth's Laketown - we got this far didn't we?" Emerie's soft tone barely carried past the hood that sheltered her from the rain. Vann hesitated with his axe, instead of splitting the log in front of him he hit the tool into the stump where it pointed its handle towards the sky, his black shirt now wet and damp. He placed one of his palms onto the edge of the axe's handle and held back the guilt that sat in his chest as his eyes watered in the rain.

Arvuria: The Ethereal Children

"The Sovereigns were supposed to get us away from Avane, the war is only days away Emerie! We didn't steal from the stock house because that noble gave us a chance to get far away from here without causing trouble. It would have paid for us to get Martell to a shelter where we could find him somewhere stable, maybe even some genuine foster parents too. It would have given Leon one step closer to getting to The Thirteen Temples, and it would have given Owain a chance to sign up to a guild. By The Pale it would have given me a chance to get you to safety. All I have ever wanted is for you to be safe and cared for. My parents tried their best with you and Tristan and now it's my turn to care for you. And I care. I cared when I put my coat around you the first time. I still do…" he ranted, regretting his final words very quickly when he saw the look that Emerie was giving him. She stood up from the pile of firewood and stepped towards him as the rain enveloped them both further. She extended a closed fist towards him and uncurled her fingers to reveal the necklace that Vann had bought for her.

"I found this in your pocket. I know it was wrapped up but the paper was all torn and to be honest I wanted to see what else you bought," Emerie spoke honestly, "This is the one that I looked at. The one like my mothers and I need to ask, did you…?"

Vann interrupted her question as her voice began to trail off and croak. He lowered her hood amongst the rain as it began to run down their skin. His hands delicately took the necklace from hers where they began to undo the clasp - he reached his arms around her and placed the necklace around her neck as he looked over her shoulder for a better view. He was proud he managed it successfully with the chain not pulling on her wild curly hair. His pride quickly vanished and turned to fear when he noticed how close his face was to Emerie's once he had retreated.

"Kiss me," Emerie told him.

"What?" Vann stumbled.

"Kiss me.

"But…the rain?"

Emerie carefully wrapped her arms around the man before her to pull him in. Her lips sang with his for a few moments where she ended by embracing him. Vann began to riddle with stress and his thoughts disappeared until Emerie released herself from him. Her eyes met his once more.

"I hope that was thanks enough. For the necklace," She quickly mumbled. Emerie was hiding her face under the hood as she hurried off towards the barn door.

Vann finally understood that he was nervous around Emerie for a reason.

Arvuria: The Ethereal Children

Luke Morgan

- Chapter 7 -
THURIAN THEO
Precipice.

THURIAN ANALYSED THE crater that stood before him. It was a clean impact that surprisingly damaged next to nothing in the surrounding area, all that stood before him was a black charred dent in the earth and the corpse of some mutilated creature that sat at the opposite side of the zone. He slid down the steep hill with ease and walked towards it with the three soldiers he had been given following closely behind him. All three were recruits, 'expendable' was the word that Commander Markarth had used to describe them, and he could see why.

He was given two sixteen year old trainees who had not even a month's training between them, but at the very least they had a good bit of muscle on them. The third was an apprentice Sensor, the type of Arcanist that was capable of scanning hints of the power in people and in the environment. Thurian wondered however, if the Arcanist in red robes beside him actually had much capability in doing so.

"My lord, what is it we are looking for?" one of the recruits asked Thurian, who met the question with silence. Thurian continued towards the corpse ahead but he stopped in his tracks when he felt an uneven feeling underneath his boots. His first thought was that it would have been some stones that were created by the comet, that would of course have made sense to him. What did not make sense to him was that he saw a series of golden sovereigns that led towards the corpse of the monster ahead of him. He motioned the recruits behind him to pick up the coins as he pointed his finger downwards towards them, he then continued to follow the small trail of gold until he found the brown pouch he was carrying yesterday, the same one that he had given to the peasants in hopes that they would make it away from the war.

He hurried over to the corpse of the arachnid monster, praying silently that he wasn't going to see their bodies - the feeling of relief swept over him when he saw tracks leading out of the crater. The Noble looked over the giant arachnid corpse in front of him and the damage that it had taken seemed odd, he could see that the impact of the inferno was enough to demolish anything that was here - so there was no way that it was the comet that killed this creature, and the dents on the humanoid torso were created by a blunt object, the decapitation was messy, not clean from a sword or an axe. Not only that, the creature had been incinerated in a flash fire after the wounds had been inflicted, but by what?

"You," Thurian looked towards the Apprentice Sensor, "What burned this creature?"

The Sensor stepped forward and removed the blood red cowl that covered half of his face, exposing the runic scars that surrounded his blind eyes. He then slashed two fingers on each hand down towards the ground to pull a purple tether of The Arcane and then placed the otherworldly power into the temples of his head - his eyes glowed a powerful violet as beams of light began to escape his sockets. The beams scanned over the monster's body and everywhere the light landed a white smoke appeared. The Apprentice fell to the ground with blood now escaping his eyes instead of the arcane essence he had created. "Divine Arcane... My liege," The Sensor answered with pain in his voice, "Whatever did this is allied to The Ethereals..."

Thurian grimaced upon hearing the words. Divine magic was an incredible rarity that could only be summoned by those who are capable of acting as a vessel to one of The Ethereals, meaning that whoever caused the attempted incineration of the monster before him was going to be one hell of a bastard for him to capture.

Thurian exhaled. He had given those peasants the gold to escape the war for a little bit longer, he had given them mercy and now he had to be the one to bring them back to Avane - no matter how benevolent of a lord he tries to act, it is as if The Ethereals are intent on making him like his father. He hurried up the steep incline to escape the crater only to be met with the faint footprints that his prey had created in their escape. Four different sets of footprints that quickly became three as the prints left the radius of the crater. He had only met three peasants the day before. His interest peaked even further. Had they been hiding an Arcanist outside of the city walls? Or was the meteor a person? A foolish thought, although it could hold some credit if the Arcanist was of Dira's capability.

Arvuria: The Ethereal Children

He followed along the tracks deeper into the woods for what felt like close to an hour with the rain pouring down onto him and his comrades, but his motivation remained as heavy tracks would appear to keep him on his path - more often than not a blotch in the mud would appear that looked as though it was created by one or two people falling over; no matter what it was it helped Thurian follow along their path with a fair amount of ease. He worried as to what was about to happen when he would find the peasants. He didn't want to have to harm any of these runaways, there was nothing more he hated than bringing danger to his own people which seemed all too common from the orders of the court these days. Orders from his father. Thurian's plan, to him, was simple. He was going to go to wherever they were hiding, be diplomatic and hope that they would swap whoever the Arcanist was for enough Sovereigns to get them a lot farther away than Beonyth's Laketown was. He knew though, deep down, that if they didn't take the offer the only thing he could do was take the Arcanist by force - he was ordered by the court after all, even someone of his status could not refuse them.

THE MOMENT CAME where his feet eventually met the path that led towards a house and a barn on the hill before him - a home far from the kind he knew, of marbled stone and echoed halls. He saw a young boy run away from two figures standing on top of the hill waiting for him, one dressed in Ideneorian red and black robes, and another in a simple green tunic with messy hair. Thurian made his way up the hill and stopped before the two peasants that stood awaiting his arrival after they had noticed him and his party. Thurian tilted his head to the robed individual, one he hadn't met, "You seem rather out of place with your Ideneorian fashion sense. You won't find much sun in the forests of the border."

The priest before him smiled and gave a nod to him, "I represent the land I come from, though it is far away, it is still a piece of me."

Thurian acknowledged the words of the young man before him, and respected the aura of honour that he carried around him. What he didn't respect was the other teen beside him, who was trying his hardest to seem natural.

"What can we do to help you, my lord?" The one in green spoke to him with a sincere plea to not cause trouble on the farm.

"I am looking for an Arcanist that came through here last night. I have tracked them here so do not pretend that you have not seen them," Thurian answered simply, "Believe me, I have no intent of violence, but if I feel it is my only option I will burn this farm to the ground."

The two peasants looked to each other as they attempted to compose the fear that they surely must have felt from Thurian. He wanted them to be afraid. If his sister had taught him one thing, it is that fear is what makes you powerful.

"It's just us and the young boy here my lord, the two you met yesterday are still in Avane," the one with the messy hair spoke once more with his hands now resting on the hilt of an old sword which had its blade buried into the ground next to him. A threat.

Thurian looked at the blade stabbed into the dirt and smiled to the vocal one, "Put that toy away, you will hurt yourself."

He then looked to the monk as he disregarded the liar beside him.

"I followed the tracks of three of your friends. One was about my height, brown hair, nervous; the other a ginger, tall, burly. And the other -"

Arvuria: The Ethereal Children

Was the girl who opened the door and walked with purpose to the confrontation that was happening on her doorstep. Thurian heard the whispers call her name from behind her, it was the same voice of the boy he had given the gold too. "The other was you," Thurian greeted with a goading smile, and was met with a beautiful smirk in return.

"I heard you're looking for an Arcanist?" the girl spoke softly to him. Thurian gently nodded a yes in reply. "Looking, hunting, it can be either depending on the next few words that come from that pretty face of yours."

"I am the Arcanist," The girl replied with a fierceness to her.

Thurian laughed to himself, and then the two recruits that stood behind him followed suit. "Sweetheart, I saw the comet as well, and I saw you before it landed. Do you really think me a fool?" Thurian asked, he genuinely wanted to know.

"No milord, I just don't want my friends to be in trouble because of me."

Thurian sighed at the now pathetic attempt to persuade him with a false tale. He turned to the Sensor beside him and pointed at the two boys almost disgustingly, and then nodded to the recruits to head towards the barn. The recruits drew their swords and began to walk towards it.

"Wait!" The robed peasant spoke, "I am the Arcanist, test me and then take me with you, just do not harm my friends."

The Apprentice Sensor tore a tether of arcane and two more purple beams shot from his scabbed eyes onto the monk where white smoke appeared the same way it did from the arachnid - it had a much weaker thickness to it but it was still all the evidence that Thurian needed. One of the recruits turned around and pulled a set of shackles from his belt and went to place them onto the wrists of the monk but quickly stopped upon hearing the sound of a group of footsteps coming up the hill. The recruits looked behind Thurian to see the towering presence of Commander Markarth and ten sleekly armoured soldiers in black and brown coloured leathers.

"Of course you followed me," Thurian goaded, "Come to claim the Arcanist for yourself? To earn your promotion that way?"

Markarth smiled at Thurian as he walked up the hill. He barged past him and towered before the three peasant teens. He grabbed hold of the monk's wrists and lifted him into the air, examining him as he struggled to get free. The boy in green drew his sword and swung it towards the torso of Markarth but the blade rebounded from the metal of his armour with a loud clang. The girl bolted towards the barn door but was quickly apprehended by the two recruits who stood between her and safety.

"Burn this place to the ground. Burn it to ashes!" The Commander ordered with a furious roar. Five of his men lit their torches and began to throw the fire all over the farmstead, igniting the two buildings and the array of colourful flowers that rode down the hill.

"Stop! What are you doing?!" Thurian shouted to the soldiers who chose to ignore him. It was quickly realised by Thurian that these men were not loyal to his bloodline, but instead loyal to the fierce character of Commander Markarth. He attempted to push Markarth, to try to stagger him such as to force him to let the monk go, but it came to no avail. His fury grew as he could not help himself in defending Markarth when the boy in green attempted another swipe towards the exposed joint under the giant's shoulders - the noble unsheathed his silver blade with blinding speed and parried his weapon against the peasant who took a step back and nervously held his sword before him.

"Tristan!" the girl bellowed towards him as she attempted to fight the two men that held her from her brother and friend. Markarth grinned menacingly towards Thurian and gave him a proud nod, but he was quickly embarrassed when the feet of the monk connected with his nose which forced him to let go.

Now, standing before Thurian and Markarth, was a scared swordsman, and a Priest with his palms open and his feet stanced.

"We do not want to hurt you, just get the rest of your friends to come out peacefully," Thurian requested. A pointless gesture, he knew it was. In typical fashion of The Theothen Empire, the soldiers would rather burn a home down than to solve things peacefully. He was furious with the Commander beside him, but he knew that if he did not side with him, it would only go one way for Thurian - he was certainly not ready to be claimed by an Ethereal.

The Commander roared forward with a swing of his giant-kin fist towards the monk who dodged it with such speed that it caused Markarth to stumble forward, and to almost lose his footing. Thurian watched for a moment as the monk exchanged blows with the veteran commander, but his attention quickly shifted as he felt the blade of the peasant speed towards him. Thurian met each strike from Tristan defensively, he was toying with him - taking out his frustration towards Markarth by embarrassing this poor boy who was simply defending his home.

"Emerie! Get out of here dammit!" Tristan shouted to his sister to only then be disarmed by a simple flourish from Thurian. The noble pressed the edge of the sword underneath the chin of the pathetic young man before him and grimaced. He heard Markarth land a thunderous strike to Leon where the body of the monk soon thudded just beside Tristan on the ground.

A hiss sounded amongst the burning wood of the barn causing Thurian to turn towards the blaze to the left of him to see a peculiar effect of thick purple smoke escape the cracks of the building and then two more random appearances of smoke followed at both entrances of the farm.

"Find the rest of these rats!" Markarth ordered his men through the natural smoke of the burning buildings and flowers, Thurian watched as the commander fixed the bridge of his nose back into place before he stormed towards the barn doors, ripping them both from their positions amongst the flames with ease and entering into the burning domain.

"Please, let us go. You helped us before! Help us again!" Tristan begged but Thurian's blade remained against his opponent's neck as he watched Emerie scream and fight to escape the recruits grip. She was begging for the lives of her friends and screaming over the death of her home.

A country dominated by those with power. This is what the Theothen Empire had become This is what *his* Empire had become.

Dira was right.

Arvuria: The Ethereal Children

- Chapter 8 -
VANN ERENDON
The Girl We Saved.

VANN RAN. He held Martell over his shoulder with one hand and in the other a rucksack with the group's emergency supplies. He had used Emerie's smoke bombs to escape the barn and to distract the soldiers into thinking they had headed towards the entrances. Owain was smart enough to have removed a part of the wall at the back of the barn a few weeks ago and placed the section back in, weak enough for it to break should they ever have needed to escape.

Vann jogged behind the redhead who was carrying the girl who still remained unconscious from the night before. He felt anger towards her, he was losing everything because he wanted to save an innocent life that day. The only reason that they had all escaped was because Emerie told them what to do before she left the barn, ignoring every plea from Vann to come with them, but she wouldn't leave Tristan.

How did it all go so wrong so quickly? Vann's legs carried him away from danger as they always did. Behind him, now nearly a mile away, was the smoke of his old home. He knew the situation was always a temporary one, but he didn't think this was how it would end for all of them. Martell's head remained buried into his shoulders as the young boy's eyes ran out of tears, all he had now to give was the silent whimper of losing Leon. Vann caught Owain looking over his shoulder to check on him every few minutes. He had never seen Owain so composed in his life, or was it seething anger that kept him calm? Vann couldn't quite tell.

The redhead led Vann to the rendezvous point that the group had all agreed upon, a small entrance into a cave that dipped into a wider area, enough to fit all six of them if they slept closely to one another. Vann placed Martell down onto his feet and then wiped the red eyes of the boy, and gave him a reassuring smile that everything would be okay, which Martell returned sombrely. Vann stepped into the drop at the entrance of the cave and raised his arms up to take the unconscious girl from Owain, and to carry her into the cave - and when she met his arms, he noticed her face stir, as if she was dreaming a new life for herself. He dipped his head underneath the frame of the entrance and stood up inside the low cave as he carried the girl towards the back of their small safe-house where he could prop her up against the semi-damp walls. The two other boys followed closely behind , where Owain pulled down the netted foliage to cover their safety.

Vann watched as Owain opened the rucksack to pull out his spare journal of paper and some charcoal. He began to stroke the charcoal onto the paper with a tender touch. His tongue began to stick out as he concentrated on beginning his art piece.

"I don't think now is the time," Vann softly spoke, not wanting to upset his friend. Owain looked towards Vann with a defeated gaze, before turning his attention back to his task. Vann didn't know what to do. He had abandoned his friends for the safety of Martell, and this damned girl who wouldn't even wake up - all at the request of Emerie. He knew that Owain would be beating himself up inside his head, he was the brawn of the group, he was the one who took the protection of all of them deep into his heart. Vann wanted to tell him that he shouldn't blame himself, that if he had stayed to help the others he wouldn't have made a difference. But how do you say that to someone? How do you tell someone that they made the right choice by running away? Vann gripped the chest of his coat tightly and then ripped the buttons apart from each other in anger. He buried his face as he lifted the open sides of the coat upwards, tears beginning to pour into the fabric, erasing the stains of soot and smoke that covered him. He held back the choke in his throat, he didn't want to upset his friends even more .

The same feeling of frostbite from the night before touched the back of his head with the cold running down his hair and into his scalp. Vann jolted his head away from the sensation to see the girl looking at him curiously - she removed her hand from him and retreated it back towards her chest.

"Thank you for saving me from that creature," The girl said. Her voice was calm and soft, it had an accent similar to the pronunciation of nobles, but a slight twang to it similar to those of the desert-landers of Ideneor.

Vann looked to her with his eyes wide and his mouth agape as he tried to reply, but his lips quivered and his voice could not escape. The girl pulled him into an embrace and held him as he sobbed on the worst day of his life. After a few moments Vann felt Owain's usually iron grip tenderly place itself onto his shoulder.

"We're going to be okay. All of us," Owain promised.

"But what do we even do from here?" Vann asked, to both him and the girl that held him, "I don't even know your name, or why the hell the Empire is after you."

The girl removed herself from Vann and stood up with her head just an inch from the top of the small cave. She looked over her body as if it was the first time that she had seen it, her sight analysing every part of her hands. Her confusion appeared further when she began to run her hands through her golden hair.

"I don't know how I got here," The girl revealed, "But I know that I am here for a reason."

"A reason? Like some sort of Divine mission?" Owain asked, curiously sarcastic.

"I think so," The girl eagerly nodded at the question. "I dreamed. For the last cycle I dreamed of a lake by a sprawling mountainous forest, where I saw my Uncle looking over his home where men and women in green stood before him. I need to find him, I know he has answers for me and I know he'll be able to help us I'm sure of it." She smiled something beautiful. "Us."

"What about Leon? And Emerie and Tristan?" Martell spoke up with his little voice. The girl dropped her shoulders and her eyebrows raised as her heart seemed to ache as she heard the young boy speak to her. Vann saw the girl float almost ethereally to the boy opposite her, her hands placed onto Martell's cheeks and she smiled once more. "If anyone can help us, and your friends, it will be Uncle Borrenthus. He's very powerful, and kind, he will help." The girl promised with one of her hands on her heart.

Owain tilted his head and Vann knew one of his well put together questions would quickly follow. "So let me get this straight. You fall from the sky, we save you and you save us, and then our friends get captured, right? So now that you have decided to wake up after our home has been burned down and our friends, once again, having been captured, you want us to travel to what I, and probably Vann as well, assume to be Beonyth's Laketown on the off-chance that your uncle will help us save our friends somehow? Is that it?"

The girl followed along with every one of his words closely, and when he finished his tirade the mysterious girl pointed a finger towards him, "That is precisely it," she answered before trying to hide her curiosity towards the use of her finger.

Vann could see the anger that Owain had clearly been feeling ooze out of him and what filled him as a replacement was utter confusion. Vann's gaze bounced between the three people in front of him before finally meeting with Martell who was waiting for Vann to come to a decision. He could see both Owain and the girl now turn to him, waiting to see what he would say next. Vann was nervous. Were all three of them expecting him to lead them to Beonyth's Laketown? He didn't want to be the one responsible for the adventure, he didn't want to be the reason to lose any of them if something would go wrong again. He could still feel Emerie force his hand from her wrist as she rushed to go and help Leon and Tristan. She had stressed to him that he and Owain needed to protect Martell and the girl, and that she would handle everything else. Vann rubbed a hand across his face to try and relieve the stress that he felt.

"Your name. May I ask what it is?" he gently asked the girl in white. She thought to herself for a few moments - the name was clearly escaping her and rattling around her brain. As Owain began to come up with one for her, her soft spoken voice sounded once more. "Arvuria," she answered with a proud and strong belief towards it.

Vann and Owain exchanged glances. They had a fast and silent discussion of how the name was awfully similar to the capital's name of Arvur. Maybe she was confusing it for her own, but it was a name, and that's what she wanted to be called.

"Arvuria," Vann began, "If you think you're capable of using your Arcane power when needed, Me, Owain, and Martell will get you to the Laketown. I don't know how much your uncle could help, so I want your word that you will use your ability to help us get our friends back, because the gods know that we are not strong enough to take on those soldiers by ourselves."

"It is a solemn vow that I will help you reunite with Tristan, Leon, and Emerie." Arvuria didn't hesitate to reply.

THE GROUP REMAINED sheltered within the confines of the small cave for the rest of the night as the torrential rain and thunder sounded over the woods. The thunder awoke Vann after a loud crash, and once his eyes were open he couldn't fall back asleep as the upsetting events replayed in his head as his remaining friends slept beside him. He remembered how Leon and Tristan had simply left the barn to place a cover over the firewood he had made, that they only did so because he forgot to do it. They were only out there because of his small error. He remembered nodding off as he was meant to be watching over Arvuria as she slept in Emerie's bed, it was his turn to make sure she was okay and because of that he wasn't there to diffuse the situation between the noble and his friends. He remembered chasing Emerie after the two of them had seen the noble and the soldiers antagonise Leon and Tristan. He believed that the two of them could handle it without Emerie, but she wouldn't listen - he had told her that she would just make it worse if the noble recognised her but she believed she could help. So he loosened his grip around her wrist and let her push him away. He sat there with nothing but the same thoughts rolling around in his head for hours, it was torture for him.

Vann hesitantly lifted himself from the thin linen beneath him that was the only comfort between him and the damp rocky mud that covered the ground. He stepped over Owain who was snoring and was surprised that Martell was able to use his chest as a pillow amongst the noise. As Vann looked around the small cave, he noticed that Arvuria was no longer sleeping beside them, his gaze quickly moved to the foliage that covered the entrance of the cave and saw that there was a gap where she had left. He hurried out the exit of their safety and looked around the immediate area before him, the dark woods moved as the heavy wind carried through them. The sound around them was the swish of the condensed tree being battered by the heavy rain.

"I am up here," Arvuria whispered gently from above him. She was sitting on top of the small cliff on top of the cave where the cluster of trees above her helped shelter her from the torrential waters. Vann looked up to see the light of the two moons shining directly onto her, her pale skin illuminating as it bounced the light back to the night light that looked upon her. Her legs dangled down from the edge, they were lightly kicking against the rock while her hands sat delicately on her knees propping up her perfect posture. Vann climbed up the rocks that sat beside the cave entrance and placed himself next to her.

"I guess you've slept enough," Vann whispered. Arvuria ignored him and continued to take in the scenery of the dark woods and the large emerald green mountains that were placed in the distance. It was where Beonyth's Green sat. Vann found her odd, she didn't seem as though she really understood what was going on, as if there was a piece missing to her view of the world. Maybe that's what made her special. He wanted to tell her to come back inside, but he relented before he began, he was sure that if the soldiers were to find them she would be more than capable of dealing with them, he half-hoped that he would find some strength too should it come to that.

Arvuria's sight turned to the sky and Vann's eyes followed suit, he couldn't tell where she was looking but he knew that her eyes had a fixed point, he could feel the sense of longing that escaped from her.

"It was you, wasn't it? You were the inferno that fell from the sky, and not just someone who fell into its crater," Vann spoke softly. The young woman beside him looked away from the cascade of dark clouds and turned her attention to him. She nodded.

"It would make sense, would it not?" Arvuria said. "I have never seen those mountains before, or the trees sitting in front of us, or even the dark clouds that hide the stars from you and I," she revealed with a sombre tone, "I have memories of before I saved you and Owain, but they are blurry and the voices that speak in them are of a language I do not understand. I want to know why I am here, I want to know the reason."

Vann's eyes met Arvuria's, she fixated on his and he noticed that her pupils weren't completely round, they were more as a thin oval, as they were enveloped by her yellow iris'.

"It's a common thing you know. You're not alone when you wonder why you're here." Vann replied to her, placing his hand onto one of hers in reassurance, "You could create a reason for yourself, or you could always find something to believe in. Whatever works for you."

Arvuria listened to Vann's words intently as he began to share how he sees the world. Vann could see that she was searching for something within Vann, but she wasn't able to see it just yet.

"What do you believe in?" she asked with an earnest curiosity.

Vann thought for a moment, and looked away from the wide-eyed Arvuria.

"I don't know," Vann answered, "I think as long as you're a good person, or you try to be, I think that's enough. That's all I want to try to be… a good person."

Arvuria looked downwards towards Vann's hand that had been placed onto hers - Vann could see the curiosity on her face as she wondered why he had put it there. He removed his hand as he worried that the girl might get the wrong idea, and he certainly did not want to upset Emerie when he saw her again.

"I think you are a good person, Vann," Arvuria spoke with her eyes directly meeting his again, this time it was her reassuring him - with a smile added extra.

"You don't even know me," Vann laughed quietly in the night.

"I know that you ran towards danger because someone might have needed help. Would a bad person do that?" Arvuria asked before she tried to figure out the question herself.

"No, I guess they wouldn't," Vann replied, "though I do doubt a good person would put their friends in danger because they were afraid of feeling guilty."

"Guilty?" Arvuria tilted her head.

"Yeah, guilty," Vann croaked as he remembered how he willingly left his village before the war began, leaving his family and his friends by themselves at the request of his parents. He was old enough to have joined the war and to be trained to defend his home, but he was scared, and his parents were scared. So when the recruiters from Theothen arrived, his parents told them they had no son as he left the walled village with Tristan and Emerie. It had been 3 months since then, even in that short amount of time he already felt like he was a different person. He found it funny that all the chores he hated and the small home he always complained about were things he would do anything to experience one more time.

"Vann?" Arvuria softly spoke.

"Yeah?"

"I am thankful that it was you who found me, I do not believe many others would have been so courageous… or stupid," The girl reassured and teased. Vann couldn't help but smile towards her, he was pretty sure it was the first joke she had ever made. The two teens laughed with each other for a few moments until it naturally died down. The air grew thick between them despite just sharing their first friendly moment together.

"I need to ask, away from the other two. Do you really think that your Uncle will be able to help us? You seemed sure down there, but up here, I mean, you're staring at a thundercloud. That's not usually what someone does when they're confident," Vann asked.

Arvuria nodded. "Of course he can help us," she answered meekly. Vann could tell she was lying, he could see that it was her first attempt at dishonesty but he didn't press the matter. She may be human, but it was clear that it was her first time being one - much like it was his, the only difference was that he had more practice than she did.

The two teens stayed on top of the cave until the morning sun began to dawn. Its rays of light managed to pierce small entrances through the clouds that remained heavy and dark - but it was enough for Vann to be awoken with a golden touch on his face. His eyes opened to see that Arvuria was no longer beside him, but she had folded his long blue coat up to act as a pillow for his head as he laid on the stone beneath him. The rain was not as heavy as it was a few hours ago, but he could still feel it drop onto his skin. Vann sat up and wiped his eyes with his wet knuckles and breathed the crisp morning air - he looked around the evergreen trees that surrounded him to see that they were still swaying amongst the wind. He wasn't sure how he and the others had all managed to have a safe and relatively comfortable sleep - he was sure that at some point they would have been swarmed by his country's soldiers.

He stood up from his makeshift bed and unfolded the coat to wrap it around his body. He slid down from the rock and dropped towards the now open cave entrance, where the foliage had been moved to allow in the golden light of the sun. He saw that Owain and Martell were still asleep and all the supplies remained in the cave still - all that was missing was Arvuria, again. He noticed her white shirt with its draping silk tail was now piled next to the supply bag, and a few of the extra shirts had been dragged from it, hanging over the straps. Vann exhaled, beginning to realise that this would be a common occurrence from the golden girl. He stepped over the cape blankets covering the other two and then reached over them to grab his fathers sword. He always felt safer with the blade around his waist, which of course is a given when you carry such a thing, but it was more because he felt like his father was always at his side, telling him that he can make it one more day. Vann looked towards the open journal that Owain had been scribbling into the night before, he had begun a sketch of Vann's sword and the rucksack that had been sitting opposite him.

Arvuria: The Ethereal Children

Vann heard the soft footsteps of Arvuria place themselves at the entrance of the stone cavern. He turned around to see the girl in one of his brown tunics that had a few different shades of the colour stitched onto it to hide the damage he had caused over the last few months. Around her shoulders were two rabbits attached to a stick via some small vines. She smiled at him and then looked towards the two boys still snoring away.

"Do they like these things?" Arvuria asked, "It was either these or one of those big animals with the horns."

Vann managed to hide his broken heart as he realised that the other option must have been a dear."Those things? You mean rabbits?" Vann asked with a small smile, "They're going to love you for getting them."

Arvuria beamed a wide smile towards him, her excitement was palpable as she pumped a fist to her side in victory. Vann walked towards her, placed the rabbits over his shoulders instead, and had her follow him out of the cave. He showed her how to prepare the rabbits and how to start the fire to cook them on.

After some time of preparation, Owain stumbled out of the entrance with his mace ready to swing, with Martell following just a few seconds behind him. Vann and Arvuria laughed as they saw Owain's eyes adjust to the sun and his pale skin fight the light that had defeated the rain.

"Careful Owain, you might get sunburn," Vann called out with a laugh - he tried to set the tone of the morning, he wanted to stop any sadness before it began. Arvuria laughed along with him but Vann wasn't sure if she understood the joke, or if it was even humorous.

The redhead mumbled something to himself as he stepped down the small hill to the campfire that Vann and Arvuria created, his groggy eyes not seeing what sat above the fire until the smell hit him. Vann waited for Owain to stop staring at the breakfast that sat in front of him before he offered him a stick with meat on it. Rabbit Meat.

"How the hells do we have rabbits?" Owain exclaimed as he stepped closer towards the fire. He bent over to examine if they were the real thing.

"I hunted them down for us to feast upon," Arvuria answered with pride in her voice as though she was a conquering hero. To the three boys that had drooled over the smell of the fire, she was just that.

"If you were my eyes Arvuria, I would ask to have your hand in marriage right now," Owain joked as he sat on one of the logs that Vann had placed earlier to act as a seat for his broader friend. Arvuria tilted her body towards Vann, "What does he mean 'my eyes'?" she whispered.

Vann smirked at the innocent question before speaking in a warm tone, "You prefer a soldier boy don't you Owain," he teased. Arvuria still remained confused, but no answer was given to her as Owain laughed as he raised a middle finger. Martell moved Owain's gestured hand down and then hurried towards Arvuria, jumping into her chest to give her a tight hug which almost stopped her from breathing.

"Thank you so much," he smiled over her shoulder. The golden girl squeezed him with her arms and moved him side to side as she rocked the delicate nine year old boy. Vann's feeling of warmth at the happy sight slowly faded away as he noticed Martell worryingly removing himself from Arvuria as his sight remained behind her - he was staring towards the treeline. Vann turned to the direction Martell faced to see a man walking through the woods with a bloodied sword drawn and his cape's hood draping over the top half of his face while a rough pointed black beard covered the lower half. The figure moved his grip on the sword so that his gloved hand held it by the blade, to almost signal that he meant no harm. An almost pointless gesture as the red began to drip from his hand too.

"Martell, come here," Owain ordered before he moved the boy behind him as he held his mace over his shoulder in a display obvious enough for the distant figure to notice. Vann stood up and placed himself between his friends and the hooded figure with his right hand sat on the handle of his blade waiting to draw it should he need to.

"Come no further!" Vann shouted. He drew his father's sword an inch out of its scabbard. The Hooded Man stopped. He stabbed his sword into the ground and raised his hands slowly. The air was thick for a few moments until he pulled down his hood to reveal his long black hair draping over the deep green cape that covered his body. He moved the cape over his shoulders to reveal dirty black coloured leathers that were vastly different to what the soldiers from the night before wore. The thick leather covered only the top half of his chest while thin chain mail sat underneath. His arms were exposed save some similar coloured leather gloves that carried it's armour halfway more up his arm where the scars of previous battles showed across his skin.

"I'm just a traveller who smelled the air," The Hooded Man called out towards Vann, "That is rabbit, isn't it?"

"It might be," Vann returned. "Why is your sword bloodied?" he demanded to know.

The Man stepped forward away from the red sword and moved towards the group of teens that had attempted to eat their breakfast in peace.

"Some soldiers attacked me when I told them I hadn't seen some runaway teenagers," he revealed, "Unfortunately for them they were a little early. Had they asked me some minutes later I would have been able to point them in this direction," he joked.

Arvuria stood up from her seat and Vann felt her hand touch his right arm to silently tell him to be calm. He turned to her to watch as she stepped in front of him towards the man just a little bit further.

"You look like one of them," Arvuria spoke. The Man carried forward until he was just a few steps away from the group. "Who? One of the gods?" the man questioned with a little laugh.

"No," Arvuria spoke with a frown, "One of the men who stood before my uncle in my dreams. You were at the front - standing before the rest."

"So the old man isn't going senile," The Man whispered to himself in disbelief. He took another step towards Arvuria which caused Vann to draw his sword another inch out of its scabbard - the man looked Vann up and down before rolling his eyes back towards Arvuria.

"What do you mean? Who isn't going Senile?" Vann questioned, "Who are you?"

The Man walked past Arvuria and Vann to then take a seat at the campfire. He pulled a rod of rabbit from the fire and began picking apart at the skewered meat, taking some of it with his fingers and enjoying it as it sat in his mouth. He pointed towards one of the carcasses with a grateful look on his face, "This is brilliant, you should try some," he complimented as he reached the food over to Owain who shrugged and took hold of the metal stick that the man handed him over the fire. Arvuria moved beside their guest and took a seat despite the daggers that Vann's eyes shot towards her as she did so.

The Man noticed Vann's fierce gaze on him causing him to sigh towards the teen once more.

"Harnon, one of Borrenthus' men," he spoke towards Vann almost with irritation but there was understanding of why Vann was wary.

"So you do know my uncle?!" Arvuria beamed excitedly, "How is he? Is he okay?"

Harnon moved his head away from the loud noise beside him and rubbed his pointed right ear. He fished out a streak of rabbit between his teeth and nibbled on it before swallowing. "That was good," Harnon said before looking at Vann, "Don't let me ruin your morning young man, eat up."

Vann sheathed the two inches of his blade back into its scabbard and sat opposite Harnon with a watchful gaze. He grabbed one of the metal rods he had prepared with some of the meat on it and took a bite, managing to hide the satisfaction of his cooking.

"I'm here to bring you to Borrenthus. It's a damn good thing he sent me too because Theothen Vanguard would have slit your throats as you slept," he revealed as if it was casual information.

Vann's eyes widened, "You killed all of them?"

"Be thankful I did. Try not to feel guilt over their deaths. It was you or them," Harnon stated as he looked over his shoulder back towards his bloodied blade that remained stabbed into the ground. Arvuria looked towards the sword in the grass and an expression of grief appeared on her face - Vann wanted to turn her away from it but a part of him knew that she was going to have to experience what the world was really like if she was going to survive. Even Martell seemed unfazed by the sword.

"So, who is Borrenthus really?" Vann asked, "I thought he'd be some powerful Arcanist so I don't get why he sent a man with a sword instead of coming himself."

Harnon looked towards Vann with his eyes squinted, the teenager wasn't sure of how Harnon had taken his statement, but it clearly wasn't good.

"You throw around the word 'Arcanist' as if it's something common," Harnon spat, "A bit of wise advice: It's a dangerous time to be saying that word."

Vann raised an eyebrow, as if to goad the man just a little bit more but Harnon simply changed his tune and smiled at him and wagged a finger instead of revealing anything else so soon.

"You're too opinionated for your own good," Harnon laughed, "I'll tell you what, when I was your age I-"

"You still haven't said who Borrenthus is," Vann interrupted, "We've just had a really fucking rough night so I would appreciate it if you stopped playing coy."

Why he was acting so blunt, Vann wasn't so sure. Was it the bravery that Arvuria said he had in him? Or was it the usual stupidity? Vann wasn't sure himself.

"Please tell me all you know," Arvuria delicately added.

The Marauder unbuttoned one of the small bags that sat on his belt and passed Arvuria a piece of paper. The girl undid the multiple folds of the old parchment until a drawing of her face appeared.

"One of Borrenthus' followers gave me this a week ago and asked me to search for you," Harnon revealed.

"Wait, so that means wherever Arvuria came from, it has only been nearly a week since she left? She was with Borrenthus?" Owain asked, trying to make sense of the Marauder's reveal. Harnon shook his head, "How are you not following this, Red? Borrenthus knew Arvuria would be arriving before she landed."

"Owain."

"What?"

"My name is Owain, not red."

"I don't care?" Harnon frowned at the teenager, "Are the two of you always like this? I'm trying to tell you what the hells is going on with this girl and you all keep interrupting me. Did your parents not teach you manners?" He questioned.

"They did, but we haven't seen them in months," Vann revealed with a sombre tone.

"I can tell," Harnon huffed in annoyance. "Now, can I speak?" he asked the group of teenagers and Martell, who was still remaining closely beside Owain. They all nodded in agreement.

"Teenagers, honestly," Harnon breathed again. "Borrenthus asked me to come here as a favour to make sure that I would be the one to find you, Arvuria. I've been tasked with bringing you to Laketown," The Marauder began as he pointed a finger upwards in front of her lips to keep her from shouting into his face again. "Unfortunately for me, lover-boy is the one who I assume got to you first. I was going to speak to you all at that farm - the one with all of them flowers, but there's not much I can do against twenty or so men and that Giant fuck in the armour if I'm trying to be stealthy. Half of Markarth's Vanguard from last night were looking for you throughout the night. Those ones I have dealt with. The other ten or so, The Commander, and The Prince have taken your three other friends to Avane. They're safe as far as I know, I heard Prince Thurian order his men to bind them, not kill them."

"I'm sorry, did you say 'Prince'? You mean Prince Thurian?" Owain immediately questioned.

"The very man himself," Harnon answered, "The man who started this war."

"We're so in over our heads Vann," Owain stressed, as he stood up from his seat to start to pace back and forth, "If the Prince is involved then we're fucked. Especially if he's looking for Arvuria! He's as psychopathic as his sister. You don't fuck with the crown!"

"Calm down, I don't want to hear whining so early in the morning," Harnon hushed, "I can get you to Borrenthus, and when I've done so his Guild will be able to protect you. Even from the Prince you're so scared of. My life will be much easier if you all come willingly so eat, pack what things you have, and let's get going. You have no choice but to trust me," Harnon ordered as he took another bite of the rabbit meat.

Arvuria: The Ethereal Children

- Chapter 9 -
THURIAN THEO
To be Civil in War.

PRINCE THURIAN STORMED upwards the spiral staircase as the stones echoed the fierce anger that he felt inside of him. He was the son of Emperor Thrane, and he would be damned if a lowly commander was going to undermine him to the extent that Markarth had. How dare he. How dare the Giant-Kin who was found homeless on the streets of Arcann of all places believe he was above Prince Thurian. The Prince barged past the guardsman who tried to stop him from entering the room and kicked open the door with his now fully armoured boot that led up to his ornate golden armour.

"Go against my better judgement once more you cretinous creature, and I will have your head! I will hack it from your neck and roll it down the mountain you were born of!" Thurian roared towards Markarth who stood at the head of a long wooden table in his office surrounded by the noblemen of Avane.

"I am Prince Thurian, Only-born son of the Emperor. You are and always will be beneath me," Thurian spat with venom as a final insult.

The Commander looked towards each of the nobles that surrounded the tables and motioned them with his hand for them to leave, which they were all too happy to agree to. They awkwardly moved past Thurian who remained just before the exit - his eyes fixated onto Markarth.

"Please, take a seat," Commander Markarth asked politely, but Thurian only took it as an insult.

"Stand up," Thurian seethed.

Markarth took a deep breath and exhaled. His annoyance with the teenager was an obvious display. The Giant-kin moved his large seat backwards and lifted himself to his feet and saluted with his arm forward, his elbow bending his forearm towards the sky with his first two fingers pointing upwards. Thurian's lips twitched as he saw the unserious eyes of Commander Markarth, but the display of power was enough to sate him for now.

"Sit," Thurian ordered as he pulled a chair out for himself at the table and dropped his ornate golden sword onto the table. The Commander followed in suit. A mutual agreement of peace. An equal threat of death.

"I will be taking the three prisoners to Arvur and I will tell my father that I was the one who found the contents of the comet," Thurian informed with an all too eager voice, "I am willing to tell him that you helped me, Markarth, on the condition that you do not dare ever treat me as you have done. I understand the hesitance of your men in following me, they are loyal to you after all, but you are a servant of the Crown, not a servant solely of my sister. You would do well to remember that fact. You are good at your job but there are a hundred men and women who are waiting replace you."

Markarth stared down Thurian, and the Prince felt all of the violent thoughts that were escaping the Commander. The Prince simply smiled - he knew that Markarth had needed a keen reminder of who he was.

"May I speak freely, my liege?" Commander Markarth asked.

"Yes."

Markarth met Thurian's goading smile with just a small furrow of his brow. "Do you truly believe that after everything you have done; After being the man who started this war, that you think you can earn redemption so easily?"

Thurian's aura dwindled. Markarth stood back up from his seat and walked to the station behind the long dining table, where a cabinet of draws stood underneath a painting of the Emperor in his youth who was clad in his onyx regalia. The Commander reached into the drawer and returned back with an opened scroll in his hand, "There was a second raven yesterday, one I decided not to share with you, for your own sake," Markarth informed as he tossed the scroll onto Thurian's sword that sat on the oaken wood.

Thurian unravelled the curled paper to see his sister's handwriting.

Commander Markarth,

I hope my words reach you in a timely manner, and with utmost secrecy. You will have been ordered by my Cousin to secure the contents of the comet and to bring it to him in Sunsrest. I have

Arvuria: The Ethereal Children

> *heard that The Empress has been awaiting its fall for weeks, and that a girl with golden hair will appear from its smoke to bring the world into new light. I have all faith that The Empress is not wrong in her expectations. Find the girl, and bring her to me. Together we will take what is rightfully mine.*
>
> *When Thurian finds himself involved, do not hesitate to end him should the opportunity arise. One more cube off the board is an opportunity we cannot pass on.*
>
> D.

Thurian carefully folded the bent paper into squares as he sat nervously, eyeing up his sword sitting peacefully before him. He was waiting for Markarth to take hold of his own weapon but the Giant-kin leaned over his large, almost throne-like chair.

"You expect me to kill you now, don't you Thurian?" Markarth asked with pity in his tone.

"Why aren't you?" Thurian asked, "You must be a fool to show this to me. To go against Dira is to go against the Emperor himself."

Markarth released a huff in agreement before reaching into one of the belt's pouches that sat on his black and red gambeson. He pulled out a bracelet that seemed to have been ripped apart, it was of blue woven rope with luminescent green and red stones placed in equal sections.

"I know that we have all lost someone due to war. Whether it was this one or the last. We all have our reasons for the risks that we take... This belonged to my daughter," Markarth calmly began, as he passed the broken bracelet to Thurian who took it with respect and grace. "She was slaughtered by the Theothen army twenty three years, eleven months, and seventeen days ago. Cut to pieces in her bedroom with my son who tried to protect her from the man who had just beheaded my wife," Markarth spoke coldly.

"I'm sorry," Thurian apologised.

"It's not your fault," Markarth quickly brushed him away.

"I ripped that man apart, I tore his legs from his body as he screamed. He wanted to pass out after I began, but I wouldn't let him. It made me feel strong. To see him trying to crawl away from me, begging for me to let him live. He wanted mercy, yet he gave none. Every man is strong when they are the only beast in the room."

"Did you give him mercy?" Thurian asked.

Markarth shook his head and his face lightened up just for a brief moment where the wrinkles of stress on his face softened. "I dragged him outside to watch me butcher his comrades that were cutting down my people. We were deemed a threat by your father simply because my people tried to become civilised. To try to choose our representative, someone of our people, not some human bureaucrat who had been brought to our home to rule over us."

Thurian sat in silence as he held the bracelet, he believed that the bracelet was easy to fix but then he realised that Markarth knew that already. He was trying to focus on anything other than the idea of his father ordering the executions of innocents but he had realised as he reached adulthood, that the man who fathered him was not the same man who ruled The Theothen Empire.

"You lost your entire family to my father's Empire, yet you wear its colours and kill in the name of it? I must ask, and I do so with respect, do you not see the hypocrisy?"

Thurian questioned as he held the bracelet back towards Markarth who took it from him and placed it back into its container.

"We all lose a piece of ourselves when vengeance is involved, and it's never a piece that we would choose to lose, I am not the man that my wife loved," Markarth muttered. He looked towards Thurian with determination alight in his eyes, "You started this war with Resnia. Tell me why you did it, and not the reason."

"What do you mean?" The Prince guarded.

"I don't care about who you killed, I want to know why you did it," Markarth demanded, "Answer me now Prince, or those swords sitting before us will be drawn and only one of us will make it back to Arvur. Now tell me. Why did you start this war?"

"I was defending this country," Thurian answered.

"You lie," Markarth spat, "Do not try me again."

Thurian's heart wanted to collapse under the stress of the situation, but every other part of his body was calm, almost content with the idea of Markarth being his end. He had been shamed for the last few months due to his actions that caused the war to begin. He was the one little spark that ignited the fire underneath the two countries.

"I didn't want to die."

"That's the why," Thurian answered, "That's why thousands of bodies have already been buried on both sides - because I was defending myself instead of someone else."

"So you are just like me," Markarth replied, "You're responsible for the deaths of many because you deemed yourself more important."

Thurian was confused. Markarth had just told him that he murdered a man because he killed his family, and then killed the fellow soldiers that raided his home. Thurian felt as though he was exactly what Markarth would hate, so why was he comparing himself to him?

"Yes, I'm responsible for it all, and not a day goes by that it doesn't weigh on me. I volunteered to come here. To come to the battlefront so that I can sneak my way to the front lines and die fighting. I was using your potential promotion as an excuse to be here," Thurian revealed, "But then I met those peasants before last night, and I saw in them, for the first time, the long term consequences of my actions. They made me realise that I could serve this country a lot more than by being a martyr who furthers the bloodshed."

Markarth walked beside Thurian and placed one of his meaty hands onto the Prince's shoulder. "I hate you, Thurian. Your empire was built upon Taundrad's natives, and your bloodline has devolved into murderers since the death of The Golden Dragon," Markarth uttered, "But I know you are the better option than Dira is. It seems you are the only one in your family who was born with a heart."

"You mean to follow me?" Thurian questioned, incredibly confused, "Then why have you undermined me since the start of our journey? Why have we captured those three teenagers when this letter says we should be looking for a girl with golden hair?"

The Giant-kin removed his hands from the prince and dropped himself back into his large seat with a thud. He took his large and thick steel blade that sat in front of him and leaned it against the table between him and Thurian. "I wanted to see if you had a backbone after all the stories that I've heard about the weak and cowardly Prince. Regarding the peasants, I wanted to see if you'd protect innocents and stand up for them where your parents and sister would have killed them without a second thought."

"So you've been playing me? You're not just a battle-hungry fool with a sword?" Thurian asked, with humour and admiration surprisingly surfing his voice.

The giant smiled and nodded downward. "There is the matter of finding the girl, which is going to prove difficult for everyone except for us," The Commander spoke, "Because we're not going to try to look"

"Why wouldn't we?" Thurian asked, "Dira has ordered the both of us to find her, if we do not then you won't become a general, and my life becomes even more difficult."

"Dira and the Councilmen are all already marching towards nearby towns and cities with the intent of searching for her because 'someone' leaked the information. Dira was just a few days ahead of the others and has already set up a war camp nearby. Nobody expects you to complete your task, and I was tasked with bringing the reinforcements to Avane, which I have done so. My men can defend this city with half of my forces while the other half heads to the battlefront to fight under Commander Krenn who has similar ideals to myself," Markarth informed, "So while Princess Dira is away from Arvur, and all heads of the court are moving their men to find this girl, you can begin to win over the nobles that remain in our Capital- undermining your sister. You will have Avane in your name with my protection while the battlefront is also yours. It is the beginning of our cause."

"Our cause?" Thurian asked, "and what might that be?"

"To build a new Theothen Empire," Markarth answered, "Under a new Emperor."

Luke Morgan

Arvuria: The Ethereal Children

Luke Morgan

- Chapter 10 -
SHIN WATERMAN.
Tethering The Arcane.

BEING A MENDER in the Theothen Empire required skill, talent, and a reliant access to the Arcane. When Shin enlisted into the Empire's Army she was brought from her basic training to specialise in healing because of her Arcanist ability, but more so because she struggled to harm others. She was soft-spoken and cared for those around her, especially the squad she was assigned to - so to be surrounded by rebels of the crown while half of her comrades were injured was the worst situation that she could possibly be in. She had enlisted to fight the Resnian's not her own people.

"Get behind me Shin!" Sergeant Brennan beckoned. He yanked Shin's arm to pull her behind him as he leaped forward with his shield to block the oncoming blade of a rebel soldier. Shin fell to the ground onto her backside and scurried away from the combat towards one of her wounded brethren.. She hurried as she crawled amongst the dirt, the blood, and the screams of battle until she picked herself up from the ground to help Markus as he held onto the deep cut that had slashed through the leather on the side of his armour, she tried her hardest to hold his skin together.

Shin ripped her gauntlets from her wrists and pointed two fingers on both hands towards the sky and ripped pink-coloured Arcane from the sky and motioned her hands to create a glowing rune with the tethers she had pulled from The Ethereals. She then delicately brought it towards the wound that slowly began to heal but around the healing wound mass bruising appeared around the area. Instead of her body taking the toll of using the Arcane, she had been using the flesh of those she healed instead - exchanging their long term lifespan with immediate healing. Although she had grown an incredible reputation for healing, many of her rank thought her rough and unlearned as she always left her men injured but alive. It was a secret she had discovered by accident in her youth, a secret healing she keeps all to herself under the guise of being bad at her job.

"Markus?" Shin hurriedly spoke to her comrade who was slowly dipping into unconsciousness. The Soldier placed one of his bloodied hands onto Shin's and smiled to her, "Help the...rest."

Shin placed two of her fingers onto Markus' neck, checking his pulse which remained stable. He was alive, though bruised still. She looked around to see many more of her brothers-in-arms cut down onto the floor - dead and injured, with the rebels outnumbering her Squad four-to-one.

She knew she had to do something but all she was was a healer - she would be executed by the rebels within a second if she were to stand up and fight. That wasn't who she was. A Circle of Defence from her comrades began to surround Shin and the injured soldiers - a shield wall formed as the rebels attempted to surround them.

"Stand firm brothers!" Sergeant Brennan roared, "Remind these bastards who we are!"

"Dragons!" The remaining soldiers roared as almost in unison they pushed the rebels back and cut down a line of them.

"Who are we?!" The Sergeant beckoned again as he booted one of his opponents away with a forceful kick.

"The Blood Dragons!" The soldiers roared ferociously as they began to fight and duel with more vigour and intensity. They were one cohesive unit. Beasts that had been cornered. Beasts that knew how to fight back.

Shin stood back up in the field of the injured and began to pull multiple pink threads of the Arcane around her, drawing up a large pink dome to surround her.

"By The Ethereals Shin I need help," one of the injured spoke to her as he held onto his bleeding chopped arm.

"I'm trying," Shin spoke firmly, "Just hold on a moment more!"

After a few more threads were pulled and the runic pattern was stable she pulled the threads of the Arcane closely towards her and then with all of her strength pushed them away from her tethering the power around her comrades with the pink light dome enveloping all of the Theothen soldiers as she stood holding the strings of the walls.

For a moment, the battle had been paused.

All of her comrades turned to her in disbelief. "Shin?" Sergeant Brennan muttered in awe - The Blood Dragons began to cheer and taunt towards the rebels on the other side of the barrier.

"Take a breath and steel yourselves, I cannot hold this for long!" Shin screamed in agony as she used her own body to tether the arcane for a little longer - her own wisp anchoring the power... one of the few things she was afraid of.

She felt her entire body, every muscle and every joint scream - every cell that made her herself buzzed in her body - she could feel the rebels and the soldiers pound against the protective dome. Her eyes opened sharply when she felt the rebels to the south of the dome begin to stop their attack against the barrier - a single pair of footsteps began to climb the dome.

"My Blood Dragons do not cower from battle! Kill these pitiful creatures!" a husky female voice ordered with all her might as the owner began to slide down towards the other side of the dome where the bulk of the rebel forces remained.

"Princess Dira is here!" Sergeant Brennan announced, "Show her what we are made of!"

Shin released the tethers and the pink light of the dome vanished as the soldiers of The Empire rallied and began to push back the rebels who outnumbered them as Dira's unexpected reinforcements arrived. The Mender's body grew weak and the view of the battle before her faded as her body gave in to the weakness it had to using the Arcane.

Shin fell to the ground.

Luke Morgan

Arvuria: The Ethereal Children

- Chapter 11 -
EMERIE HERENE
Falling Upwards.

EMERIE WAS SPRAWLED across the mattress, it was the most comfort she had ever felt lying down her entire life. The blanket beneath her was soft and inviting, and the room's hearth slowly burned, giving her the warmth any home should give. The events of the previous night played over and over in her mind - she couldn't stop thinking about how she yanked her arm away from Vann, and how she left the barn believing that she was going to either watch her brother die, or for him to see her be killed in front of him. Yet here she was, in a room fit for a Princess.

The bed she laid upon was the size of the small horse stable she had been sleeping in for the last few months - on each side of the bed were curtains that she believed she could drape down if she wanted to, to allow her privacy in her sleep - but the idea of it scared her. It reminded her of the black door.

On the other side of the room was the hearth that provided her the summer warmth she had been looking forward to. Sprawling away from the fire and the chimney was ornate stone tiling that displayed the emblem of Avane which was three golden coins interlinked with rope. Emerie smelled her brown tunic that belonged to Vann, it still reeked of fire and smoke, with the dirt sullying the pristine white bed sheets sitting below her. She moved herself from the edge of the bed and looked at the bruise that surrounded her wrist - Vann had left her a sign of him. She brought her wrist to her lips and delicately kissed it. The faint pain it gave her was a reminder that she was still alive, and that this room wasn't part of the judgement she would receive in The First Layer.

A knock sounded at the door, it was a commanding three hard bangs followed with a muffled voice. "Are you decent?" It asked her.

Emerie remained quiet and looked around the room for something she could use as a weapon, something, anything. Her eyes darted around to see that there were no loose items scattered around the room, that the four walls only included her, the bed, the fire, and some wooden cabinets. Unless she would be able to rip one of the cabinet doors off its hinges quietly, she didn't think she had much chance of fighting anyone, especially after feeling the effect of hunger and stress on her body.

"I'm decent," Emerie replied after the three knocks sounded again.

The door opened and following it were two maids and the young noble who was there when the Giant-kin burned down her home and captured her and her friends. Anger swelled up inside of her. She wanted to lunge towards him and strangle him. But before the urge overcame her, she remembered how he defended Leon and Tristan from the giant soldier after they had been defeated. That this noble had stood between them all and ordered the Commander to capture them, not to kill them. For what reason, she didn't know. What she did know was that she didn't like how the maids were looking at her as if she was an animal beneath them.

The Maids walked around Emerie and began to change the sheets of the bed that were now covered with soot and dirt with only Thurian standing before her in this moment. His ornate golden armour was removed since she last saw him and all he wore now was a silk white shirt with black trousers tucked into his black boots that were laced on the side. His arms were hidden behind his back and his posture was perfect, he smiled at Emerie, who only met him with a scowl.

"Did you sleep well?" he asked her in a clear and brisk manner. Emerie couldn't figure out if she hated it or loved it, it was a new tune in her ears, different to what she had heard from him twice before.

"As well as I could after having my home burned down," Emerie quickly snapped back. She knew the noble was expecting some level of defiance after he did not react to her attitude.

"You will be glad to know that Firven and Clarissa are still alive. It was their home after all. Am I mistaken?" Thurian asked her.

"They're alive with nowhere to go, because of you," Emerie replied.

Thurian removed his hands from behind his back and walked to the fire at the hearth which hand begun to dwindle. He moved the metal guard from it and began to place more coal onto the small embers which began to smoke the black rock a few moments after it met the orange glow.

"The farmstead is going to be rebuilt, and I will be paying the couple a monthly sum until their home is returned to them better than before," The Noble informed as he stood away from the fire where he now seemed content to watch it crackle.

Emerie was confused. Why would the noble care about the damage that he caused to peasants? This was the second time that he had shown her charity, something that she grew up believing was a myth.

"Why?" Emerie questioned, "Your men burned it down, and now you want to rebuild it? What was the point in doing it in the first place?"

"That is how this world works," The Noble replied matter-of-factly, "It is easier to rebuild than it is to be careful, don't you think?"

"Maybe," Emerie agreed, "But just because you have the ability to rebuild, that does not mean you have the right to tear something down."

Emerie noticed a small smile curve at the handsome noble's face as if she had said something he was waiting to hear. He looked towards the maids who had finished changing the sheets of the bed to signal them to leave - they ever so quickly hurried out of the room but not before Emerie saw the maids looking towards her nervously, a change to their expressions just moments ago.

"What would you change about Theothen? As someone who has lived at the bottom, do you think the Nobility are acting how they should?" Thurian asked her. Emerie considered her answer for a few moments. She was never one who listened to her father's political lectures, and her village at the border had no nobility, so her interactions with them had only ever been with the man who stood before her. Her lifestyle, and the help she had received from the start of the war was a clear indication to her as to how much the rich cared.

"I think 'Nobility' is a term coined by egotistical men who were born into an easy life," Emerie answered. "People like you, you don't know what life is really like for normal people. You don't have to worry when your next meal might be, or how you'll survive the night in the cold, or how you will ever afford to have a family or home of your own. You have everything given to you - you have no idea how difficult life is. If I could change anything, it would be a change of leadership. The Emperor, his family, all the 'Noble' councillors who were born into their position need to step aside and allow people like me to choose who represents them."

"You would want to elect the councillors? What makes you think the people you choose wouldn't end up tainted by their newfound political power? What's stopping them from being worse?" Thurian asked her with curiosity. Emerie stumbled for a moment, she couldn't deny it was a good question, and wondered herself if she would be the type of person who would get used to comfortable beds and warm fires at the expense of other people.

"Hope." Emerie answered, "I would hope that they wouldn't."

Her heart skipped a little, either in fear or in nervousness when the noble turned to her completely and smiled. "Your honesty is quite admirable. Anyone else in this Keep would have told me what I wanted to hear."

"Exactly my point," Emerie replied, "You're a noble, everyone is scared of you while you think they love you."

"I'm not a noble Emerie," Thurian replied with a small laugh.

Arvuria: The Ethereal Children

"What are you then? The Emperor in disguise?" Emerie taunted, "I heard he was an old broken man but by the looks of it you're far from it."

Thurian laughed at Emerie's taunt. She didn't quite understand the Noble's game that he was trying to play with her with all of his questions that seemed to lead nowhere, but for a moment she appreciated seeing a human side of him with the way his laugh had some warmth to it.

"An 'old and broken man'?" Thurian repeated, "I've heard my father described as worse things but I think you have nailed it perfectly."

Emerie was pretty sure her heart was about to fail. She analysed the man standing in front of her and she realised how stupid and ignorant she had been. He was wearing the finest quality silk, his skin was clean, his smile was perfect, and his lengthy obsidian hair tied neatly back. Around his neck was a golden chain that glimmered against the fire from the hearth. The pendent was a golden dragons head with amber in its eyes and teeth. Emerie looked down to check she still wore the necklace that Vann had gifted her, before looking back to The Prince before her.

"You're Prince Thurian?" Emerie stammered, "The Son of Emperor Thrane?"

"I am," The Prince replied. "And I would appreciate your help."

Emerie was even more sure that she was about to break down in stress. She wanted to run away from the situation. What could he possibly want her help for? She had to figure out a way to get herself, Tristan, and Leon out of this Keep. She had played the Prince's game so far but she also knew she needed to use his apparent need of help to bargain for her brother and Leon's lives.

"What for?" Emerie replied quickly, "Do I even have a choice?"

"Since I like you, I will give you two choices. You can leave this keep with your brother, and your pious friend, or you can stay with me and help me change the Theothen Empire from the inside out. It is your decision," Thurian spoke, offering the options to Emerie calmly. Emerie took a deep breath and rubbed the bruise on her wrist.

"Your friend Leon has already been released. He was not the Arcanist we were looking for. We offered to escort him to the Grand Temple in Arvur but he insisted on continuing his journey as a pilgrimage. Your brother however said he will follow whichever decision you choose," The Prince added to the offer.

"What did you offer Tristan?" Emerie asked.

The Prince smiled at Emerie once again. Emerie ignored the charm it exuded this time. "He asked that I not tell you, should it sway your own decision," Thurian answered honestly.

"Tell me," Emerie demanded. She wasn't going to make any decision that would affect her brother, she never wanted to do that in her life - she was just like Vann in that sense. They both would allow Tristan to guide them ever since they left their village. She wondered if this time, Tristan had made a decision for himself, instead of the both of them.

Emerie felt Thurian's eyes wander across the details of her face, before finally meeting his eyes with hers, "I offered him the same deal. To leave this Keep or to help me change the country that you both believe does not care about its people. I intend to train your brother in swordsmanship personally - The Ethereals know he needs it after his poor display last night. And as a show of good faith, I will even have him be one of my personal guards to learn from some of the best warriors in Arvur."

Arvuria: The Ethereal Children

"What's the catch? How do I help you then? I don't know how to fight," Emerie questioned. She still did not understand what the Prince wanted from her. Thurian hesitated when he opened his mouth, Emerie knew right away she wasn't going to like what he was about to say.

"You will be engaged to me," Thurian answered.

"What?" Emerie answered in a deadpan voice.

"The Court and the Nobility below me are hesitant to follow me in regards to my involvement in the war's beginnings. They favour my sister. I am sure you have heard stories of her. There are people in this Empire who believe in me, people who want things to get better. And it is as you, and probably all 'normal people' say, the Nobility does not care unless it is about themselves. I intend to win the hearts of the people, for them to want me to become the Emperor when my father dies. I need him to see that I am like the man he used to be. That he needs to reinstate me as his rightful heir. Him, The Nobility, and The People... I believe they will be more supportive of me for their own gain if they see that I have fallen in love with you." Thurian explained.

"You want to use me because I am a peasant?" Emerie laughed loudly at the foolish idea. She could not believe the offer that was being made to her, she thought it was some sick joke. He was going to use her because she was a commoner, maybe even less so than that at this point. He was going to trick her people into believing that he was one of them, that he cared for the lower class - but her mind wandered, would he even be rebuilding the farm and giving them a chance to go free if he didn't, at the very least, care about them? He did give them the bag of sovereigns for nothing more than an honest conversation with Vann.

"What of my other friends? The ones who ran away from the farm when your partner burned it all down?" Emerie questioned.

Thurian shook his head, "You mean the child and the two boys with you the other day? Unfortunately I do not know their whereabouts, but should they be found and should they be willing to talk, I am inclined to offer the same to them if I deem they have the abilities to help our cause. If not, I will help them find a home in Arvur nonetheless."

Emerie wanted to ask him about the blonde girl, the Arcanist who was in the comet. She wanted to know if his soldiers had seen her in the barn, even if in passing, but she figured if they didn't know where Vann and Owain were, then they mustn't know that the girl was with them. That's what she hoped. She wanted Vann and Owain with her, her best friends, but she knew that they would not align themselves with Thurian. They had a keen hatred towards royalty and nobility. Vann's father was a politically motivated man with rash ideals, ideals that had been passed down towards him; and Owain, well, he only believes in his friends and his fists.

"I want to see my brother before I make any decision," Emerie demanded with her fingers nervously intertwining with each other. The Prince smiled at her and accepted the request.

"I' will have someone send for you in a moment. They will bring some clean clothes for you to wear - do you have a preferred colour and style?" He asked her.

"Seriously?" Emerie questioned. She hadn't even accepted his offer yet and she felt like it had already been made for her, or maybe Thurian could read her face pretty clearly. Who would say no to the offer before them? She grew up on stories about women changing the world for the better, as well as stories about handsome Princes sweeping women from their feet. But more than that, Thurian was promising her a life that was the complete opposite of the one she has had, she wondered if it was possible for Thurian to bring Uncle Vernon and Aunt Jessy to the capital too - she was sure he'd say no right away but maybe it was something she could order when she was his Princess.

"I like green and yellow," Emerie spoke softly, "And I'm only going to wear a dress on the important occasions. Everyday wear needs to involve trousers, and they need to have pockets."

"You are already acting the part," Thurian smiled. He looked her over once more and Emerie could have sworn that his face went just a hint pinker before he turned to walk towards the door, "I'll see what the maids have for you," he announced as he left the room. Emerie stood before the hearth that Thurian had made warmer for her, the fire crackled slowly and calmly but the heat felt as though it was a message for a brighter future. She walked towards the window of the room to see the sprawl of the trade city where the late morning trade had begun. Where the long road of market stalls ran directly towards the room, Emerie wondered if Thurian had given her this view on purpose, to remind her of the generosity he had shown her yesterday.

After nearly a quarter of an hour quickly vanished, a girl younger than Emerie stood at the doorway with clothes folded in her arms with the pile ending just underneath her eyesight. The small framed girl struggled with the clothes as her quiet voice spoke up, "Lady Emerie, I have your selection."

Emerie hurried towards the girl and took the pile of clothes from the small maid where she then moved them to the bed for the girl who apologised profusely for having Emerie help her.

"I'm sorry. I'm so sorry," the maid apologised, "I will resign and tell the Prince to find a replacement."

"No you don't have to do that, don't worry," Emerie quickly said, attempting to calm the maid down, "It's fine, honestly, I'm happy to help."

The maid looked at her with a quivering lip before composing herself. She stepped past Emerie and began unfolding the clothes on the bed to show Emerie the selection of outfits all in different shades of green with trousers that coloured black and brown.

"Prince Thurian asked me kindly to find a green outfit for you. He said that it had to be green or yellow but I didn't think yellow was the colour of the day so I picked some green garments and some black trousers. But then I didn't know if you liked black so I brought some brown too to give a forest theme - but then I saw this really beautiful all-as-one outfit that was this deep green that I thought would go with the hair Thurian said you have and I wanted to-"

"Calm down," Emerie laughed, "I'll take that one."

The maids' eyes widened just a little bit as she held the all-as-one in her hands. "This one?" she asked nervously.

"Yes," Emerie laughed again, delicately taking it from her maids arms. "What is your name?" Emerie asked.

"Candle," The maid replied, "I know it's a foolish name but it's the one mother gave me."

"It's a lovely name, Candle." Emerie smiled and took the maids hand with one of hers and rubbed it gently with her thumb, "May I ask, what do you think of Prince Thurian?"

Candle pressed her lips together and forced a smile, "I dare not say," she spoke, "He informed me that you two intend to marry. Though I can say the maids are all quite upset by it," Candle snickered a little before remembering Emerie was her boss.

"Why?" Emerie asked.

"Because he is the best looking man to ever step foot into this keep? Have you seen him?" Candle blushed. Emerie began to laugh at the trainee maid and the two of them shared a moment of camaraderie, even if Emerie didn't admit it, she was hesitant to agree with Candle's opinion.

Candle corrected herself, "Do you need help dressing yourself my Lady? Or are you like me and hate when people are watching?" The Maid asked with humour in her tone.

"I'll be fine on my own," Emerie smirked, trying not to enjoy her conversation too much with Candle so as not to potentially get her in trouble. The Maid bowed to her and began refolding the outfits she had displayed on the bed and once she had done so she took the pile and informed Emerie she would return momentarily to escort her to 'Sir Tristan.'

After Emerie had gotten dressed Candle soon reappeared with Tristan's sword in her hands. Before Emerie was able to question it she explained that Thurian was returning it to him, and that he had sharpened and cleaned it for him personally. Emerie was led through a few winding halls and down a staircase, the journey she was taken on was a strange one - each time a maid saw her they would bow towards her, and when she walked past a soldier they would salute with their fingers pointing upwards while saying firmly, "My Lady."

She knew Thurian had gotten the word out intentionally to show her what her life could be like with him, and because of this, she knew the decision that Tristan had made. Candle gave Emerie Tristan's sword and opened the door to his room, "I'll be just outside with these two," she spoke softly as she pointed towards the armoured guards outside of Tristan's room.

Emerie stepped into the room where she saw Tristan run towards her to hold her tightly. He placed her head into his chest where she began struggling to breathe, "By The Ethereals you're alright, you're here. I said I wouldn't make a decision until I saw you."

Emerie let her older brother fuss over her for a few seconds more before she forced an escape from his arms. She looked over him to see that he was also wearing fine clean clothes. He wore a long sleeve white tunic, and a black tabard with the Princes' emblem - the golden skull of a dragon.

"Are you sure you haven't made a decision?" Emerie asked him as she pointed towards his clothing, Tristan in return did the same as he saw his sister in the fine clothes Candle had given her.

"Have you seen Leon?" Emerie asked her brother, "Thurian said he had been released."

"I haven't. Thurian told me the same thing, but I don't see any reason to argue against it when he's offering what he is to us. And besides, Leon has wanted to leave the farm for a while," Tristan spoke, picking at his fingernails.

"The Prince told me what he was going to offer you," Tristan began again, "You would suit being a Princess," he spoke fondly.

Emerie took a seat on the comfortable bed beside her brother and fell backwards into a groan. "Any way that I think about it, it doesn't make sense to not accept the offer. I would be a Princess Tristan, and you would be the Knight that you have always wanted to be. Why would we say no? We even get to help change our country for the better," Emerie answered.

"It isn't like the fairy tales Em, it's going to be dangerous in Arvur. Especially for you. A commoner turned Princess is bound to upset a lot of people," Tristan replied with worry in his tone, "On the other side of the sovereign, you would be a hero to people like us. You would be an idol for them, something to tell them that even the lowest born people can rise to the top. I think it's something admirable if you were to take the offer."

Emerie huffed and sat back up on the bed.

"You say all of that about me, but you would be a commoner who becomes a Princes' Knight. I bet there's a lot of soldiers out there who would try to prove themselves against you," Emerie cautioned.

Tristan nodded. He released his sword from his scabbard and let the sunlight that cascaded across his room bounce against his shining blade.

"Everyone has something to prove," Tristan replied with purpose.

The door to the room opened slowly and Candle's face peaked past the wood cautiously, "I've been told the Drakeship will be arriving soon," she whispered in an attempt to not undermine their conversation which had paused upon her entrance.

"Drakeship?" Tristan questioned with panic.

"They're actually real?!" Emerie questioned with excitement.

Candle took a step back as Emerie raised her voice, catching her off guard. "It's how we will all return to Arvur quickly. Are you scared of heights?" She asked the two of them.

"Heights? Of course not! I've always wanted to go on one of those," Emerie replied, excitement appearing from her even further. Tristan however was growing pale at the thought of riding a ship that sails through the sky.

"Can't I just walk to Arvur?" he muttered.

Candle inhaled with her lips together and cringed, "I'll request a bucket to be placed into your quarters on the ship."

THE DRAKESHIP BEGAN to slowly descend into the open field just outside the Legion's encampment. The hum of the Arcane pipes that ran along the outside of the hull grew louder the closer it came to where Emerie and the others stood waiting. The metallic hull was shaped closely to that of a ship that would sail the seas but where the sails would pull the ship along, the Drakeship had a series of canopies that allowed the wind to pass through them and would move according to the Captain's directions. On the side of the ship were a series four large wings that were flapping to help the ship stay afloat and near the back were a series of exhausts expelling smoke and fire created by two Arcanists firing their power into the pipes that were attached to their arms. The galleon sized ship extended some metallic legs so that the ship would stand flat onto the emerald green grass.

Emerie covered her eyes with an arm as the wind being created battered her face with grass and small stones, "This is incredible!" she shouted to Tristan beside her, her voice just barely carrying amongst the gust before the hum of the ship softened as the ship finished its landing. Tristan was gripping the handle of his sword tightly, Emerie could feel the fear of her brother escape him.

"How high did Thurian say we were going to be?" Tristan asked, his lips quivering, his breath inhaling and exhaling slowly as he tried to remain calm. Emerie took his arm in hers and she began to rub it gently, "As high as a bird flies," Emerie answered with hesitance, "At least you've seen that it's able to land, right?

Arvuria: The Ethereal Children

"Right," Tristan replied.

A metallic ramp unfolded towards the ground where a woman dressed in a red jumpsuit, similar to Emerie's but less fashionable, and a black leather coat with fur in-lining began to saunter towards the royal party. Thurian stood ahead of Emerie, Tristan, and the soldiers and maids that surrounded them. Emerie couldn't hear what Thurian was saying to the peculiar woman but it seemed that she was explaining quite a few things to him, with Thurian only nodding in agreement to what was being said. After a few minutes Thurian led the woman towards her and Tristan. The woman raised her goggles to her forehead and removed the plugs in her ears as she extended a handshake towards Emerie. "Admiral Jaine Holloway, I'll be flying you to Arvur should the Red Dragon permit it. I see you're dressed for the occasion," She introduced herself.

"It's a pleasure to meet you," Emerie answered as she continued to try to comfort Tristan, "This is my brother, one of Princes Thurian's Guardsmen-in-Training, I think. He's nervous, could you say something to help him find some comfort?" She almost begged.

Thurian didn't manage to hide his smirk to Emerie which almost caused her to share one in return at the almost funny sight of Tristan's panic. Jaine smiled at Tristan and wrapped her arm around his shoulder to begin to lead him ahead of the party towards the ramp, "There's nothing to worry about mate. Being on a Drakeship is the safest form of travel, there's no highwaymen to rob us or trees to crash into, right?" she asked Tristan.

"Right," Tristan answered with his nerves still remaining.

"And besides, it's not like we're flying over Ideneor. We tried that once and let me tell you, Zergrath wasn't too happy about it and he ended up incinerating our ships!"

Jaine laughed. "It's Dragon-free land my friend, we'll be fine as long as those slaves pumping their Wisps into the engine don't kick the bucket too soon." she pointed towards the pale and malnutritioned Arcanists whose arms were attached to the engine pipes.

Their voices carried away from Emerie far enough for her to no longer hear them - she could tell, much quicker than Tristan could, that Jaine was trying to get him on the ship before he ran away from it. Thurian watched the comedic view beside Emerie for a moment before an honest laugh released from him. Emerie found it endearing to hear the Prince show a moment of normality, even if it was at the expense of her brother.

"When I spoke with Tristan before I came to you, he seemed so well composed and confident. I did not expect him to be like this so I am sorry for laughing," The Prince apologised to Emerie who stifled her laugh at the comparison.

"Don't apologise, it is pretty humorous seeing him like this for once," Emerie admitted, "And this sounds strange, but it's nice to see that Tristan isn't as perfect as he seems."

Thurian turned to look at her where his smile appeared once more, "We should probably follow them. Should we all get left behind."

Emerie looked over the Drakeship before her - she built up her excitement for her coming life and then took her first step towards it. Thurian followed her closely, and then Candle, and then the rest of the soldiers and maids followed suit. Emerie was surprised to hear her footsteps sounded differently as she walked up the ramp. Instead of the clack on stone or the soft press of grass, her steps sounded like a blacksmith's hammer against metal. It was a new sensation for her, a strange one. Once she and Thurian made it to the deck of the ship they were met with the crew all saluting to The Prince, and to her. Although their uniforms were not clean and certainly not up to regulation, it was inspiring to Emerie to see that they believed in the crown.

"Welcome to the D.S. Fire-Cloud," Jaine spoke loudly, "This is the crew that will be looking after you over the next few days and this handsome gentleman is Esteraswain, my esteemed Co-Pilot," She introduced with admiration in her tone. Beside her was a tall and slender humanoid with grey skin and two pointed prongs on the tip of his ears, his eyes were luminescent blue and he had a sharp bone sticking out from his chin.

Esteraswain removed his tricorn hat and bowed differently than what Emerie had seen before, deeper and at an angle.

"It is an honour, my royalty. If you have any questions regarding the D.S. Fire-Cloud please come and ask," Esteraswain offered.

Emerie watched as Thurian took a few steps forward to shake Jaine's hand, and then Esteraswain's to thank them for welcoming him and his group aboard. After he had done so Jaine hurried up the staircase towards the wheel and the controls that stood beside it.

"Stations!" the Sky-captain roared, "We have been tasked to bring the Prince home. And by The Ethereals that is what the Fire-Cloud will do!"

The crew mates all quickly left the rows they had been standing in and scurried off to their designated stations to perform their tasks. Candle stepped forward to take Emerie's arm to escort towards her quarters, with the other maids quickly hurrying behind them, "There's not enough straps for us to stay on the deck," Candle warned before Emerie could complain that she wanted to watch the take off.

Emerie was led to a small room that sat a bed beside a wall with a circular window sitting just above where the pillows were. She hurried past Candle to jump onto the bed to look out the window, "Come on Candle! This is going to be brilliant," Emerie called over excitedly to her personal maid.

Candle slowly closed the door to the room to remain professional to the guards outside before leaping onto the bed beside Emerie. The two of them shared their view of the small windows and yelped when The Arcane began to move through the pipes outside. Emerie was able to angle her view through the window to see the wing on their side began to slowly flap, pushing and pulling the trees that circled the Fire-Cloud. After a few minutes passed their room began to shake and the view of the ground beneath them began to disappear. Emerie felt Candle's hand envelop hers where she then looked to her maid to see the girl's wide-eye's stare out of the window, "Is this what it's like to be a dragon?" she asked Emerie.

Emerie thought for a moment. It had taken humanity over several hundred years but they had finally equalled themselves to one of the legendary beasts. She wondered if that's why only one of three remaining dragons ever showed itself.

Arvuria: The Ethereal Children

Luke Morgan

- Chapter 12 -
SHIN WATERMAN
How To Send a Message.

Dearest Mathane,

How is your work in Laketown? I hope, despite the war, that tourists are still coming to the beaches of the lake. Is the boat still holding on strong? I must admit that despite how much I complained about our lives, I do miss seeing people enjoy themselves on the boat. Do you remember when a Rhenn visited from up north and gave us some of their liquor while we were supposed to be sailing the rotten thing? I never expected you of all people to laugh at the capsizing of our livelihood - but then again it was your error. I miss those days. As much as I love what I do now, fighting those who would do our old country harm, I think I will always look back to our youth on the crystal blue lake. It keeps me going knowing that I am making you proud Matty.

I know that I have sent you a lot of letters, but this one is important because something incredible happened! I can't tell you all of the details for the safety of myself - but let me tell you this: My Unit fought off against a band of rebels, we were four-to-one at least and when all hope seemed lost Princess Dira herself came to our aid. Princess Dira. Can you believe that?! I knew I was lucky that I was stationed under her banner but I am pretty sure that she even looked at me. She must have looked at me! Maybe this is how I get a promotion. I can't stop thinking about her, I want to be just like her one day.

Anyway, I will write again soon, little brother. After we have destroyed the Rebel Sect near Avane, I hear we might be heading up north so maybe I might be granted leave to visit Laketown on the way. We'll see.

All my love,
Mender S. Waterman.

SHIN PUT DOWN her quill and looked over her written words wondering if what she said was too much or not enough. Every soldier is given an allowance of one letter every two weeks, any more than that comes out of their wages to cover the cost of travel for the Postmasters of The Empire, or to feed the pigeons that they use. Shin would be lying if she told you that she hadn't spent a lot of her wages on keeping her little brother up to date, to let him know that she was still alive.

Luke Morgan

She had cared for Mathane since they were children, but he was the one who forced her to follow her dream of serving as a soldier in The Theothen Empire. If he hadn't, she would have spent the rest of her life selling rides on their small boat that had belonged to their Uncle.

Shin finished reading her letter for the fourth time and rolled it into a scroll and attached some lace around it, adding her name tag and rank, and then finishing it with a cute red bow - she smiled at the thought of her brother sighing at the addition. She then stood up from writing on one of the crates of medical supplies in her room and pushed the entrance flaps of her small tent open, exposing her to the morning air. Before her stood a grand display of The Blood Dragons, Princess Dira's grandiose army of handpicked soldiers, as they went about their daily chores within the campsite that almost rivalled the scale of a small city. The war camp had been set up between Jhonston, Avane, and Beonyth's Laketown so that Dira had the capability of manoeuvring her troops to the many battlefields on the border, while also being close enough to most of the rebel activity near Bayton.

As it was Shin's final day of recovery she was still free of all chores and tasks. She was in her casual clothing, unarmoured with no regalia stating her position - Just a pair of work boots, brown trousers, and her black undershirt. She walked through the many working soldiers who were lifting heavy items and shouting to each other in frustration and jest, and some even fighting to both train and to settle their differences - this army was filled with some of the most vicious warriors in the entire Theothen Empire which Shin always found some kind of twisted humour in as she struggled to even harm a fly. It was her job to keep these adrenaline addicted warriors to live another day, and ever since she had been garnering herself a reputation of being kind and reliable, everyone who knew her had grown to be protective of her. Even the stern and hardened Sergeant Brennan, one of Dira's most trusted Soldiers.

The Mender walked towards the Western stables of the war camp where the postmasters of Theothen were attaching scrolls to their selection of birds and loading up crates of paper to their horse wagons. Shin stood in the small queue of people awaiting her turn to post her letter to her little brother. After a few minutes of waiting she heard a commotion down the main pathway she had just walked through - a crowd of men and women cheering and clapping as Princess Dira once again appeared, dragging a large man behind her as she pulled a rope connected to his legs over her shoulder. She waded through the mud in similar clothing to Shin, but instead wore a red vest exposing the well-trained muscularity of her body. She could meet the strength of a bear with ease.

"Traitor!" Some of the soldiers shouted to the man that Dira dragged through the mud - some spitting on the man and throwing food and other unwanted items at him.

"What's going on?" Shin turned back to the postmaster as she stepped up for her turn. The older man with his brown singlet uniform and white beret took her scroll, read the name tag, and threw the paper into a sack behind him.

"He was leaking information to the Resnian's," The Postmaster said, "That's what someone from the Northern section told me anyway."

"So Princess Dira is dragging him throughout the entire camp?" Shin asked astounded, with admiration.

The postmaster scoffed and laughed, "Indeed. She is drowning him in the mud. If she is trying to make an example out of the traitor, it is most certainly working."

"Yeah…" Shin agreed as she took delicate steps away from the postmaster, towards the large crowd that cheered for their Princess. She couldn't help but keep her eyes on the woman who had saved her and her Squad two days prior - it felt like she was watching some kind of mythical creature right in front of her. Shin's eyes were piercing through the crowd to get a glimpse of Dira - she ran ahead of the groups and lined up amongst the men who were pushing and shoving each other to also catch a glimpse of the notoriously brutal Princess - Shin pushed her small body through to the front where she saw the woman just a few feet ahead of her. Her clothes wet, muddy and becoming baggy; Her scars were placed all over her exposed arms, neck, and face - her blind right eye prominent white against the dirt that had been splattered over her face. The determination on her was extremely prevalent underneath the short black hair that ruffled over her sight. She was going to kill the traitor this way. No matter how long it took.

Shin's nerves shocked her entire body when Dira's gaze strayed from its constant path forward to look at her, where a minuscule hint of a smile appeared on the lips of The Princess.

Shin stood as a statue amongst the ruckus of the crowd around her that continued to enjoy the display of the slow murder. The Princess had just acknowledged her. This was the greatest day of Shin's life.

Arvuria: The Ethereal Children

- Chapter 13 -
VANN ERENDON
Cold-Blooded.

VANN LOOKED INTO the sky to see the metallic black ship in the distance had grown smaller. He had heard rumours in passing, when he had visited Avane, that the Empire had created weapons to rival dragons - and a way to finally meet the aerial challenge of Resnia's Lyger Riders. Looking at the aerial fortress before him, he wondered if the war that Theothen had been losing was now going to turn itself around.

"They call it a Drakeship, they believe themselves on par to a Dragon," Harnon announced as he led the way through the path in the woods. He carried over his shoulders his longsword that was wrapped in dirty leathers instead of it being placed in a scabbard.

Arvuria: The Ethereal Children

"Don't you think they are?" Owain asked curiously, "Look at that monster, we can even see it from here."

"Nothing compares to one of The Five Dragons. Only one of their Chosen could do harm to another."

"A Chosen?" Owain asked, "They're just fairy tale horseshit."

"An open mind would do you some good, Red. You are a strong man, with what seems to be a stout heart. Do not waste it on being a fool," Harnon spoke clearly as he led the teenagers.

Before the redhead could retaliate Vann patted Owain on his back to silently tell him that they needed to not piss off the man trying to take them to safety. They had been following the Marauder known as Harnon for three days; He hadn't spoken to them much other than a few statements and insults that were passed their way. Vann had come to the conclusion that Harnon didn't care about him or Owain, but was simply putting up with them because he knew that Arvuria would not leave them behind. He had tried speaking to the older man a few times but was usually only met with a cold stare, but then again, Vann knew he hadn't given the best first impression at the campfire.

Vann's worries were focused elsewhere, he did not spend his feelings on the dislike Harnon openly shared. Arvuria had grown less confident and outgoing each day that had come and gone - despite Vann's attempts of cheering the girl up it was obvious to him that she felt as he and Owain did. They were all worried about what would happen when they got to Beonyth's Laketown. Arvuria was insistent that 'Borrenthus' was powerful enough to help them but Vann and Owain had been wondering if she hadn't remembered her unclear dreams correctly. An easy assessment. Vann's worries were for Arvuria herself more than anything at the moment, he didn't want her to be disappointed with the man they were all now seeking aid from, he had found her innocence endearing at the beginning of their friendship but at some point the harsh reality of the world was going to crash around her - there was only so much that he could do to protect her from it.

Vann's eyes raised from the ground beneath him where he noticed that Martell was dragging his feet behind Arvuria. He was sulking. The young boy had asked Owain last night if he was ever going to see Leon again. Owain promised the Martell that they would all see each other very soon but the boy had only seemed more solemn since then. Vann scurried behind Martell and lifted him from the ground, the squire giggled as he was placed onto Vann's shoulders where the teenager began to spin around in circles causing Martell to giggle in excitement as the world spun around him.

"Stop it Vann, stop it!" Martell laughed, his hands beginning to cover the eyes of Vann.

"Oh no it's a magic tornado," Owain called out, "I'll save you!" he shouted quietly before lifting him from Vann's shoulders to begin carrying him in the air as if Martell was flying.

Martell continued to laugh as he outstretched his arms as if they were wings, "Look Arvuria, I'm a Lyger!" he cheered.

Vann's heart warmed as he saw that Arvuria was smiling again at the sight of the boys having fun. Harnon however stood with a tired face, waiting for them to end their distraction. The Girl walked towards the flying Martell and took him from Owain's arms where she began to cuddle him, "You have found safety," she laughed as she lifted him up a little bit to carry him more comfortably. The two solemn Wisps were happier now, for the moment.

Arvuria: The Ethereal Children

Vann caught Harnon's drooped pointed ears perk up as he heard something in the distance. Vann followed his guardian's gaze as it turned to the East side of their path where the older warrior lifted his longsword from his shoulders and let the wrapped leathers unravel around the blade.

"Protect the kid and stay hidden," he pointed Vann and Arvuria to the western side of the dirt path. Arvuria carried Martell to the largest tree near them and Vann followed suit with his hand on his sword's hilt as always.

"I can help, what's coming?" Owain asked Harnon as he placed the large rucksack onto the ground and pulled his Mace from the side of it. He gently jolted the heavy weapon into the air instead of lifting it and caught in his meaty palms. Vann watched Harnon shrug towards Owain before motioning with a hand for him to stay back a few feet.

"It's Levia. It's chasing the footsteps of four men, you should see them any moment now," Harnon informed. The Marauder then looked over his shoulder and pointed to Vann once more, "Anything comes near Arvuria or the kid, you kill them or we're fucked. If the Empire finds out we have the girl, they will stop at nothing to retrieve her."

A few seconds passed. Just a few moments of silence until, through the tree line, four Theothen soldiers being chased by a giant brown-splotched Reptile arrived with speed. The Levia towered almost as high as the trees it ran through. It was barrelling towards them on its hind legs as its arms attempted to reach out towards the soldiers in front of it- it succeeded in grabbing one of its prey to take one large bite from the body it claimed before it slurped the rest of the body down its gullet with ease.

"Help us!" One of the soldiers called out to Harnon. The Marauder waited for the soldiers to run through the treeline before he bolted towards the Levia. Owain stayed behind to make sure that the soldiers were okay and unharmed - two of the three collapsed to the ground in exhaustion as they tried to reclaim what energy they could while Harnon began to engage the monster.

The Levia stepped over the small dip that ended the treeline where Harnon met it with a clean swing of his sword. His blade glided across the tough hide of its left hind leg and ran up the scales causing barely a scratch. Vann watched as the Levia stumbled forward at the dip where it collected itself just in front of Owain and the soldiers, it could have claimed all four lives there but it was clear that Harnon had succeeded in getting the Reptile monster's attention. Harnon braced his longsword in front of him with the sword pointing towards the monster - where Vann then saw a genuine smile on Harnon's usually grizzled face. The Levia stepped forward and went to swipe Harnon with its long spindly arms which Harnon managed to duck under it with haste, tapping his blade onto the Lizard's skin multiple times, creating small irritating cuts. The sound of his sword clanging against the scales rang quietly underneath the roar of the Levia.

"I can help him," Arvuria whispered to Vann. Vann pressed a finger over his lips to hush her as he watched the Marauder do battle with the monster before them.

"The soldiers can't see you," Vann answered quietly, "He has me and Owain if he needs us."

The Soldiers that were retrieving their own energy beside Owain began to stand back up from the floor causing Vann's attention to shift to them, they began to push Owain towards Levia, "Go help him!" They ordered him, "Cover our escape!"

Owain, being Owain, pushed them backwards with his mace in hands.

"Fucking Cowards, help us!" he spat back at them. He hated soldiers. All of them knew the extent that he would go to avoid them because he could not hold his anger in.

"Not now Owain," Vann muttered to himself, hoping that his friend wouldn't have to defend himself. Vann's gaze turned back to Harnon who was now mounting the Levia with his longsword in one hand and a dagger indented into its back as he was flung around the air as if he was riding a steed that was sick of its rider.

"Go! Do your duty, peasant!" One of the Soldiers shouted towards Owain. He drew his blade towards the teenager and pushed him one more time towards the Levia -all the while the other two soldiers began to move in the direction of Vann, Arvuria, and Martell. Owain's mace connected with the head of the soldier pushing him, knocking him towards the ground and splattering his face. His brain met the stones beneath them. One of the remaining soldiers in anger at the sight unsheathed his sword and began to duel the redheaded teenager who parried and began to meet the blade. The last remaining soldier ran towards the group behind the tree. He was trying to flee.

"There's no honour in this," The fleeing soldier bellowed as he ran.

"Keep Martell with you," Vann ordered Arvuria as he prepared himself to draw his fathers sword. The blade escaped its scabbard a few inches before he hesitated using it once more, he couldn't. He instead opted to try to tackle the fleeing soldier as he ran past the tree they were hiding behind. The soldier spotted the group and stopped in his tracks with recognition in his eyes as he saw Arvuria.

"A blonde girl…" the soldier muttered - but before he had a chance to draw his own weapon to secure the target he had stumbled upon, Vann speared forward and tackled the soldier. The victim yelped and began attacking Vann with his fists, clobbering and scratching at the teenager who was trying to subdue him without the need of violence.

"Calm down," Vann ordered as he grappled the frightened man, "I'm not trying to harm you!"

"Get off of me you little rat, I'll kill you!" The soldier threatened, his right arm reached downward towards a dagger at his belt. Vann struck the soldier's bruised face with a clean punch as he heard the dagger begin to escape the leather it sat in. The small blade dropped from the hands of his enemy where he followed by lifting the soldier up a few inches from the ground as he held his collar, "Fucking stop!" Vann warned, a scratch bleeding from his cheek.

"Let me go," The soldier begged, "I won't tell anyone about this I swear. It was the Levia who killed them, not you. I never even saw the girl!"

The Levia screeched in the distance as Harnon wounded it further.

Vann looked over his shoulder to see Arvuria staring at the battle between him and this man on the grass while she hid Martell's face against her chest. He wanted her to tell him what to do, as Tristan would have, but he couldn't read her face. He didn't know what the right option was. He felt his quarry's body move once more underneath him to see the dagger in the hand of his enemy once again. Vann grasped the forearm of his opponent and twisted it backward, almost snapping the arm from the elbow with strength he didn't know he had - the blade of the weapon sliced into the top of Vann's arm, giving him a flesh wound as it fell into the grass once more. He picked up the weapon and roared as he buried it into the chest of the helpless man underneath him. A man who moments ago was running away from a monster.

Arvuria: The Ethereal Children

The world slowed down at that moment, everything but the soldier became blurred. He felt every vibration of the blade shattering the bones of the soldier's chest, he felt the steel pierce the organs inside. His gaze met the frightened eyes of the older man underneath him, whose hand reached to Vann's head, grasping his hair but he was not able to wield the strength to raise the arm for long. Vann couldn't hear anything other than his breath which was hesitant to leave him after what he had just done. He didn't have a choice. No, the soldier didn't give him a choice. So it couldn't have been murder - it was self-defence. If the soldier had escaped he would have told his superiors that he saw Arvuria, and then they would know where they were and where they were headed. He could only find Emerie and the others if he got Arvuria to Beonyth's Laketown safely, and he knew that he would have to do things that he didn't like. He had to steel himself, it was self-defence, there was justice in killing this man, he needed to die or Vann was at risk of losing everything.

"Vann," he heard a muffled voice say.

He then felt the unfamiliar touch of Harnon who rubbed his back as he tried to console him. "You did well," Harnon spoke.

Vann's vision became clearer once more as he looked at the grizzled man who had slain the Levia, with his friends standing behind him.

"Are we all safe?" Vann asked his friends with a croak shattering his voice. Harnon forced a smile to him, "We're safe. Are you okay?"

Vann nodded. His eyes were dry but they wanted to burst into tears, the urge to vomit sat in his stomach but he managed to at least calm that part of himself. Harnon and Owain lifted him from the corpse and placed him at the tree beside Arvuria who enveloped him with her arms.

Vann could feel the stare of Harnon as he cried into Arvuria's shoulder - he couldn't tell if the Marauder was disgusted by his heartbreak or somehow admired it. Harnon knelt down next to him, "I know it's hard to cross that line, but if you're going to keep your friends safe, you need to come to terms that you will kill others - whether they deserve it or not is not up to you, it's up to them," he pointed towards the sky, towards the The First Layer where the Ethereals live. "There is no story that you can write in this land that isn't inked in the blood of your enemies. Remember that, and you might keep your friends alive."

"I didn't use my fathers sword," Vann mumbled, "He would have been ashamed of me."

"Kid, no father would be ashamed of their Son protecting others, believe me," Harnon shook his head in disbelief over what Vann worried about. "If you're so concerned with using your fathers sword, take mine," Harnon offered, holding out the longsword that was covered in the black blood of the Levia. "This blade has already been stained by countless lives, there is no legacy for you to tarnish," Harnon whispered to him.

Vann held out his hand dismissively towards the sword that Harnon handed towards him, "You honour me but I can't accept it. I must be the man my father believes I am... I want to be who he believes I can be."

"I understand," Harnon nodded respectfully, "But the more you respect your father's sword, the more you will be hesitant to use it. Do not make its legacy one of loss. Make it one of protection."

Arvuria: The Ethereal Children

Luke Morgan

- Chapter 14 -
VANN ERENDON
Beonyth's Laketown.

DAYS OF TRAVEL passed until they saw the edge of Anelli's Tears, the lake aptly named after the event that gave birth to The Golden Dragon over six-hundred years ago.

The group travelled an hour further up the pathway where they followed and crossed paths with merchants and travellers who were looking to flog their goods at Beonyth's Laketown before the war had a chance to hinder their trade. Beonyth's Laketown sat at the base of a green mountain where the lake's shores rested as an amenity for the beach-goers that would lie underneath the Spring sun. Around the white-sand beach were wooden houses for the tourists and travellers to use, but further into the Laketown was where the Limestone buildings began to appear - Laketown was known not just for being the birthplace of Arvur, but also as an architectural marvel with how condensed the city was with such a large population.

Vann had been under the watchful eye of Owain who had been spending the days following the Levia's attack trying to cheer him up. Vann appreciated his friends' attempts, and he appreciated how they got worse as the days went by, but Vann knew that he had to come to terms that he had killed someone and that would forever be a scar in his heart. He knew that he would have to take more lives to save the ones dear to him. Harnon had started to grow just a little bit more caring towards him and Owain. He could see why Harnon liked Owain since he was ready with his mace right away and had no trouble fighting when the need called for it. Whereas Vann considered that Harnon simply worried over him because of how he acted after the death of the soldier. He felt weak. Vann almost wanted to prove to Harnon that he could be a warrior like he was - a man capable of fighting a twenty foot tall reptile and come out unscathed.

As he was deep in thought, he felt Arvuria's hand carefully grip the sleeve of his coat as she stood beside him, "I think I am scared," Arvuria whispered to him.

Vann turned his head to Arvuria and gave her a meek smile, "I think I am too, to be honest."

The two teenagers walked beside each other until the end of the road where they were let into the city with no check after the section of guardsmen saw that they were all with Harnon. Vann wanted to question it after being so used to the hassle of queuing up and having your location verified at Avane but he was far from the mood of being inquisitorial. Harnon was Harnon - it was easier to leave it at that. After just days with him Vann had realised there was a lot more to the man than he was letting on.

The Marauder led the teenagers and Martell through winding alleyways and compact bustling streets until he stopped at a tavern with a sign that had a dragon's eye amongst some leaves - Melodies of Trees was the name that sat on the sign. Harnon opened the door and motioned for the teenagers to enter the building. Vann walked into the tavern before Arvuria and the others, he turned from the hot and stuffy entrance way and walked through the second door where he was met with music, dancing, and revelry. Something he had never experienced all at once, especially to this scale. It was overwhelming, his heart began to pulsate and his chest grew tight.

The bar was the length of the entire wall to his right with at least fifteen bar workers all attempting to serve the swath of crowds gathering along the wood. There was a section of tables to the left of him stationed on a platform three steps above the floor where groups of families and friends were feasting on all kinds of meals. In the open space of the centre was a chandelier providing light for those opting to dance underneath it with a performance of bards on stage at the far side of the room. Behind the bars stood triangular boxes of metal amplifying the sound of the vocals and the strings of the bards to fill across the room that was louder than the hustle and bustle of the city outside. Around the high ceiling were platforms running along the sides where more tables and stools were placed for those who wanted a good view of the fun underneath.

"Never been to a Tavern before?" Harnon asked as he patted Vann on the back to gently push him forward.

Vann looked at Harnon with a hint of concern, "Borrenthus is here?" he asked.

The Marauder scrunched up his nose and sniffed, turning his head towards the bar, and then to an open table to the left, "I'm hungry. Go sit over there," he pointed. The Teenagers followed the Marauders orders and took a seat at the sticky table. Beside them was a family enjoying a meal together and on the other side of them was a rambunctious group of lads just a few years older than them enjoying their evening a bit too much volume for his liking..

Vann looked to Owain whose energy seemed to have perked back up by being surrounded by the happy energy of the people around them, "This is incredible," Owain gleamed, "Do you think he'll let us dance?"

"Dance?" Arvuria asked, "I do not know how to do that, but I will watch."

"You don't know how to dance?" Owain looked at Arvuria, his mouth agape with surprise on his face, "I could teach you!"

Martell pulled on Vann's coat, "I don't like the music. The beat doesn't make sense," he complained. Vann gave the boy a little laugh and ruffled his hair, "Try and enjoy it nonetheless. We are used to Tristan's singing, I'm sure this must be better."

"Did Harnon say to either of you why he was going to bring us here?" Vann questioned Arvuria and Owain, "It seems a little strange to have us enter a tavern when The Empire seems to still be after us. That soldier I…he recognised Arvuria, they must know she came from the inferno," Vann theorised but regretted doing so when he saw Arvuria's excitement fade a little upon hearing that she was a danger to her friends.

Owain tapped his finger to his cheek as he thought of an answer to Vann's question, "Maybe he really is just hungry? Besides, he killed a Levia single-handedly, I'm sure he could fight half of this tavern before breaking a sweat. He's insane."

Vann looked behind Owain's seat to see that Harnon had been served ahead of the crowd by a barman and had now begun to walk towards them with three tankards in one hand and two cups stacked onto each other in the spare hand. He walked up the three steps towards them and then placed the drinks heavily onto the table.

"Your parents let you drink before?" He asked Vann and Owain - the two boys nodded. Harnon moved a tankard to Owain and then to Vann, where the latter held onto the handle and swigged a sip of the beer quickly, his top lips grimaced to his nose as he tried to enjoy its flavour. Vann placed the tankard back onto the table to see Harnon hand a cup to Martell and two Arvuria, "One is strawberry juice and the other is Wine. I doubt the Wine will affect you no matter how much you drink," Harnon slipped up to Arvuria.

"Why wouldn't wine affect her?" Owain asked, curious as to why it wouldn't get Arvuria tipsy at the least, not because Harnon seemed to have messed up.

"Because it is just one cup," Harnon replied, "I'm sorry it's not in a glass, I couldn't carry it all if it were. It's a bad idea to leave drinks alone here because some scavenger will drink it for you."

The group of five sat quietly and awkwardly for a few minutes as they all attempted to enjoy their drinks. Harnon finished his quickly and replaced it with another - once again being served right away by the same Barman.

"Why does he keep serving you despite the large crowd waiting before you?" Vann asked with an innocent tone but one clear enough that it was obvious he was trying to figure Harnon out.

The Marauder sighed and polished off his new tankard quickly. He then stood up and motioned with a flick of his hand for the teenagers to do the same, "It's about that time anyway," he complained, "Bring your drinks if you want to finish them, just don't spill them on anyone."

Vann followed Harnon with Arvuria closely behind him with Owain holding Martell in his arms as they followed in suit. They were taken through the edge of the dance floor and led to a singular door that was placed in the left corner of the room where one large built man was stood on one side, and a slender grey-skinned Rhenn with his long pointed ears and boned jawline stood on the other side. Harnon walked past them, leading the teenagers through the door as the bouncers stared them down. Following the doorway was a small staircase that led down to another room, it was quarter the size of the room they had just left, with only a few people sitting down at the small bar and a group of three people discussing something around a round table in the centre. All of the patrons in this lounge turned to look at Vann and his group as their footsteps sounded onto the stone floor once they had finished their descent.

Vann noticed that everyone in this room were wearing emerald green pieces of armour and all wore a brown cape similar to Harnon's. His curiosity peaked and his mind began to search it's echoing depths for the familiarity it gave him.

The long blonde-haired man behind the bar whipped his small towel over his shoulder and leaned against the counter in front of him, "Lyra's furious with you Harnon. You've really mucked things up," he announced with his enunciated words.

Harnon laughed and walked over towards the barman, clapping their hands together as they greeted one another, "Where is the tyrant?" He asked the barman.

"The Tyrant waits for you to introduce your friends," a commanding voice spoke from the table shadowed in the corner. Vann's gaze cautiously turned towards the corner of the room where a series of dim candles along the stone wall illuminated the Ideneorian woman in the corner. Her emerald green leather armour hugged her silhouette and her black locks of hair draped over her shoulders - her armour was sleeveless, much like Harnon's and though the style of the armour had similarities, the woman wore no chain mail underneath. Her leathers were a verdant green of such colour you would only find in the most beautiful of forests. Vann recalled what he was trying to remember now. A group clad in green. Only a certain group of people in Beonyth's Laketown were spoken of to wear such a colour: 'The Glades' an incredible guild that have stood as staunch protector of Beonyth's Green and his Laketown. Vann was never sure if they existed but he grew up on many tales of their valour - stories that his father would tell him when he was young and could not sleep.

"Lyra, sweetheart," Harnon called out to the presence in the corner, "Your voice seems as though it is filled with more stress than usual."

"It's been five months," Lyra stated, "You left us with no warning and I had to step up. We almost lost everything we had built."

Vann felt the urge to step forward, to introduce himself and his friends before Harnon would cause problems with his newly witnessed diplomatic skills. Vann had been travelling with Harnon for nearly a week and he hadn't mentioned what would happen when they got to Beonyth's Laketown, only that he would get them to Borrenthus.

"Is that the girl?" Lyra asked out loud as she directed her tone towards Vann and his friends just as much as she was speaking towards Harnon.

Vann stepped forward in front of Arvuria, "Where is Borrenthus?" he demanded, "My friend is trying to get to him. She says he can help us."

The Ideneorian in the corner stood up from her seat and moved out of the dim light. Her gaze was threatening, an intentional display as her eyes peered towards Vann underneath the lines of her green face paint that drew horizontal across her eyes.

"You must be the boy who discovered her first," Lyra spoke with a monotone voice before she stood in front of Vann. She extended a hand towards him, "You have my gratitude," she thanked, waiting for Vann to grasp her hand which he did so earnestly.

"So, where is Borrenthus?" Vann asked her.

Lyra's eyes turned towards Arvuria, she ignored the question and stepped past Vann before she looked the girl up and down, analysing every inch of her, "You are as Borrenthus says you would be."

Vann smiled when he saw Arvuria's worried face grow confident, "I want to see my Uncle," Arvuria demanded. "We have travelled far and without much rest for my friends. They are hungry and they are tired. I ask that you feed them and give them a place to stay for the time being. While they remain here Harnon will take me to my Uncle."

"I will go with you two," Vann added. There was no way that he was going to let Arvuria be alone in the city, even if it was with Harnon who had proven his worth to them. Vann was unsure as to whether Lyra could be trusted, but he was even less certain about this mysterious Borrenthus - and he partly wanted to be there with Arvuria to ask for this man's help in finding his friends in person.

Lyra released a huff and reached into her pocket where she passed to Harnon an Emerald-like gem that had been shaped into a thick triangle. Harnon hesitated to take it from her for a moment before taking hold of it, "I was told that all I had to do was bring them here, and that you would bring them to him. You know I want nothing to do with that old lizard, and I want nothing to do with The Glades. The Guild isn't mine anymore, it's yours."

Lyra smiled to him as if she had finally caught him out, "You have a habit of finding strays - you've earned their trust as you did mine. So make sure you bring them to Borrenthus for they will not go otherwise. A word of warning, he's been asking about you ever since you left."

VANN'S CURIOSITY WAS ignored by Harnon for the rest of the night after he had quickly relented to Lyra's order of bringing them to Borrenthus. Harnon left the teenagers to their own entertainment or rest and headed back to the revelry upstairs. Lyra brought them through winding hallways that sat underneath the tavern; it almost felt like an underground city to Vann, but Lyra described it as a secret community for her guild. She didn't answer any of Vann's or Owain's questions either. As soon as Lyra had given them all a room to sleep in, they were left alone - they had the freedom to leave which Owain and Martell tested when they needed to relieve themselves of the drinks Harnon had bought them earlier; so they didn't feel as though they were being imprisoned in any way. Although, they certainly didn't feel like they had many options.

Vann unbuckled his belt from his waist and placed his father's sword next to the frame of his chosen bed. The sword sat beside the wood of the furniture and the damp stone of the wall. His father's gift was a standard issue sword given to the common soldiers of Theothen, differing only from the regulation as his father and wrapped a blue-dyed leather around the handle of the sword. He compared it in his mind to Harnon's, whose weapon was notched and scratched with history along the metal, with the handle of the sword having a dark wooden finish and a green gem, similar to the one Lyra had given him, sitting in the pommel.

"Do you think I will need to learn how to use a weapon such as those?" Arvuria asked as she sat comfortable in her bed with the sheets covering her. She had created a little wall of safety from the world outside her shelter.

Vann looked over to her and shook his head, "I don't think so. With the power you have, I don't see why you would need to."

Vann's mood grew sombre as he heard Arvuria's next words escape her, "But what if I hurt someone with my power? I've been scared ever since I saved you from that monster in the smoke. My fear has become worse since I saw you fight the soldier. I wanted to help you, but what if I burned you? Or our friends? I would never have forgiven myself."

Vann walked over to Arvuria and sat just beside her on the mattress, "You haven't hurt me, Owain, Martell, or anyone else and we'll find the others we just need-"

"I am the reason that you have lost the other half of your friends. I may likely be new to this world, but I am no fool. It is my memories that blur, not my Wisp." Arvuria interrupted.

Vann tilted his head, "What do you mean you might be 'new to this world'? You are as aged as I am. Yes, you came from the meteor, but you're as human as I am."

Vann couldn't quite understand Arvuria's meaning. The sheets she was using to protect herself from the cold underground moved tighter around her body as she attempted to find some shelter from Vann's questioning.

"Arvuria, you can talk to me," Vann whispered as he tried to invite her confidence

Arvuria buried her face into her hands and groaned in frustration. After she had complained to herself in this manner her eyes met Vann's, "Remember the lake we walked past earlier? When I saw the water of Anelli's Tears, a feeling of longing washed over me of a home I had lost, deep within the waters - and part of my memories returned to me. I remember watching the land we stand on now - I remember watching it from a platform far past the sky with a woman whose face I can recall yet her name escapes me Then you walked in front of me, and in that moment I sought your comfort in the stead of my longing."

Vann listened to Arvuria intently, it was the most she had spoken about herself since the cave. She had been reluctant to act or to let any of them in after that first day she had woken up - Vann didn't quite believe that this was the only memory that she had collected since then, but the information that came with it was too much for Vann to conceptualise. Was she really telling him that she was from The First Layer? It was the only land past the barrier of the sky.

"So you're saying, you were raised by one of The Ethereals?" Vann asked her with weight in his voice, but Arvuria gave no reply to him. The girl simply shook her head and turned away from him to begin facing the walls.

"Do you want me to come with you when you will meet your Uncle?" Vann asked delicately. Arvuria's silence remained but he saw her nod her head. Vann in return placed his hand onto her covered arm and patted it awkwardly as he sat unsure of how to act.

Arvuria: The Ethereal Children

- Chapter 15 -
VANN ERENDON
Tears in The Water.

A DAY TO themselves, a day to be teenagers once again with their worries at the back of their minds - buried deep away as much as possible. Harnon and The Glades had offered them a day of rest, some time to enjoy themselves while they planned the journey to Borrenthus.

Vann walked behind Arvuria and Owain and smiled to himself. After all that they had been through so far, they were finally safe. They had made it to Beonyth's Laketown.

Vann's eyes scanned the surroundings of the limestone buildings that glowed brighter under the warm blanket of the sun with the heat that emanated from the stone walls and the roads seeping into him, forcing him to feel a sense of happiness - he couldn't help it. Ahead of the long cobbled road, down a bouncing road, you could see Anelli's Tears in the distance once again where the crystal blue lake sat calmly with its colour clashing against the orange stone buildings before them and the dense forest of Beonyth's Green in the background of the blue.

The sight grew more beautiful when Arvuria looked over her shoulder to him and smiled something delicate. After their conversation last night, he was so glad to see she was feeling better - she always seemed to live her life to the fullest. Vann's chest swelled but he quickly collected himself as Arvuria nodded her head towards the lake, "Shall we go there?" she beamed with a smile so wide it closed her eyes.

He wondered if it was a good idea after what she had told him the night before - and it was quite a ways out, if they were to go there they would not get back to the Inn until nightfall… but wouldn't it be fun to swim in the lake? He smiled back to his friend, "If Owain wants to, sure."

The broad redhead raised his arms in triumph "I knew he would say yes if you asked him Ria!"

"Ria?" Arvuria asked, "Are you giving me a new name?"

Owain laughed, "It's your same name, it is just that 'Arvuria' is quite a mouthful sometimes."

The Meteor Girl quickly stepped towards Owain and jumped onto his back with laughter, "I like it Owa."

"Owa is absolutely not sticking."

Vann hurried to be beside the other two, and lightly slapped Owain's shoulder as he caught up, "Come on Owa, I think it suits you," he teased.

"By the Thirteen…" Owain rolled his eyes and lifted Arvuria more comfortably on his back, "Fine… But only Arvuria is allowed to say it."

"Deal," Arvuria and Vann laughed together.

Luke Morgan

This is nice. Was all Vann could think to himself. He felt swelling in his chest once again and he wasn't sure if tears were going to arrive to his eyes or if he was just content. Though, this feeling soon stopped when he remembered the last time he felt like this in Avane… instead of being with Arvuria, he was with Emerie. His brow furrowed as was his habit when he became deep in thought. He was still going to find her, Tristan, and Leon. Arvuria was going to help him after all, but he didn't want to feel guilty by being able to enjoy a day of respite - they would have wanted him and the others to take a breather. Emerie would have told him to enjoy himself, she had always been the one to try to get him into Avane more than the others. She always tried to bring him out of his shell. He smiled to himself again when he remembered their kiss. He will find her again. He had promised her though she hadn't heard it.

"So where to go first? Shall we head to the lake or shall we get some food, maybe even buy some trinkets?" Owain asked with a grin that silently informed the others they would be doing all three no matter what their answer would be.

"I am interested in trinkets!" Arvuria announced, "I would like to purchase something to remember today by."

"Owain is in charge of the coin," Vann responded to her, "You will have to persuade him, or he will spend it all on fried pork."

"I see no issue in pursuing my culinary favourites," Owain answered. He looked above his shoulder to see Arvuria's mischievous smirk as she remained on his back, "I have never eaten Fried Pork…"

Owain was shocked, "You are absolutely going to try Fried Pork!"

Vann's stomach grumbled at the thought of the crispy outer layer of the meat. "I will have some too," he spoke in agreement as his nose led him towards the market stand at the bottom of the cobbled road where tourists would purchase overpriced food and items before heading to the white sanded beach around the lake.

The group of three eventually found themselves at the stone arch that separated Laketown and the beach of Anelli's Tears where Vann looked around to see all sorts of people and markets. There were stalls selling Ideneorian clothing which were perfect for the summer heat, they were always the most breathable under hot conditions. There was also Everrian sea jewellery, created with shells and gems found in their waters, and then you had the standard Resnian and Theothen styles of clothing and trinkets that you could find most in most cities for sale too.

"This is just like Avane," Vann said to Arvuria as they waited for Owain to grab some Fried Pork Skewers from an Everrian stand.

"Owain, ask if they can wrap some so we can take some back to Martell!" He called over towards his friend as he queued up for the food. Owain lifted a thumb in the air as he waited to order - he was looking at the at the menu sign where underneath sat a flyer for what Vann could make out to be for a performance for some musical band.

"I never got the chance to visit the City of Avane, but I am glad to spend this moment with you and Owain,," Arvuria smiled, "For me, this is my first experience being a normal person."

Vann hadn't even realised. He had been so inside his own head trying to ignore his guilt, that he hadn't focused as much as he should have on giving Arvuria a day for her to remember. He was getting very tired of his own worries encroaching on how he would treat his friends.

"I didn't see!" Vann blurted out, his voice loud for the first time in quite a few weeks. "Owain and I will make this the best day. I promise," he apologised, bowing his head a little as he waited for Arvuria to accept his apology but all she did in return was tilt her own head down to look up to him.

"There is nothing to apologise for Vann, if you did not realise then that means I am doing a good job in being normal. Isn't that so?" She smiled thinly.

"Yes," Vann answered as he lifted his head back up, "You are doing better than I at this moment that's for sure."

The two of them stood awkwardly for a few moments, as if it was the first time they were meeting one another as they both waited for the other to speak.

"I leave you two alone for five minutes and you get weird. It ain't that hard to use your words," Owain teased as he slowly moved the Fried Pork Skewers in front of their faces. Both Vann and Arvuria's faces lit up in excitement as they took hold of the two skewers he had got each of them, as he held four for himself.

"I won't lie to you, I may have spent a few too many Drakes on these, but they're good," Owain mumbled with a mouthful of food.

Arvuria bounced with joy as she bit into the first chunk she had ripped from the wooden rod, "This is so good!" she pumped her fist downwards imitating what Martell would do when he ate. She was right, it was good. Vann took a moment to enjoy the succulent taste of the meat with its crispy outer shell, he almost couldn't stop chewing it, he didn't want to. It was the best taste all three of them had had in months, well, for him and Owain at least.

Arvuria: The Ethereal Children

"Get me on that beach now," Vann sighed happily as he finished his pork skewer alongside Arvuria, and Owain who had managed to devour four of them at the same time.

Arvuria linked her arm with his and pulled him through the stone wall arch that led towards the white sand, "Come on Owain!" she shouted over her shoulder. Vann stumbled for the first few steps as his friend led ahead of him where he struggled to match her pace for a few moments, but when he collected his footing their stride was almost perfectly in sync as their collective boots hit the soft silky sand of Anelli's Tears.

"Wait!" Arvuria stopped quickly as she finished her first five steps on the sand. "I do not like this. The texture of this ground feels weird."

"It's Sand, Ria. It's soft," Owain stated.

"I know this now, but I thought it would be like soft mud. I have been enjoying walking on that," Arvuria announced, "This feels as though I am to sink into the depths underneath."

Vann couldn't help but release a genuine laugh as he stood a few steps before her. Everyday Arvuria would come across something in their world that would confuse her, and for the most part it would make sense. It reminded him of when she came across a Snail for the first time - she thought it was a wandering merchant in the animal world, but when she saw that it was incredibly slow, she started talking about how snails do not make sense as a merchant. Vann had been finding the strength to not laugh at her so far, but in this moment it had all finally boiled up to the point where tears of happiness and humour were forming in his eyes.

"What is happening?" Owain asked Arvuria worriedly.

"I think... Vann is laughing?" her words followed slowly as her eyes watched curiously.

Vann wiped away the small tears from his eyes and his cackle died down into a chuckle, "I'm sorry Arvuria, but you are so innocent sometimes."

"Well, I only arrived a week ago," Arvuria answered with a slight laugh of her own, "I am enjoying our time together. I think being with the two of you and Martell has been the most entertaining part of my life... from what I can remember anyway."

Owain and Vann exchanged glances as they both wondered again what her life had been like before the meteor - they were so close to the answers yet they were still focusing on having a day of enjoyment.

"Are we going into the Lake or not?!" Owain cheered gleefully as he tried to distract Arvuria from the thoughts of her past. The large lad thundered onto the white sand, leaving deep footprints into the silk which quickly filled back in to recreate the white blanket before the blue of the water. He headed towards the far corner of the beach where there seemed to be nobody around.

Vann kicked off his well worn boots towards the Lake, removed his shirt and chased after Owain, "You aren't going to beat me!" Vann challenged as he ran from Arvuria, leaving her to make her own decision as to whether or not to follow the two of them. He focused on following Owain, watching him run towards the water in an excitement he hadn't seen from the usually pessimistic redhead before. He had been so happy today, Vann couldn't help but feel his bond with Owain grow stronger. Their time at the farm had been a difficult one for him, Owain hadn't spoken much about his past but he had mentioned before a large family in the west, but anything west of Theothen would make him a Resnian. Owain hadn't escaped the war, he was already far from it to begin with - Owain was a runaway. For what he was running away from, Vann wasn't sure of, but in this very moment he could see that Owain was running towards something he had wanted for so very long: Freedom.

Vann caught up towards his friend halfway towards the Lake and nudged him as he ran past, "You could run through a door, that's all you'd be good for!" Vann teased as he sprinted forward further past his boots that had landed and stepped into the warm sapphire waters of Anelli's Tears. It was a strange sensation as the liquid touched his bare feet - the water could barely be felt, as if he was floating on absolutely nothing, it took a few moments for him to correct himself in the water as it quickly deepened as the shallow end finished with a ledge underwater. Owain jumped in a few moments after him upon seeing that the shallow waters didn't last long - he lept into the air and tucked his feet to his chest, "I'm good for this you asshole!" he cheered with a crash into the Ethereal's tears... backside first.

The two teenage boys began to wrestle and splash each other amongst the water and laughed as they did so, but Vann calmed down when he saw in the corner of his eyes Arvuria standing on the shoreline with the soft waves crashing against her feet with her boots placed carefully just before the shoreline. Her blue tunic that was originally his was a vast contrast against the white sand behind her.

"Are you okay?" Vann asked cautiously, "The water is lovely to swim in," he smiled.

Arvuria took a step further into the water and then stopped, "Vann... I do not know how to swim," she replied nervously. Vann saw on her face the same caution and worry that she would have every time she would come across something new - she always seemed to be afraid of failing to be normal, or to be embarrassed of not understanding something. He had learned however, that she was always brave enough to beat her fears, she just needed a little help sometimes.

Owain swam towards Vann, "Go on, help her. I'll grab our stuff from the beach" he whispered to him, "I'll leave you two love birds alone."

"*Love birds?*" Vann quickly hissed towards Owain who had already taken off back towards the shore, "*Owain!*" he whispered heavily again as he followed his friend once more who hurried from the waters to slowly pick up his and Vann's discarded clothes from further up the beach. Vann lifted himself from the water to meet Arvuria, who looked him up and down with wide-eyes as the water dripped from his toned body.

"Sorry," Vann apologised as he saw her eyes wander. His face grew red.

"Will you teach me to swim?" She quickly requested.

"Of course," Vann smiled at her as he took one of her hands to lead her towards the water. His heart pounded, he could only imagine how red he was getting.

"Do I not need to-"

"No!" Vann quickly rejected, "You can keep your clothes on. You can wear mine when we get out."

Vann walked slowly with his friend into the warm waters as her hand held tightly to his. He dropped past the shallow platform first and kicked his feet softly amongst the deep calm waters as he slipped from the underwater ledge.

"You just have to kick your legs a little, see?" he instructed her as she lowered herself down at the drop before the water deepened. Vann waited for the courage to build up in Arvuria for a few moments before he smiled and pulled her into the deep.

"Vann!" She screamed as she fell into his arms, both of them sinking for a few moments before their heads lifted up back towards the air - the two of them floated as they held each other where her legs kicked Vann a few times as they tread together, his arm around her waist.

"You fool!" Arvuria lightly slapped Vann's chest as she laughed at his moronic way of getting her deeper into the water.

"You would have taken a while to come to me," Vann laughed unapologetically as he held her.

"But I would have eventually!" Arvuria laughed along as she moved herself closer into his arms where their faces became but an inch apart.

"Yes… you're right…" Vann mumbled to her.

The two looked into each others eyes. Vann was terrified.

"I want to kiss you," Arvuria spoke. "Something in my chest is compelling me to do so."

Vann didn't hesitate. For some reason or another, his body betrayed his anxiety.

He closed his eyes and leaned in towards hers. His eyes were shut tight as the nerves of his body buzzed. He could feel her breath on his face but in the darkness of his closed sight, a bright light began to shine, blinding him past the shelter of the woman in front of him. He opened his eyes to see Arvuria looking into his as her hair began to shine a blinding white as if she was lit alight. Her hair cascaded down onto the waters and sat on top of it as strands of white fire floated upwards in flickers of ember. It was as if the sand in her hair was kindling the fire that her hair had become.

"Arvuria?" Vann spoke in worry, "What's going on?"

"I do not know," Arvuria replied as she moved her burning hair with her hands, "I feel as though I am surging with Arcane."

"We need to get you out of here, right? This isn't good," Vann held her tighter and began to pull her closer to the shore as he kicked his feet under the water. Arvuria's muscles began to contract, first it started faintly and continued to become worse and worse. The fire in her hair grew larger - she screamed in agony as her body began to pulsate and shake. Her body began to curl and twist horrifically as the sight of an almost transparent second Arvuria escaped from her being as if her Wisp was escaping as it tried to keep up with her.

Vann tried to keep hold of her but his hand slipped causing her to dip under the water for just a moment but that was enough for her hair to begin to heat the waters underneath. The liquid around them both began to boil and turn a hue of white. Vann grimaced through the growing pain of the heat around his skin and dived into the water to reach for Arvuria's hand as her body continued to convulse.

He clasped her freezing hand amongst the heat and pulled her back to above the water - he held her tighter than before as his skin began to sting and burn as her pain continued.

"Owain!" Vann screamed for help. The Redhead turned from collecting their clothes and immediately began to sprint towards them.

"What the fuck is happening to her?!" Owain shouted as he stopped in the shallow to grab her from Vann. The immense heat of the lake quickly dropped as Arvuria left Vann's arms - he then lifted himself onto the ledge under the water and scurried forward along the sand as Owain placed the girl down. The two of them tilted her onto her left side and moved her right leg forward and tucked her arms under her head.

"Arvuria, focus on my voice. It's me, Vann. You're safe. You're out of the water," Vann spoke carefully as his hands hovered over her. He didn't know what to do. He didn't know how to help.

Arvuria's convulsing stopped as her body sprang to lie on her back. Her eyes shot out a beam of white light that faded as it hit the height of the trees - her hair burst in white flames once more where one final scream of pain sounded before it ended.

A few seconds passed and she tried to sit up as if nothing happened.

"Don't move!" The boys spoke in unison.

"What was that?" Owain questioned, "The fuck is going on?"

"That was... strange," Arvuria shook her head, "Memories returned to me. That was... it was too much for me. I need to process this."

"You're telling us," Owain huffed in disbelief. He ran his hands through his red hair and groaned out the stress he felt.

"We thought you were going to die," Vann mumbled as he knelt up beside her. His heart had never beat so fast. After all that had happened he couldn't bear to lose her too.

Arvuria tried to distract from what had happened with a smile, "I am well. That is all that matters," she disregarded but Vann could see that something was still wrong. The usual light in her eyes had faded for now.

"You can't be well, after what that was we need to-"

"Would you for a moment *stop* hovering over me? I am not a child who must be cared for constantly, Vann. I know that you have lost your friends but do not put your guilt onto me," Arvuria snapped. "I must return to the city. I should not have come here. It is too soon."

"What the ever-loving..." Owain stopped himself.

Arvuria turned away from Vann and lifted herself from the white sands with a struggle but she disregarded the help that Vann offered her once more.

"I speak in riddles for I must. You are not ready to hear the truth - nor do I want you to be part of it. To be around me is to die. That must not be your fate," she muttered as walked away from the two boys who had saved her from drowning,

Vann stood dumbfounded as he watched her abandon him and Owain. They remained in silence - that wasn't the Arvuria that they had grown to know.

"So…"

"Don't."

"Didn't kiss her huh?"

Vann stood up from the sands in frustration and barged past Owain to stride back towards the waters, "Now isn't the time for your foolishness Owain. Everything is always a fucking joke with you."

The teen stopped a few moments away as his feet met the shallow part of the beach again where he began to look towards the other side of the lake at the emerald trees of Beonyth's Green which towered in the distance. He could feel his friend looking towards him. They had argued a lot at Firvan's Farm, but both knew that they never meant any ill-words - they always had each others back. Vann hoped that his friend knew this still.

"I'll go after her," Owain called to him, "I'll take her back to Melodies and leave your clothes here - take as much time as you need brother."

Vann exhaled. Relief.

He watched the lack of ripples in Anelli's Tears. They remained still. The world was falling to shit, yet the lake remained untouched - a gem of beauty in a world about to be smothered in darkness.

Arvuria: The Ethereal Children

Why did you make me leave? I should have stayed to fight - I wanted to stay and fight. You should have let me help you protect our people. I'm a fucking coward. I want to make you proud but it is just so damn hard to help people and to be there for those who need me - you always made it seem so easy. I want to come home, father. I can't do this shit anymore...

"It is easy to believe things would have been better in the past for we always know what we could have done differently - that is why we fear the future. *What could have been* is the curse of man. That is what I have found at least, dear boy."

Beside him was a middle-aged woman. He did not hear her walk beside him, and he did know who she was or how she got there. Vann looked her over with a quick glance - Her hair was blonde and it flowed beautifully into the yellow of her silk dress as if they were one and the same. Her aura was comforting and her smile was warm. Vann felt as if he had always known her.

"It's not a curse. It's hope. I look back in the moments I wish I could change and believe I could have been a better person," Vann replied.

"Would you rather be a better person back then, or would you rather be that man you have grown to be through strife and struggle?" The Woman questioned.

"I will never be the man I wish I could be, but these passing days I have learned that I can at the very least try to be the one I am today. They are two different people - yet I am still alive. That has to count for something."

The woman nodded. "You are doing more than you believe you are, Vann Erendon. You have changed the world already. The choices you have made have already saved countless lives, but I need you to understand: You will lose people. People dear to you. People you have not even met yet, and people you will never know existed. The choices you are going to make in the future will cause you great pain - you must always remember your humanity."

Vann turned to her once more, but where she stood he could see no remnants of her.

Humanity. If only everyone else remembered such a fickle thing.

Arvuria: The Ethereal Children

- Chapter 16 -
THURIAN THEO
The Five Dragons.

THE DAY THAT they arrived at the golden city of Arvur, Thurian was summoned to his father as soon as he stepped from the Fire-Cloud's ramp. He had apologised profusely to his bride-to-be that he wouldn't be able to show her the Five-Spire himself, but he had summoned one of the veteran butlers for her alongside his personal guard to give her a tour and to keep her safe.

Thurian walked through the white and gold marble hallways on his own after choosing against being brought to his own father under armed protection. He didn't want it. Why should he have to require protection in his own home? He had walked these halls alone as a child during the time of peace, he would be damned if he was going to admit to others, and himself, that he was a target for his own people. The Prince had followed this pathway many times in his life, the way to the throne, and it was rarely ever for good reason.

He left Arvur weeks ago for what he believed was going to be the last time, and he still wondered if it would have been better to die on the battlefield, to give Resnia what they wanted - but Markarth had lit a fire under Thurian's heart, one that ignited from the small ember of belief in himself. The Prince may have caused this war, but maybe it was a design from The Ethereals, a way for him to finally find himself on the throne to make the world a better place. He wanted for his people to not have to worry about the wars that may come in the future, or worry about when their next meal might be or if they can survive another day. He wanted his people to wake up in the morning to see that his Empire would be worth living in.

What Thurian wanted could only come true if his father were to give up the throne willingly, to rename him as his heir, and for him to then secure peace with Resnia.

Thurian stood before the titanic black doors before him. Cascading over the door were images of gold that told the tale of The Five Dragons. Beginning with the two human blood-brothers, King Theo and King Herreken, who arrived at Ideneor with their fleet of settlers from lands lost to history. They created an alliance with the many clans of Ideneoran's who looked just as they did, but they had a vastly different culture and darker skin, they were a few generations behind in terms of physical Arcane use, but they were more in tune with their spiritual side believing that their Wisps and kindness is what mattered most, with their ideals leaning towards a collective of people helping each other, instead of one ruler. King Herreken wanted to subjugate them, for the Ideneorians to become citizens under their rule but King Theo talked sense into his friend, explaining that they could barely support and rule their own people, and that ruling those whose society worked was not their mission.

The two Kings, with the aid of willing Ideneoran's who wanted leave of the arid lands made their way to the large landmass to the East of Ideneor where they discovered the Rhenn's, a people who had a vast civilisation along the coast of Taundrad. King Theo and King Herreken created diplomatic ties with the Rhenn's and were allowed to create their first city in their lands. The city that would become Ressoran which was named after King Herreken's wife: Resso. It was the first new kingdom of the human race.

Upon seeing the humans settle their newly discovered lands, Grenden the Ethereal of The Earth created Beonyth, The Green Dragon who was tasked to protect the nature and wildlife of Taundrad - and then came Mitrand, The Blue Dragon who took host near Everria to protect the seas between the settled lands. She was born of Henoite and Ibris, The Ethereals of Knowledge and Freedom.

Last of all, Zergrath, The Red Dragon who was manufactured by Orus and Dhulo, The Ethereals of War and Chaos. He was a titanic force of nature who was born with a darker heart - he went against his task of blocking the skies from The Ethereals and instead chose to rule Ideneor as its God-King, protecting the desert land from outside wars and threats.

The Three Primal Dragons attempted to keep peace with each other despite their differences, but the world began to change rapidly after the human settlements aimed to expand. The two kings began a war against the Rhenn's and defeated them with ease, pushing them north until only a small part of their civilisation remained. With the Kingdom of Humans established, the two kings began to disagree with the ways they should rule. King

Arvuria: The Ethereal Children

Herreken believed that there should be ministers in charge of the largest regions that answered to him, while King Theo believed that too many minds leads to destruction, that there needs to be a single uniting force to lead their people to a brighter future.

The Fourth Dragon was born amongst the growing discord between the ideals and beliefs of humanity. Brigir, The Pale Dragon. As the legends tell Thurian, Brigir was not born from The Ethereals above but from something much darker. Something from below. The Pale Dragon's schemes infected the heart of King Herreken causing a civil war between the new human kingdom. King Theo and almost half of the human race left the established lands in the west and moved further east in search of safety.

With King Theo's righteous heart he was able to be the pillar of light to his people that he dreamed of being and managed to begin the creation of an incredible white and gold city.

Thurian took a moment from reading the final parts of the story. He wondered where it had all gone wrong, where his bloodline had begun to fall from the example that his ancestor, King Theo, had set for them. He looked back to the golden art in front of him to see The Golden Dragon appear in the story.

Anelli - The Ethereal of Life - sent The Golden Dragon known as Arvur to the land of Taundrad to help King Theo fight against Brigir and Herreken, to give the brave people that followed him a uniting force to stand behind. Arvur and King Theo became incredible friends, they became brothers as Theo had once been to Herreken - and in this newfound brotherhood Arvur lent his powers to King Theo creating history's very first recorded Chosen of a Dragon. With the unity of the golden dragon and the righteous king, they warred with Herreken and Brigir's forces - they defeated them in a horrific battle where Arvur sacrificed himself to kill Brigir, ending the existence of the Light and Dark forces of Taundrad. Humanity was left to trudge its own path.

Thurian laughed. The art on the door had been created years after the end of Theothen's victory. He wondered if the artists actually believed that their peace would last. No true peace would ever last if there were two opposing beliefs, there would always be someone else to challenge what the right thing to do is. Rebellion is natural of course, and so is wanting to be the one to change things for the better. Thurian knew he was that type of person right now but he stood there, before the story of The Five Dragons and swore on his soul that he would create True Peace. Whatever the cost.

The doors before him slowly opened where the golden pathway lined with the Scaleguard in their matte black dragon-styled armour led him towards his father; The Emperor of Theothen. The Emperor sat on the glistening golden throne which had ornate and delicate art chipped into it of dragons and cities and the history of Arvur. Surrounding those residing in the room was the usual white and black marble mixed into the floors and walls.

Thurian's footsteps echoed as he walked the path towards the throne - each step an announcement of his return.

"You have returned home. Entered my domain once more. I half-hoped that you were going to kill yourself like you intended, yet here you are." The Emperor muttered with disgust.

"Here I am."

Thurian looked over his father to see that his illness had grown rapidly worse. Along his chest to his enlarged right arm the infection had become even more prevalent since the last time Thurian had seen him - The infected parts of his body had grown scabbed and repulsive with purple and yellow pus dripping from the rotten meat that had become reliant on The Arcane to sustain it. His skin sagged from his face causing the sockets of his eyes to almost appear exposed. The Emperor took laboured breaths, and moved his hand from his infected chest wound that was exposed to Thurian and The Scaleguard where the pus from his hand dripped onto the cloth that covered the arm of the golden throne.

"Why have you returned to me, my son?" his father spoke with a warm loving tone, a different person to the fiend he was moments ago. Thurian's heart almost broke, hearing the words of his younger father.

"I have come to request Ceremony to a woman who has claimed my heart as her own," Thurian said confidently, "Though her blood may not be noble, her heart is as righteous as Anelli's."

"Righteousness leads to zealotry!" The Emperor spat.

"But a woman's love rivals that of The Ethereals," his father smiled.

Thurian stood concerned with the behaviour of the man before him; he had grown much worse within the last few weeks, his mind addled with more poison and rot than ever before. Maybe Emerie and the rumours of the peasants were right, his father was a broken man.

"I know you and I have had our differences, Father, but it would mean the world to me to have your permission to marry her, and to throw a Masquerade in your honour. I remember how you and mother loved celebrations and parties in your youth - allow me to create a love like you had," Thurian forced a smile.

His father remained as Thurian watched him remember the memories of his youth, before the last decade took its toll on him.

"We loved to celebrate," his father smiled, "I remember a time where you hid under a table, hiding from a Councilman who wanted you to marry his daughter."

"Councillor Lerren. What a horrible man," Thurian laughed.

"Wasn't he just?" His father laughed alongside him.

"That is why I executed him, vile, ugly, rancid man," The Emperor beckoned down his domain. His scaleguard continued to ignore his lunacy, standing frozen at their posts.

"I should split you down into two pieces for starting this war, one for me and one for The King," The Emperor seethed, "Someone seize this traitor! He is no son of mine!"

Thurian remained strong as two of the Scaleguard closest to him stepped forward and forced him to his knees. A third walked behind him and placed their sword's edge at the top of his spine to prepare to slide the blade deep into The Prince's meat.

"You killed Resnia's most-loved Princess, you ended the chance of peace. You slit her throat and ran," The Emperor muttered, "I raised no Prince to kill in cowardice."

"There is no such thing as cowardice when your life is at stake," Thurian answered. "I awoke to see an assassin's knife pressed against my throat, and one against hers. I loved her. You know that I did. I tried to save her but I wasn't strong enough. All I could do was butcher her attackers and by the Thirteen Ethereals I wish that I could relive killing them all over again," Thurian seethed. "I loved her more than you could ever understand. I will not be charged with cowardice when I watched my love die because I knew less people would suffer if I lived. You would have burned Resnia to the ground - At least with their dead Princess, they still have honour enough to not harm innocents."

The Prince forced himself to his feet with the intent of feeling the blade enter his skin. He didn't expect for the Scaleguard behind him to move the sword an inch away, surprising Thurian to see one of The Scaleguard going against the Emperor's wishes. If there was one, there would be others.

"Emperor Thrane. You are an old, frail, broken man whose time on this throne is coming quickly to an end. I want you to know that before this illness had taken over you, you were the best father that I could have asked for and that is the man who will remain in my heart. I ask you, from son to father, allow me to marry Emerie Herene, and in return I promise to you that I will create lasting peace from the war that I began," Thurian swore with his arms remaining in the hands of the two Scaleguard's.

The Emperor leaned back and breathed in heavily, Thurian's father reappeared once more, "You have my permission, my beloved son."

"Thank you," Thurian smiled, hiding the pain he felt to see his idol in such a way.

"Thurian?" His father croaked.

"Yes?"

"Be aware of those around you. *Be aware of what lies below,*" his father murmured before the exhaustion of their conversation took its toll, forcing a slumber to overcome him.

Luke Morgan

Arvuria: The Ethereal Children

- Chapter 17 -
EMERIE HERENE
The Five Spire.

EMERIE AND CANDLE were split apart from Thurian and Tristan upon arriving in the Fifth Spire of the Capital. It was the tallest beacon in Arvur, the singular tower attached to the four below it. It was as high as the clouds and as wide as Avane. They were both taken to a room where Emerie would stay until their day of Ceremony, as was Theothen tradition for the engaged to be separate under the idea their love would grow stronger. Emerie stood before the window in front of her as the view of the Spire's colourful garden in the sky sat beautifully before her. It reminded her of Firvan's Farm... before the Theothen's burned it to ash.

She wondered for a moment if Thurian had yet sent men to rebuild her caretaker's home but a part of her, as guilty as she felt, did not think of it as something that would hinder her willingness to stay here.

"I am sorry that we are cooped up in here like pigeons Lady Herene. I was told we would be given a tour of the spire but it seems that will have to wait until Thurian approves it. Where he is and what he is up to, I am unsure of," Candle informed her.

Emerie's eyes remained fixed to the outside. She could see the green lands of Theothen in the distance as far as the eye could see, almost an endless land of soft rolling hills and small villages and towns.

"Our country is beautiful," Emerie muttered to herself, "You do not appreciate it when your feet touch the dirt, yet in the eyes of a bird you see the beauty The Ethereals created. Do you think they still pay attention to us?"

"My Lady, they must surely pay attention to you. A commoner who won over the heart of Prince Thurian. You are surely in the design of The Ethereals," Candle answered with belief.

Emerie exhaled through her nose. If only Candle knew of The Black Door she had been raised by. It had taken Emerie eighteen years to receive any good luck at all - maybe where she stands now was due to being owed that many years of favour from those who watch above.

"If The Ethereals placed me here, then I might as well see what I can do with such a grand design. Don't you think so?" Emerie turned to Candle with a smirk. It took a moment for Candle to catch on to Emerie's intent, but the moment she did she tried to hide her smile of approval.

"I will fetch for some maids," Candle smirked as she turned to leave the doors that kept Emerie inside.

EMERIE WAITED NEARLY an hour for Candle to return. She found barely anything in the bedroom to keep her entertained in that time apart from a book titled The Histories of Theothen Bloodlines in which she brushed up on her knowledge on the previous generation of noble families. Although it was ten years out of date she was sure she could find some more use for it politically - or at least that is how she assumed politics worked: To know which noble families aligned with you. The only politics she ever knew was how to ask Uncle Vernon to buy her some sweets without doing chores. Emerie smiled, she missed Vann's father. Her mind went back to the last night she spent with her own - what a bastard he was. Her throat tightened and she felt nauseous as the image of The Black Door appeared in her mind -

"Lady Herene, I have returned with an escort for you to bathe," Candle interrupted her thoughts. Her small servant brought with her two women dressed in black robes with lace masks covering their eyes - only their pale mouths were visible - they were dressed in no sort of way as Candle was.

"I informed one of The Matriarchs that you have been given a room with no bath - I find the lack of preparation disgusting," Candle turned a scowl towards the taller women, "So these kind beings will be escorting you higher up the spire, closer to Thurian."

"I am glad," Emerie answered politely, and gave a nod of acknowledgement to The Matriarchs who in return stood in silence awaiting her to walk towards them.

Emerie followed the two women ahead of her with Candle two steps behind. Each soldier that they walked past saluted to her and some even spoke her name. Lady Herene. She knew hearing her family name would be a thing of the past soon enough but for a moment she wished that her mother could see her now - she always believe Emerie would become somebody.

"Emerie," Candle whispered, "When they turn the corner we run, okay?" Candle almost snickered as did Emerie herself. They both waited for The Matriarch's before them to turn the corner before shifting their feet and bolting into the opposite direction, past all the soldiers they had seen before who did not leave their stations to chase them. Emerie's adrenaline shot up as the small girl in front of her led her through hallways, down spiralling staircases, and through rooms that they had no right in accessing.

"I've been planning an exit since we arrived!" Candle called out ahead of her as they ran through a series of small rooms with the final one being filled with gardeners tools. "It made sense to do so since you are in my protection," Candle announced with triumph as she pushed a small door open as they ran through the tool-room.

"Welcome to Arvur's Garden," The Maid introduced.

Emerie paused. Her eyes had never witnessed such vibrant colours before. The Garden was akin more to a forest - one that was a culmination of all the nature in the world of Taundrad. Immediately there were plants she never knew existed, there were sculptures in stone that she had never seen before - there were trees in colours that her eyes could not be removed from.

"If I am in a dream, Candle, I do not ever want to leave," she whispered.

"Come," The Maid ordered excitedly as she grabbed her hand and began to lead her through Arvur's garden.

"History tells us that this garden was created and maintained by The Golden Dragon all those centuries ago. He took inspiration from Beonyth to take notice of the beauty that Grenden had created when he made our world. I find it fascinating that The Ethereals see a wonder like this yet remain in their domain above - it makes me curious as to what their world looks like," Candle rambled as Emerie tried to listen but the beauty of the world before her could not escape her attention.

Emerie followed along the cobbled-stone pathway with her arm linked with Candle as the two new friends enjoyed the scenery around them. She couldn't help but genuinely smile to herself, she was so happy, she was so content. She felt as though she was owed this moment after everything that had happened.

"Vann would have loved this," She spoke before her mind could keep herself silenced.

"Vann?" Candle asked earnestly.

Emerie had given Candle what trust she could as she had felt that the two of them were in this situation together - they were both lost in this new world they had never been in before. At least, Candle had told her she had only ever been in Avane. She didn't want to share much of her past with Candle, and she didn't want to put any of her friend in danger but there was something about the maid beside her who invited comfort. Emerie had never had a friend like her before.

"One of my best friends," Emerie replied, "He was a hunter. He spent a lot of time in the Verdant Forests around Avane - I think the two of you would have been great friends."

"What makes you say that?" Candle asked as she tighten their linked arms together and rested her head onto Emerie's shoulder as if they had known each other for years. Emerie tilted her eyes to the friend beside her and placed one of her cheeks on top.

"He is kind, especially to those he cares for but he is shy around new people. It is quite endearing to see a man so worried about upsetting others that he doesn't act on what he wants. You know, the type of man where you must give him a million hints for him to know you are interested," Emerie remembered her friend too fondly for the moment and quickly tried to correct herself - she was to marry Thurian after all. "When we were last in Avane I had to force him to speak to a barmaid he had been in love with for years. It went ever so terribly for him," Emerie laughed. She remembered his face after she had kissed him.

"I was like him once. You cannot always live your life worrying about your love scaring others - at some point you just have to believe you are worth it and make the leap. You will either find happiness in the one you wish to give your heart to, or you will find someone else after that. There is always someone else," Candle laughed.

"Candle, are you a man eater?"

"Of course. Have you seen me?"

The two women stopped in the cobbled path and looked at each other in disbelief until Emerie snorted a laugh causing both of them to interrupt the serenity of the garden.

Around them they heard the silent mutters of other Noble's as they walked past the teenagers giggling with tears in their eyes. Emerie felt at home.

"Tell me why you are already getting in trouble?" Tristan questioned. Emerie's eyes widened and her body straightened upon hearing her brother's voice.

"Shit." Spoke Emerie.

"Shit." Added Candle.

Tristan sighed and motioned Emerie forward with the flick of his hand, "You are going to be a Princess Emerie, you cannot and should not be causing a scene such as this," he spoke sternly, "You must realised that people are going to talk about this."

"Then let them talk. What better way for the Empire to know my name than hearing tales of my laughter," Emerie retaliated. "I will not be cooped up in a room as mother was."

"That has nothing to do with this Em. Thurian was summoned by The Emperor, he was keeping you safe for the time being but you decide to run through the Fifth Spire and into The Golden Dragon's Garden. We are still commoners - the people here do not like us. We are still the bottom of the food chain. You are lucky that the two Matriarchs you ran away from sought me out."

Emerie huffed. He was right. Tristan was always right and nothing pissed her off more than that. "Fine. I'll go back."

"Stay in your room for only today. Thurian has sent word to me there will be a masquerade in honour of your engagement. You have to be there, as do I," Tristan ordered.

Emerie noticed Tristan analyse Candle with interest.

"The troublemaker can watch from afar, with the rest of the maids," he pointed before ushering them both to follow him back to the room.

Arvuria: The Ethereal Children

Luke Morgan

- Chapter 18 -
SHIN WATERMAN
White Sand.

SHIN SAT JUST on the outskirts of the war camp with her legs dangling from the makeshift walls that encircled its defences. In her hands was her tin bowl of meat-scrap soup which was her favourite meal of the week - she always liked the surprise whenever she got to chew on a genuine chunk of food instead of gristle and fat. She dunked her piece of bread into the soup and bit into it after the liquid had made the snack softer after being stored for so long - as she ate her food she pondered for a few moments as to what was to come.

Many of her comrades and others within the camp had heard rumours that they were to head towards Beonyth's Laketown in search of a rebel leader; which wouldn't necessarily set any bells off in people's heads should a small party head there, but the worry with every soldier was that it were to be at least be three squads of The Blood Dragons that would be going. With Beonyth's Laketown being its own City State, and a neutral territory for all those who reside in Taundrad, it was an act of war should Dira march her whole army into their borders. A gigantic risk, especially considering hundreds of years ago a King of Resnia tried the same thing, only to be thwarted by The Green Dragon.

The Mender held her hands underneath the warm bowl after she had finished her supper to keep her fingers safe amongst the cold evening air where she protected herself further with her black hood sitting on top of her long brown hair which coiled together in a messy bun. Shin knew that this small part of the wall was the least defended, which is why she would sit there most nights but it was more so that it was also one of the closest parts to the woods which allowed her to hear the woodland melodies. She could hear the howls and roars of the creatures in the forest, and hear the songs of the birds and other little creatures.

Her peace and her listening to the songs was abruptly interrupted when a hooded figure leapt past her over the wall and hurried into the forest before her - Shin released a fearful yelp and dropped her warm bowl down to the grass below.

"Halt!" She beckoned to the cloaked figure who ignored her and continued into the treeline. Shin's body carried her forward before she could think as she pushed herself off the wall, falling near ten feet to then roll as her body landed - she picked herself up from the ground and chased after the runner.

Shin, for once, had been brave enough to engage in a potential confrontation but she didn't quite understand why she was doing it when she would normally have ran to one of the soldiers to inform them of danger. Shin was a Mender, not a Warrior. A Mender - naturally - without a weapon, which was the last thing she realised as her feet continued to carry her forward.

"Stop right there!" Shin shouted with her fearful voice as she leapt over a log, and ducked under a tree branch where the figure had now vanished amongst the density of the trees. Shin stopped in her tracks.

"Hello?" She asked aloud, hoping that she hadn't lost the figure. She turned around continuously to scan her surroundings, but all she heard was the sounds of the forest once more as the noises called out to each other to speak about the happenings in their home.

Cold steel pressed against her neck.

"Why do I keep seeing you?" It asked her, with its husky voice that Shin would never have forgotten.

"I did not mean to anger you Princess Dira," Shin quickly apologised as she held her empty hands outwards. "It is only natural that I chase a hooded figure that hurries out of our camp."

Shin flew towards the ground as Princess Dira pushed her away in frustration.

"You are the Mender from three days ago, aren't you? The one who formed the dome of Arcane," Princess Dira questioned, placing her knife back into the row of blades that sat on her upper left arm.

The Mender turned around onto her back and lifted herself to her feet from the fluffy grass below, "Yes my Princess," Shin muttered. She was afraid of the woman she had been admiring, but she understood The Princess' frustration with her - whatever reason she had to be out in the forest was of no concern to a lowly soldier such as herself.

Princess Dira walked towards Shin, "Come with me," she ordered as she bumped past her with a nudge of her shoulder. Shin's eyes widened and her heart fluttered - The Princess had just asked for her help in whatever she was doing. She asked her. Every bad day she had had in the army was all worth it for this very moment. Shin didn't know how to react in fear of saying the wrong thing so she nodded with a grunt and walked a foot behind The Princess as they moved swiftly through the forest.

After nearly ten minutes of silence and tension, The Princess looked over her shoulder to Shin with a curious look. The Mender's heart swelled again.

"I am sorry," Shin quickly apologised.

"For what?" Princess Dira questioned.

"I do not know," The Mender answered, "I do not wish to upset you Princess - you've been my hero for as long as I can remember. Stories of you are why I enlisted."

Princess Dira laughed. "How can a woman such as I be a hero to a woman such as you?"

Shin stopped walking, causing the Princess to stop in turn. "You are the first Princess to ever be named Heir to The Empire. You are the undefeated, unstoppable Warrior who improves every piece of land you step upon, and you improve every life that you touch with your presence. I wish to one day be like you. I want to be sure of my strength... of what strength I do have."

Shin's words rattled from her tongue quickly with her adoration coming off as borderline obsession. Her chest tightened as if a sharp object was digging deep into her as Dira looked at her with pity.

"If you want to be strong, you cannot imagine to be anyone else but yourself. Do not wait for me to inspire you, find your own courage or you will be weak forever."

"You think I am weak?" Shin spoke before thinking once more, expecting the quick blade of Dira to slice her upon speaking her mind, but The Princess instead turned back around and continued her desired path through the dark forest.

"If you were truly weak, I would not be asking for your aid," Dira answered, ending the conversation as the two returned to their journey through the green.

Shin smiled to herself for the rest of the journey that Dira was taking her on. The Princess of The Theothen Empire herself had not only spoken to her, but had also complimented her strength, there was nothing more that Shin could ever ask for. Her life felt complete - right up until the moment Dira moved a bundle of tree branches to see three of her men dead alongside a Levia.

"By The Ones Above…" Shin croaked at the brutal sight. She hurried towards the corpses ready to pull the Arcane so that she could heal them but as she got to the first body she could tell that the soldier had been dead for close to two or maybe three days. Dira stood behind her as her fingers and sight analysed the wounds on the body, the two closest to her had no wounds created by the teeth or the claws of The Levia, but had instead been bludgeoned to death. Perhaps by a mace or a rock.

"This makes no sense," Shin muttered. She hurried to the corpse of the large Levia. Its wounds were specific and each cut was deep into its tough hide. She climbed onto the body to see that there was a slit in the shape of a long dagger, with the skin around it ripped and peeling as if the weapon that impacted this site had been moved around with vigour.

"Someone was riding this monster?" Shin questioned herself.

Dira jumped up from the ground onto the monster and scouted the wounds herself, "Harnon," she whispered to herself.

"The scales are hardened you're right," Shin answered, "I think with the irritation of the blade that did this, the scales must actually harden as studies suggest."

Dira slid down from the nape to the snout of the Levia and returned to the bodies by the treeline. Shin stood upon the scales and watched Dira analyse each of the corpses again before taking from their necks their pillars of service: necklaces made of fine rope that held a stone with their names on. Shin hurried down from the monster and began to speak a prayer for them, "In the name of Riteus, I return your Wisp to The Ethereals. In the name of Irren, I pray you pass judgement, and in the name of Anelli, I pray for your loved ones a long life. May your soul be claimed by those you believed in. May your body return to Grenden's soil."

"You are a religious woman?" Dira questioned as she delicately untied the knot of the first soldier's necklace.

"I put my faith into Anelli, as most do," Shin answered, "If I may ask, who do you put your faith towards?"

Dira removed the necklace from the first body and looked it over, reaching into the pockets of the corpse to find a small portrait sketch of a man where on the opposite side of the paper it read: To Lee, I am always with you. Forever yours, Stefan.

"People say there are Thirteen Ethereals above us, but I truly believe that Valen is the only one who matters." Dira spoke honestly as she folded up the sketch with Lee's pillar inside of it and placed it into one of her pockets.

"Valen? The Ethereal of Destiny?" Shin spoke curiously.

Shin continued to watch as Dira walked away from the corpse towards the final one of the two where she once again tenderly undid the bindings of the rope around its neck.

"If we all have a path laid before us that leads to one big crescendo - where the meaning of our life on this world is shown to us... is that not the only thing that matters? I wake up every day and wonder if today is the day that I meet my destiny, yet each night I go back to sleep awaiting the morrow. I survive battle after battle, each as important as the last but here I am still walking my path of blood. I put my faith in Valen because all the death and the destruction that I reap has to lead to something greater. My actions have to mean something in the end."

"They will," Shin's belief riding along her tone, "Everything matters."

"That is the last thing I wish to hear with what I have done. I just want my death to matter," Dira brushed off with a surprisingly pleasant laugh.

Shin hurried beside Dira with her best intentions, "I do not believe there are things you regret so much."

"My father will be dead soon, by steel or by illness," Dira looked up towards the night sky and took two deep breaths, "And so I ordered the assassination of my little brother to secure my seat on the throne. I regret that he is going to die, we were close once. This war doesn't end without his death - with him gone, maybe the Resnian's will listen to sense."

Fear ran through Shin's body within a second of hearing those words, The Princess of The Empire just openly stated her treason towards the Crown - if Shin didn't take action now, she would be a traitor too. But she didn't care. Strangely, pity towards The Princess began to appear in her chest as she looked at the war-torn warrior in front of her, where her facade of constant strength dropped for a moment as her face softened and her body language relaxed.

"I don't know why I'm telling any of this to you," Dira sighed, with a hint of embarrassment.

"I'm just a single soldier, whatever you say to me doesn't matter," Shin tried to brush off Dira's worry.

Shin gave Dira a meek smile as The Princess' eyes moved from the stars back to her. "Do you have any family? It seems everyone has lost someone during times such as these," Dira asked sombrely.

Shin's smile grew as she remembered her time growing up with her little brother and her Uncle, how they spent nearly all their lives sitting at the beach of Anelli's Tears.

"My little brother is living in my Uncle's old home. My Uncle passed away seven months ago, but Mathane is continuing our boat lending for visitors," Shin answered, "We earn quite some Sovereigns after the Winter months where tourism picks up. People want to escape the war somewhere pleasant, which is the only benefit we receive when war comes, as sick as it is to say."

Dira frowned at the words but then shook off her guilt and forced a smile. "I always enjoy being on a boat. There's something peaceful about it that I can't quite put into words."

"I know what you mean," Shin responded eagerly, reaching into one of the pouches on her belts, struggling to find what she was looking for for a few moments until she unbuckled the correct one - where medical supplies should be, she had a small vial of white sand, "I want to give this to you," she spoke softly as she held out the vial towards Dira who looked at it almost concerned.

"It's sand from the very centre-bottom of Anelli's Tears - The Lake created by our Ethereal of Life," Shin smiled again, "If legends are true it is the closest point you can get to where The Golden Dragon was born!"

The Mender watched The Princess with warmth as she slowly reached her hand out and took the vial of crystal white sand. "What do I do with it?" Dira asked curiously, "Does it heal?"

Shin laughed, "My Princess it is sand. Just sand."

Her laugh stopped abruptly when she felt the piercing gaze of Dira.

"Oh," The Princess answered with her face growing red… right up until her laugh escaped her pressed lips where a delicate giggle turned into a genuine laugh - Shin could help but join her.

She felt honoured to stand with the Princess in this moment - to see that she is more than just her legend. That she was a person too. One that seemed to struggle to interact normally with someone, whether because she hadn't the opportunity that often or because she was afraid to let someone in was something that Shin couldn't quite figure out. Nonetheless she was happy to hear this incredible warrior show her that she had some humanity; enough for her to laugh at something simple.

Their shared moment of laughter died down after a few moments where shin watched Dira place the vial of sand into one of her pouches attached over her leather chest-piece and then received a final warm smile from Dira, "Thank you…" she trailed off with guilt appearing on her face.

"I have shared an honest moment with you yet I do not know your name," Dira mumbled.

"Shin. Shin Waterman."

"Well, Shin Waterman. Thank you."

The Mender shook the hand of Dira who had outstretched it in thanks, and when the moment had ended Shin noticed Dira's sight had turned past her as she saw something in the treeline. Shin followed Dira as she hurried up the small ledge to see a third and final body lying on its back with multiple stab wounds in its chest. It was another soldier with his own dagger embedded into his torso.

Shin muttered the same prayer she spoke earlier in her head as she witnessed the sight of the brutal murder. Whoever had killed this man seemed very desperate to do so.

Dira walked around the body and noticed the grass and the mud at the base of the tree and seemed disturbed by what must have been two bodies at the base of the tree.

"Whoever killed this soldier was defending two people," Dira called over to Shin. The Princess ripped some Arcane from their surroundings without tearing the air with her fingers - red Arcane seeped into her eyes before a beam of Arcane ran over the base of the tree. As the Arcane met the ground a white mist began to appear - Divine Arcane.

"She was here," Dira spat in anger as she closed her eyes, cutting the beam of Arcane off from her gaze.

"Who?" Shin asked nervously as the usual behaviour of Dira appeared again.

Dira scowled towards Shin, "The Golden-Haired Girl that my mother seems so desperate to capture. She is the reason every fucking noble in the court is heading north to hinder my efforts in finding her. If she is with Harnon he will be taking her to Laketown. I cannot allow the death of our brothers to go unavenged. They killed our people. We will kill theirs."

"We?" Shin asked Dira.

Shin saw Dira's hesitance with her next words before she spoke them to her.

"Tonight we march. The Blood Dragons. All of us."

"My Princess… Beonyth's Laketown is its own state. You have no right."

"My blood is my right."

Arvuria: The Ethereal Children

- Chapter 19 -
EMERIE HERENE
Masks and Blades.

EMERIE HAD NEVER been to a Masquerade before, not that she would ever hide that information from anyone. When would she ever have had the chance to go? She was a peasant, born in a wooden hut that just barely passed as a house, yet here she was, in the Five Spire Castle, waiting for the Theothen Prince to collect her from the entryway as the party went on inside. A party dedicated to her and him. She felt like she was going to puke. The nerves inside her ravaged what confidence she had mustered over the last two days but she found some comfort in fiddling with the necklace Vann had purchased for her.

She had barely seen Thurian since she arrived at the castle so Candle had been looking after her, but Emerie had noticed that Candle had been making everything up as she went along - she had never been to the Capital City of Arvur either, let alone the Five Spire Castle. Emerie had Candle promise to her that they both were in it together, and that if either of them had problems they would try to be there for the other. Emerie felt a sense of sisterhood with Candle, something she had never felt before, all she had ever been is protected by Tristan and Vann, especially over the last few months - well, she was still protected by Tristan at least, who arrived beside her as she played with the hem of her red dress, looking towards the high quality fabric with her golden mask covering her eyes and cheekbones. Her brother was clad in black and gold ceremonial leathers with two silver plates of armour running down his black jacket.

"Excited?" Tristan asked as he pecked Emerie on her cheek as he hugged her. Emerie wrapped her arms around her brother and embraced him tightly, "This doesn't feel real."

"No shortening words, remember? You're a soon-to-be Princess," Tristan laughed as their embrace ended - Emerie saw a wide smile beam from his face and his eyes water just a little bit.

"At least mother taught us both how to dance," Emerie smiled, "I remember she did so to entertain my idea that we would ever go to one of these. Yet here we are."

"Yet here you are," Thurian's voice sounded from the entryway of the hall towards the door. Beside him were two Scaleguards that were matching his footsteps precisely while their Swords stood linear as they pointed them down from their chest. Emerie tried to hide her attraction to The Prince who was wearing his ceremonial regalia, a suit a shade of green similar to what she had been wearing when they met near the blacksmiths. The suit jacket was patterned with a series of golden dragons placed strategically, one on each arm descended from his shoulderpads where red tassels dangled. Underneath the bold jacket was a silk red shirt with only a small collar riding up, it remained unbuttoned to reveal some of his chest where a scar that ran down from the lower part of his throat, down his chest, to then hide underneath his shirt.

Emerie now refrained from picking at her dress, "My Prince," She bowed to Thurian, where Tristan then followed behind with his salute towards the sky.

Thurian lifted her face up by placing his fingers underneath her chin and met her with a smile, "You do not bow to me," Thurian spoke delicately to her, then interlocking the fingers of his other hand to Emerie's, "Are you ready?"

"Yeah," Emerie nodded with a frown, "But, could you please look after me?"

Thurian tightened his grip onto her hand, "Only if you do the same for me," he smiled brightly before donning over his eyes a golden mask similar to Emerie's, though with more masculine accents.

Emerie's stomach issue solved itself for that very moment, but it quickly returned when she saw Thurian wink at her brother underneath his disguise, instructing him to open the ballroom doors. Tristan stepped in front of them and pushed the two ornate doors open to reveal ahead of him the masked guests dancing with their bright colours alongside angelic music that played around them. They danced amongst the ballroom, its white and gold marble structure glistened against the moonlight that was cascading through the towering windowed wall at the other end of the hall from where they entered - the landscape of the city below was on the other side of the window, and Theothen beyond it sat. Just in front of the space of the large windowed wall was a stage where the royal orchestra played, and sitting just above them from a floating platform with Arcane running underneath its pipes was Emperor Thrane who was sleeping on his mobile wooden throne while surrounded by his Scaleguard.

The centre of the room was the dance floor and running along the inner-sides of the grandiose hall were pillars with multiple circular platforms around them where party-goers sat and drank and cheered and laughed. The feeling of walking into the room almost overwhelmed her, she felt as though she had walked into The First Layer and been claimed by Anelli herself.

Tristan stopped before the two of them and readied himself to introduce their arrival, but was stopped by Thurian giving him a light tap on the shoulder and a shake of the head, "This is a masquerade Tristan, they will know who we are despite the masks, yet we do not announce it - let us not worry your sister too much," he whispered to him. Emerie's nerves dwindled a little bit further to see that Thurian was taking her worries into account, that he was a gentleman.

Tristan stood to the side as they met the edge of the dance floor where Thurian began to lead her towards the centre of it, where each person they walked past stared at them with either shock or admiration. Once they reached the centre, the dancers had naturally formed a circle around them to give them space to let them enjoy themselves. Emerie noticed that she was the only woman wearing red, maybe that was why they were looking at her, there was no way it could be because she was going to be marrying the controversial Prince. Thurian moved his placement of her hands so that they rested on his shoulders, and then he placed his hands onto her waist, "Shall we start and end like this?" he asked her with a whisper into her ear. Goosebumps scattered across her body.

"If you insist," she whispered back, trying to force confidence.

Emerie felt Thurian begin to sway them both side to side, and then begin to turn around with her as they moved around the space that had been given to them. The music that had been playing flowed into a new song almost exactly as they took their first steps. The orchestra had taken note of the 'hidden' Prince and his future bride entering the ballroom, and had been waiting for their first dance together. The music followed Thurian's lead, its tempo picking up with each foot he placed onto the ground. The Prince soon enough released their arms from being locked against each other and the music followed along still, beginning to sound upbeat, as though the players of the music could feel the swell of Emerie's heart as happiness began to overtake her.

She interrupted Thurian's lead and began to insert some of the moves that Aunt Jessy had taught her; she had her man twirl and flourish her around the circle of party-goers watching them. Thurian lifted her up into the air and placed her back down, where they both clapped their hands twice, then doing the same move a second time where the orchestra inserted a beat similar to the rhythm of their clapping hands. Thurian and Emerie danced for a few more moments until Emerie separated herself from him, where she began to pull in other party-goers, busying the dance floor. She laughed as she pulled Tristan to the floor alongside a woman who she knew was his type of attraction. Her brother reluctantly began to dance the same way she did.

After a few moments Thurian found his way back to Emerie amongst the now busier dance floor, "You're incredible," he gleamed towards Emerie as the party's atmosphere returned to how it was when they entered. Emerie smiled at him and placed her arms around his shoulders with a flirtatious smile, "Pretty good for a peasant girl, right?"

"Pretty good for my future Empress," Thurian answered before he leaned into Emerie and kissed her lips.

Emerie's heart wanted to explode, she couldn't believe this was happening. This was everything that she ever dreamed of and more. But she couldn't help but feel guilty. All she could think of was Vann, about how she had felt towards him her entire life. She wasn't able to call it love, she didn't know if that was what it was, but she knew that Vann was important to her, and he was out in the wild somewhere more than likely trying to look for her. Yet here she was, in a Ballroom kissing Prince Thurian, the man who broke them all apart. Here she was, feeling a sense of completeness as her lips locked with his, a feeling that she didn't feel when she kissed Vann. Her mother always told her that when she met the right person, she would feel it in her heart. She knew that every parent said that to their child, and every child would ignore that dream - but to her, it was true. With Thurian, it felt right.

Emerie pulled her lips away from the multiple exchanges they made with each other and she expressed a meek and tender smile to the man who had been caring for her, "You're a better man than what I imagined you to be."

Thurian's eyes locked with hers, and his brow furrowed, "I hope that I can remain this way, but remember what we're trying to do. Everything I do from this point on will be for you, and for our people."

Emerie hesitated for a moment, she closed her eyes and nodded, "It's going to get more difficult from this moment on, isn't it?"

"It is," Thurian kissed her forehead and then placed a hand against one of her cheeks, "If you look after me, I will look after you."

The two danced for two more songs before they decided to take a momentary break. Thurian had explained to Emerie beforehand that this Masquerade was more about sowing doubt against his sister than it was about celebrating their marriage. That in this time of war, Noble's were looking for allies within their own borders to see what they could gain from the hardship of their people - and although the idea of this disgusted Emerie, she knew that this was a task that they were capable of.

Emerie stood with Thurian against one of the centre pillars as the Prince explained to her who the most important targets of their charm would be. There was the Duke of Sunsrest, a jolly round man who oversaw the farmland of Theothen's most bountiful region - he cared deeply for people of his city and always represented their best interests. There were also the Three High-Bishops who ran their respective faiths of the High Three: Zaer, God of The Light. Kanir, Goddess of Darkness - And Grenden, God of The Middling.

Thurian then pointed to a woman who wore a suit similar to those that Noble Men had been wearing, she had a black half-mask on the left side of her face - with a small chain drooping down from the eye socket of the mask. "That's Harriet Thorunburg. She is the Grand-Warden of Irren's Prison." Thurian explained. Irren's prison, aptly named after the Goddess of Judgement, was homed on an island that sat between Ideneor, Resnia, and Theothen; and was agreed by the Old Kings of Resnia, the Ancient Emperors of Theothen, and the Rusted

Speakers of Ideneor that the prison would be ran independently and would house the most vile and insane prisoners of all countries. Many were sent there to die in the most inhumane ways possible, but many others were sent there to live in the most inhumane ways possible.

A man in the distance, wearing an Ideneorian style of clothing of comfortable yet elegant robes stood out to Emerie as he took a seat on one of the gallery platforms that sat high amongst one of the pillars. He wore comfortable colourful robes primarily of white and red yet there were designs of stories of old embroidered across his garments. Around his flowing black hair was a red headband which dangled jewels and metal from it. He wore no mask revealing his handsome roguish face.

"Who is that?" Emerie asked Thurian.

Thurian chuckled to himself before he answered. "That is Sebastian Mirahana. He is the current Speaker of Ideneor - and the Chosen of Zergrath," Thurian informed, "Take a look at his left hand, you should be able to see it from here I think," he added.

"See what?" Emerie asked as she tried to focus on Sebastian Mirahana's left hand. He eventually raised it to wave at a group of women trying to get his attention from the ballroom floor. She then noticed a constant orange glow that pulsated from the centre of his palm, "What is that?"

"That is one of Zergrath's scales. The tale he tells is that he plucked it from the Dragon himself and seared it into his hand for power. Many people believe it yet I don't think it to be true. It is hard to pick his story apart when he is indeed the second Chosen of the Red Dragon," Thurian answered.

"A Chosen? Like what happened with the first Kings of Humanity?" Emerie asked as her eyes remained on the Ideneorian Noble. Thurian turned her face to his with his finger, "The more you stare at him the more likely you are to get his attention."

"Isn't that a good idea? Surely having someone with a dragon's power would help our cause, right?" she whispered.

"Believe me, he would be of no help, he only cares for Ideneor. He rules his country alongside Zergrath, he is a tyrant and has been so for hundreds of years," Thurian explained quickly with a hushed voice.

Emerie wanted to question what was just said to her, how could a man live for more than one generation? But before her words could escape her an older gentleman interrupted them with a cough. He was slim built and tall, with a side-part in his hair and a moustache that sat firmly on his top lips, just underneath where his green mask ended over his nose. Emerie and Thurian turned to him and they both smiled at almost the exact same time.

"Forgive my interruption, but I was wondering if I may have a word with you, my liege?" The Gentleman asked the Prince. "Of course Lord Wolten," Thurian stepped forward. The Prince then placed his hand on the lower back of Emerie and had her step forward beside him, "This is my betrothed: Emerie Herene."

Lord Wolten evaluated her for a few moments before bowing deeply to her, "Your aura of beauty has not nearly been stated enough."

"Thank you Lord Wolten, that is very kind of you," Emerie smiled graciously. Thurian nodded to her in approval. He then moved his hand away from her waist and motioned it towards Lord Wolten, "Lord Wolten and I will just be a moment. Try and find Sir Tristan to look after you," he instructed towards her, "If you cannot, hail a Scaleguard. They will be lurking nearby."

"Of course, my love," Emerie answered. She had no intention of listening to Thurian. She knew exactly who she was going to speak to: Sebastian Mirahana, Chosen of Zergrath.

Emerie and Thurian walked away from the pillar they had been standing beside and split up, Thurian was led to a group of nobles a few feet away and Emerie began walking into the sea of people that spread across the centre of the ballroom. She felt the eyes of every person she walked past turn to her, and heard their quiet jealous words directed towards her, insults that Emerie had heard from people above her in status many times before. This time however, it didn't feel insulting to her, she found it oddly funny. She was going to be a Princess, she was going to be able to tell every one of these people what to do and how to act, so she thought to herself to allow them a moment of superiority, for she would remember the voices of who was calling her a peasant now.

She looked up towards the platform that Sebastian Mirahana had claimed for himself and was thankful to see he was still there sitting alone, but now he was watching her as she made her way towards his column. She was allowed past the Scaleguards who stood by the bottom of the stairs where she began to ascend the golden spiral staircase towards the Speaker of Ideneor. She didn't feel nervous which seemed strange to her. All of the most powerful people in the land are in this very room, yet she was more worried about whether her presentation had been good enough so far than she was worried about meeting this man.

As she reached the final step and walked onto the marble platform, Sebastian had stood up to place a seat next to his. He smiled at her and nodded his head towards the comfortable chair, "Please, young one."

Emerie walked to the front of the chair and moved her skirt forward as she took a seat, with Sebastian moving it forward to line it beside his. "Are you enjoying your first royal engagement?" He asked with his smooth and charming accent. It had a griff to its tone, and he chewed a few words as he spoke yet it sounded as if he was trying not to sing.

"To be honest with you, this is the closest thing I would imagine to being accepted by Zaer, my lord," Emerie spoke, not trying to hide her happiness as she had done so when she moved through the crowd.

"I'm not your lord sweet girl, if anything I am your enemy," Sebastian spoke honestly, "So imagine my surprise a moment ago to see you swimming through the sea of vipers to speak with me."

Sebastian leaned beside himself towards the small round table that sat between him and Emerie, Emerie watched as he poured a vintage of red wine into his glass, and then into one that sat beside her.

"Do you partake?" He asked her as the liquid filled near the rim. Emerie leaned forward and took her glass, sipping it away from her body with as much class as she could while trying not to spill the wine onto her dress. She finished half the glass before setting it down, to then meet Sebastian small chuckle, "Oh there will be stories of you being an alcoholic from now on my dear."

"What do you mean?" Emerie asked innocently.

Sebastian moved a hand with dramatic effect as it brushed over the crowd of party-goers beneath their platform, "Every single person here is watching you and Thurian, they are trying to judge you. Some want you dead already, and some find you endearing. But then there are those such as me, who aren't quite sure how to take you. You are a peasant girl, one who lost her home due to the war that your betrothed started - so I do not see a situation where you could fall in love with a man who simply gave you a grander home than the ones he burned down because he discovered what guilt feels like."

"What do you mean? Prince Thurian and I met in Avane where we fell in love quickly, a whirlwind romance," Emerie spoke in a way that she was obviously reciting a fake story to the Red Dragon's Chosen. It was clear to Emerie that Sebastian already knew way more about her than she had expected.

Sebastian took a sip of his wine and released a laugh, "Oh I like you. You are one of those girls that are secretly in it for themselves, aren't you?"

"No, I would not say so," Emerie quickly replied, "I am making a good life out of a bad situation. Thurian is kind, smart, sweet, and very handsome. He's been good to me these last few days. And the home that he burned down, he is rebuilding, he said he would. He is a good man, and he will make a great Emperor"

"Emperor?" Sebastian snarked, "Your betrothed does remember that he has become second in line? Dira is to be Empress when that rotten carcass over there finally dies," The Chosen spoke with a disgusted voice towards the Emperor that remained sleeping on his throne. It had almost become a sick display of the broken ruler, his almost-corpse rotting in front of his people who ignored him, dancing their problems away.

"You make it obvious that you know who I am and my history, yet you pretend that you know nothing of the conspiracies within the court, why is that?" Emerie asked innocently.

"Because I'm trying to teach you how to act," Sebastian revealed, "Being pretty and well-liked will only get you so far - you need to understand when to speak and when to keep your mouth closed shut. Anything that you say will lead to somebody being killed, and everything you do will also lead to a death. So you might want to take that into account next time you speak, even to me."

The Dragon's Chosen made a display of swapping his glass into his left hand where the orange glow continued to pulsate from his palm. The light shone through the wine glass and created a beautiful display onto the white table between the two of them. He looked towards Emerie and she could feel his gaze analyse her like everyone else's had ever since she had stepped foot into the capital.

"I was like you, three hundred and seventy-something years ago," Sebastian sighed.

"You were?" Emerie questioned with a little chuckle, still not believing his age. She reached to her glass of wine and took a sip, keeping the glass in her hand as she relaxed herself into the padded chair.

"I was a gambling addict, I spent all of my earnings trying to end up rich so that I could go to places like this. I spent too many sovereigns that did not belong to me and so I ended up in a labour camp - searching through blistering hot sand where my skin peeled, all to find scrap metal that remained from an ancient battleground," Sebastian reminisced, "and then I found this," he pointed to his left hand holding the glass of wine.

"The vintage?" Emerie asked. Sebastian rolled his eyes.

"A Red Scale that belonged to Zergrath, and with its power I became so much more than I could ever have dreamed of. And I believe that your friend Vann is about to walk down the same path as I," Sebastian smiled as he watched the dancers below him still.

"Vann? What does he have to do with any of this? How do you know about him?" Emerie questioned. He had to be bluffing, there was know way that he knew anything about him. She had to try and play Vann down from this point on, she didn't want to put him in danger. Nor Owain, Martell, or even the blonde girl.

Sebastian released a very audible laugh that caused a few looks from below to appear their way. He polished off his glass of wine and poured another one, then silently asking with a wiggle of the bottle of Emerie wanted a refill to which she declined.

"Your boyfriend has associated himself with a very dangerous man who goes by the name of Harnon. I guess you could call him a brother of mine, or at the very least we are in the same club," Sebastian smiled to himself once more, trying not to laugh. "And I have recently discovered through a much worse person that there is a girl I should be worrying about."

"So you're telling me Vann is friends with a dragon called Harnon?" Emerie asked, her confusion towards Sebastian continued to grow as she tried to ignore his query towards the blonde girl.

"Oh gods no, that man does not know how to bathe, there is no way he was made in an Ethereal's image," Sebastian finally released his second laugh, though it rang much quieter than the last and ended in a drunken snicker. "Regardless, you might want to find yourself looking towards Beonyth's Green when your Prince completes his little plan of Regicide. There's going to be one grand war when he begins his rule, I cannot tell you how excited Zergrath and I are. It is quite a nice thing to see, he is usually a very vicious monster so seeing happiness in my dear friend is quite uplifting."

"Of course there is going to be a war," Emerie replied , "We're already in one, it's just going to get worse before it gets better."

"His words?" Sebastian asked.

"No, mine," Emerie snapped, "My family and my village were the first to lose everything. I am no fool, I know that Thurian somehow started this war, but I am just me. I cannot return to the past to change things, all I can do is help him make amends for his actions. He is going to change Taundrad for the better, including your desert land."

"Be careful Princess," Sebastian tilted his head and raised an eyebrow to her, "That sounds like a threat towards my country. A dangerous thing to throw about when darker things lie below this castle."

What did he mean? Was he once again trying to tell her in a roundabout way to watch her back? Her entire interaction with Zergrath's Chosen felt like he was talking in riddles, trying his hardest to confuse her and make her doubt herself

"Now, if you will excuse yourself, Future Empress, I have other appointees to attend to, they have been staring at me for quite a while," Sebastian waved towards a group of men and women below him.

Emerie stood up from her comfortable seat and looked across the ballroom to see if she could find her brother, and after scouting almost half of the crowd she managed to spot Tristan dancing with the girl she had set him up with.

"May I ask one more thing?" Emerie looked to Sebastian as she walked towards the staircase, "How have you lived for so long?"

Sebastian Mirahana's eyes met Emerie's with a cold stare, as if his entire life was flashing before him. The persona he had put on for the party, and for her, faded as he considered an answer for Emerie.

"It's easier to live when you have nothing to lose."

Arvuria: The Ethereal Children

Emerie left Sebastian on his platform to his weirdly adoring fans and made her way down the spiral staircase. She counted her interaction with the Chosen as a success, she had made a good enough impression towards him for him to give her advice, and to show that he was interested by her situation, which she surmised that getting his help in the future could be an option. She walked through the crowd of people once more only this time not one insulting word was whispered her way, and in their place were words of admiration about how she had just spoken with the Speaker of Ideneor. She had no idea that it was a good thing when Thurian had warned her against doing so.

Emerie managed to find Tristan who was now hurrying between the crowd towards her with a panicked expression underneath his mask with sweat dripping from his skin. He barged the crowd out of the way towards Emerie who noticed another masked man heading towards her to the left of the same direction. The masked man's eyes were locked upon her - his eyes were glowing and when his lips moved a spark of green light escaped his lips as he spoke quietly. Fear blasted through her body, she began to tremble and her feet remained attached to the floor, she couldn't move.

"Emerie!" Tristan shouted as he continued to barge his way through the crowd. The masked man dropped a knife into his hand from the sleeve of his black coat and began to thrust it towards her throat - however, just before the blade met her skin, a sword penetrated through his chest where blood spurted over Emerie's red dress, with the crimson landing on the skin of her face and neck.

Behind the would-be assassin's neck appeared Prince Thurian who's mask had been broken, now hanging down from his neck. He pulled the sword from his enemy's chest and swung the blade towards the assassin, beheading him. The head rolled into the now scarce crowd where it created a trail of blood leading towards the Emperor.

The fear that Emerie felt disappeared, and in its stead became anger. Everything that she had done so far felt like the correct thing to do - she hadn't personally angered anyone, and she did not feel as though she had offended anyone either. So why had an assassin already been sent to claim her life?

Thurian's footsteps echoed across the ballroom floor that had grown eerily quiet. He was the only person in the room moving. He lifted the bloodied head with his hand and paraded it around the circle that had formed around him and Emerie.

"This is your attempt?!" He shouted towards the masked attendees of the party. "You think I would allow one lowly Arcanist to harm her?" He spat with venom, "I know that there are more of you in this hall. So eager to be the one to kill me, to earn the favour of my sister and of the vipers that surround you. I warn you now, I am not the man I was when I left this city. I left a broken man, like my father, who you laugh at and mock as The Emperor's rot takes over his mind," Thurian pointed towards the Emperor's platform.

Thurian pulled his arm back and launched the assassin's head towards the Emperor with such ferocity that it managed to sail onto the floating platform. "It was that creature up there who wanted to kill her, to kill the woman that I love!" Thurian roared, "That is the Emperor that you follow today, one who harms innocent people to please the many of you who are so focused on what is only good for you! So focused on how you will line your pockets with Sovereigns and blackmail, so that you can climb the ladder of nobility on the chance that one day you might sit on my rightful throne. I will not allow it. I will not allow it any more."

Arvuria: The Ethereal Children

"Thurian, what are you doing?" Emerie whispered to her partner, who met her eyes with his. She could see his broken heart glistening amongst his iris'.

"What I am doing is fixing this gods-forsaken country," Thurian replied, "I will bleed each and every one of you who dares oppose me. I will create the country that The Golden Dragon Arvur, and our first Emperor dreamed of: I will create a bastion of hope. A land where people help each other because it is the right thing to do. I am going to be The Emperor who creates True Peace." he finished, his voice broken over the seethe of his anger.

"Enough of this!" A matriarchal voice beckoned from the entrance of the ballroom. An army of twenty Scaleguard stood behind this older woman. Her hair long and grey draped over her abyssian black dress with ornate pale-silver metal protecting her chest and shoulders.

"Prince Thurian, I remind you of your place in this court," the woman walked into the hall. The crowd parted her way as they squashed against each other in the crowded room.

"You disrespect your father in such an open manner as if you had no blessing from him to marry this woman that you bring into our home," She began once more, "You have been second-in-line to your sister in recent months. A shameful Prince, shunned by the court for your actions in Resnia, yet here you are protecting a would-be Princess in place of where you failed last time. A Princess of Theothen. In my eyes, my son, you have redeemed yourself. What is a Resnian dog compared to the beauty of one of our people?"

The Empress. Thurian hadn't mentioned his mother to Emerie more than once, all she knew about the Empress was that she was always so focused on ruling in The Emperor's stead that she rarely ever left her office which was placed so far below in the caverns of the castle.

She would deliver her husband's mad rule of Theothen, but doing so in a way where the country wouldn't fall apart. She had been The Shadow of Arvur for many years, and some might even have called her the true crowned monarch.

"I have not redeemed myself, and I will not have done so until peace has been established," Thurian muttered to his mother.

The Empress looked towards the red streak of blood that ran away from them on the white marble floors, "Peace? A fool's dream. Though I wonder, and I am sure so do your patrons here tonight, how would you establish peace, Thurian?"

Emerie watched over Thurian, his fists clenched as he held in his anger. He looked towards her, asking for her help, but all she could do was give him a meek smile and mouth an almost silent, "Show them who you are."

"I would weed out those of you who would dare undermine me, and I would rip your titles from you, I would claim your lands, and I would replace you with people who give a damn about their country - about their people," Thurian answered, his voice travelling through the now cold air of the hall where voices began to mutter to each other.

"And what happens when the civil war begins?" The Empress asked, tapping her foot into the red blood she had been admiring. "Do you think your Noble men and women would allow you to take their homes so readily? All because you disagree with how they run them?"

"They would, or they would die. If that isn't enough for them, then their families would join them in judgement. It is not about disagreeing, it is about the greater good of all," Thurian answered calmly.

Arvuria: The Ethereal Children

Emerie frowned at the words, but she knew it must be a necessary evil. It's like her mother would say, if something is rotten remove it from the rest, lest it's corruption spread.

"So you, a man who believes he is of noble heart, would quiet opposing beliefs so that you can instil your own will on the people - all in the goal of 'true peace' ? Do you not see the hypocrisy?" The Empress questioned further.

"It needs to be done!" Thurian shouted to his mother, "It needs to be done!" He roared again to the crowd around him. "There is a blight in these lands, of selfishness and greed, and it needs to be dealt with. Your Emperor is a rotting corpse with the mind of two men, how can you believe that he cares for you? Dira is a blood-soaked psychopath who cares only for war, do you believe that she has Theothen's best interest at heart? Tell me, please, Anyone. Tell me that what I believe needs to be done is wrong," Thurian begged.

"I am Theothen's last hope in this world gone mad, I am the only man who can fix what you have all created. A country where everyone hates each other, where people only care for themselves. I am the only man who can create the Utopia that Arvur believed we could be. I am a descendent of the Golden Emperor! His blood runs through my veins, and I swear to you that I will live to his ideals!" Thurian pointed towards the ceiling, towards the artistic display of the golden dragon above him.

Emerie stood in the silence of the hall for what felt like a lifetime, but one voice appeared that broke the spell of uncertainty. "Emperor Thurian! Long live Emperor Thurian!" One voice cheered for Thurian. That's all it took for opinion to sway behind Thurian. The entire hall of Theothen's and other supporters all began to cry out in support of Thurian.

Luke Morgan

One voice created the song of his name.

One voice of a random patron had changed the course of history.

Arvuria: The Ethereal Children

- Chapter 20 -
THURIAN THEO
You and I.

THURIAN HAD PULLED her from the White Hall and escorted her to her room following the assassination attempt on her life. She didn't know how to feel, she didn't know how she should feel - the only emotion that was coursing through her soul was anger. Pure radiant anger. She was an innocent woman, she had never caused harm to anyone in her world, all she had done since the day she was born was simply exist, taking one day after the other - keeping herself to herself so that the aim to live unto the next day would come true.

She had been naive, of course she had. The Prince of the most powerful country in the known lands asked her, a nobody, to help him take control of his father's Empire, and she believed she had the capacity to aid him with no harm coming to her. She could still visualise the knife coming towards her throat at this very moment, the man's eye's filled with venom as he stopped her movement with a simple yet powerful Arcane Tether. She had no chance to change her fate in that moment, yet Thurian saved her from the anger of those who did not see her as human but instead a lowly peasant girl who was out of her depth. And she was. If there was one thing, however, that Emerie knew she was; it was that she was so much more than what she believed she was even if these 'Noble' people were incapable of seeing that. She was so much more.

Everyone is.

She sat on her bed as her body trembled in Thurian's arms as the scene of her near-death continued over and over. He leaned her head against his chest and stroked her hair that began to return to its wild curls as his hands unravelled it from its tangled prison. She felt a comfort that she hadn't had in a long time: Someone caring for her out of the kindness of their heart - this man who had just declared war on many noble families; The Emperor himself would rather be here, with her, making sure that she was okay instead of having someone else take her to safety.

She delicately pulled herself away from Thurian's chest and looked up to him where his tired eyes met hers, "Thank you…" she croaked, the remainder of her fear slowly escaping her. He placed a hand on one of her cheeks and gave her a tender smile, where a splatter of dried blood remained across the left side of his face. "I am here. I will not let harm come to you while you are with me," he promised to her.

There it was again, that feeling in her chest while he looked at her, with his kind words flowing into her ears. Emerie leaned upwards and kissed him another, where the same feeling as hours ago cascaded through her. She didn't have to be the abrupt girl who had to keep her friends in line, she didn't have to force herself to be strong within the wilderness anymore, she knew that she could let her guard down with him... but within these walls she also knew that he was one of the only three that she could trust.

Everything Sebastian Mirahana had tried to get across to her was now sinking in.

Thurian returned her kiss as tenderly as she asked for it, but after a few moments he pulled away from her and began to slowly pace around the room.

"What is it?" Emerie asked him, disappointed that he had shied away from her for the first time. Thurian removed his green suit jacket from himself and threw it to the floor unveiling his red shirt that had darker crimson spots now etched into it.

"I have been here before Emerie, and it scares me," The Prince revealed, "The last time that I loved another, her throat was slit as we awoke in the morning. I fear for you, I truly do. I am scared that the feelings that have quickly appeared for you will grow into something that I cannot stop. An ember that turns into a roaring blaze. You are a kind person with a good heart - I should not have brought you here."

"I want to be here," Emerie quickly retaliated, "I want to help you fix the land that we live in."

Emerie watched as Thurian ran a hand down his face in stress and turned away from her, looking towards the mirror placed in the corner of the room. She could see his eyes didn't have the warmth that usually lit them, and instead was a pain of knowing what he had to do - his hair, usually kept and styled, was now dishevelled and messy. Emerie stood up from the bed and floated towards

Arvuria: The Ethereal Children

Thurian, with her red dress flowing behind her, leading the crimson river towards him.

"We have both spoken of our fathers very little. But mine was a good man in past times, he was a soldier of your Empire in his early years and managed to survive many battles. He never ascended the ranks, nor did he want to - yet he always told me that he had lost count of the number of men he killed... as well as women and children. He and his best friend moved to a small village at the border between Resnia and Theothen, it's called Orans, a place I would not be surprised if you were unaware of. The houses and land down there are cheap enough for a retired soldier to make a home for himself," Emerie spoke quietly as one of her hands slowly stroked the back of Thurian.

"When Tristan and I grew in age, we noticed that his habits were not of a normal man when we compared him to most. He would wake up in the night screaming, and he would always have a bottle of alcohol within reach - where our stomachs would hunger his would be lined with strong liquor. In these moments, should you dare to disagree with him, or even ask for a bite of something he would meet you with his fists and then lock us behind The Black Door. Tristan would always be the one with more bruises than I, and when our friend Vann noticed this he would always come to our home every day to find an excuse to take us away from it. Not one day went by where I wasn't thankful to see Vann's face, but now I do not know where he is. He saved us from a lot of hardship by braving our doorstep, and I look at you now and I see that you and he share the trait of caring for others when it is not asked of you. You are willing to stand up for those that you should see as beneath you. That is what will make you a great Emperor."

"Vann is the one that I gifted the gold to?" Thurian asked with a soft tone.

Emerie moved the hand that stroked Thurian's back tenderly into one of his hands, and gave it a light squeeze, "That was him. "

"He was the son of my father's best friend. Who gave all three of us supplies and a kick up the ass to get ourselves towards Avane before the war would reach our village. I don't know what has become of my father, or Vann's father in these last few months, but I hope that they are both okay."

"You hope for fortune towards your father despite him starving and beating you?" Thurian asked bluntly towards Emerie, who was now meeting his sight through the mirror.

"Yes," Emerie answered, "And I know that deep down you still hope fortune for your father. Though I must not lie, every single day I wished that I met my father's rage with my own - as does Tristan, who has vowed to never tolerate such a thing again from anyone. That's why he wishes to be a Knight , to protect the innocents from monsters like him. I have come to learn that when it is people we love doing us harm, either small or large, it is easy for us to turn a blind eye to their actions because we deem them good people, we have to, because nobody should love a bad person. If you love one, then surely that makes you one too, right? That's what I used to think, that I was an evil girl because I loved an evil man, it made me sick to my stomach. But now I don't believe it. Not one bit. I am not evil for showing sympathy. It makes me feel good knowing that despite all the bad I went through I can still come out smiling at the end of a dark road. Compassion is a trait of your own, it doesn't tie you to anybody."

Emerie tilted her body in front of Thurian to get his attention from the mirror, where he then turned his body to meet hers. "You are not a bad person for still loving your father, Thurian."

"My father is no longer the man sitting on the Throne," Thurian answered to her. "I love the man that he used to be. Before the rot of his addiction took him from me."

Emerie remembered the image of the rotten man sitting on the floating platform in the Masquerade. She remembered all the stories she had heard of The Emperor all his life and the atrocities he had committed in recent times compared to the honourable decisions he had made as a Prince. Emerie compared her father with Thurian's, and the next words out of her mouth were the ones that she had always wanted to hear.

"Then you must avenge the man that your father was. Become a better person than he could ever have been - that is your responsibility."

Luke Morgan

Arvuria: The Ethereal Children

- Chapter 21 -
THURIAN THEO
The Crown Sits Heavy.

WHAT DOES A man do when the only option they have is to commit the greatest sin? It was a question that Thurian asked to himself over and over again as he stood before the great door once more - with the story of The Five Dragons displayed in front of him once more. His gaze lingered onto the image of Arvur, The Golden Dragon and wondered if he would give him his blessing, to do what must be done to bring The Theothen Empire back to the roots of its creation.

A part of him didn't want to succeed in his plan, he didn't want to be the one to kill his father… if his father was even in his own mind anymore. The rot of his body began with his over-abundant use of The Arcane during his Princely years battling Resnia in the previous war. It

Arvuria: The Ethereal Children

was always something Arcanist's feared when using their power, to use the power of The Ethereals you must in turn give to them a part of yourself, an exchange between you and The Ones Above. His father was a prime example of what addiction to the Arcane can do to oneself - and in his addiction his personality had split, The Emperor became one half of him, and his true self was the other - the good and the bad of his soul split right down the centre of his heart. Some would call this a mercy killing, many even called for this years ago but The Empress decreed him sound of mind. So here stood Thurian, Prince of The Theothen Empire in nothing but his casual clothing of boots, black trousers, his red shirt and his silver sword in his hands.

He climbed the stairs to the doors and pushed them open to see the same view as he did yesterday: The grandiose white throne room with rows of the black armoured Scaleguard leading to The Emperor.

As Thurian took his first step into the large room every single one of the thirty Scaleguard turned towards him leaning forwards as they half-drew their obsidian black blades. The Emperor came from his slumber to greet his son with a drooling smile of saliva and pus, "My dear boy you have finally arrived to take me from this world. I waited all these many hours after your display in Theo's Hall, why did you keep me waiting?"

The doors slowly closed behind Thurian who began to take deep calming breaths as he stood before the incredibly threatening army of thirty of the most Elite soldiers in the entire Empire. "I was debating whether my goal was worth it. To kill my father so that I can lead our family's Empire to what it should be - to what it was," Thurian announced with sadness in his tone, the hesitance of his soul seeping into his words.

"You never unsheathe your sword if you do not intend to use it," his father said to him, "So it seems that you have made your decision. You will kill me tonight. If you do not, I will parade your traitorous body among the streets and slaughter all the people that you hold dear. I am done playing games with you, you pathetic child, I would gladly be rid of all memory and knowledge of you. You utter Disappointment," The Emperor spat, lifting himself off his Throne an inch in anger with his unrotten arm.

Thurian released a breath and tightened his grip around his sword. He looked to the Scaleguard in front of him, "I know you have all sworn a sacred vow to defend the Crown of my Ancestors from those who would do it harm, to defend the wearer until their dying breath. But I ask you, do you see The Emperor as he once was? An honourable man who would put others first? A brilliant father who loved his children dearly? Or do you see the rotten carcass that I see? A vicious monster who has done nothing to aid our country within the last decade. A husk of evil who has murdered lords, burned villages, and taxed the poor into oblivion. You are the greatest warriors in all of Taundrad, some of you are of noble kin, and some of you were ordinary men - yet you all became extraordinary. I am asking you now to make a decision. You can side with me and together we can return our Empire to its former glory, or you can fight me, here and now, as you defend what we have become. The choice is yours, you have my eternal respect no matter which side you stand upon in this moment."

The silence from The Scaleguard was ever present and the tension in the air thickened as each of them considered their options.

"For the first time in many years of your lives, you are allowed to make a choice of your own. I beg of you to make one," Thurian pleaded, "That's what I am promising for your future: A Choice. Which is more than he has ever given to you."

The Scaleguard remained as they were, ever watchful to a threat to the Crown, but the Prince could feel the hesitance radiate into the air. Thurian steeled himself and began to walk down the red pathway towards his father. He stepped past the first two guards who sheathed their swords as he moved past them, and then same for the next two. Thurian remained tense around the blade he held as he remained keeping his eyes locked onto The Emperor who continued to taunt with a smile that begged for death. When Thurian heard the first blades to be drawn amongst the fifth and sixth Scaleguard he met their blades equally in a cross as they both aimed to decapitate him with one fell strike. Thurian pushed the blades away from him and stepped back as The two Scaleguard stepped in between him and The Emperor. In this moment the heavy footsteps of all the Elite Soldiers moved from their line towards The Emperor into two opposing factions as they drew their weapons against each other. Ten beside Thurian, and twenty against him. To Thurian, it felt almost unfair that they only had ten more than his aides, for he entered this room ready to fight the entire thirty of them.

Thurian looked to the two Scaleguard who had drawn against him first, "Cross blades with me," he smiled as he stood unarmoured. And in that moment a loud clang of metal echoed across the White Room as all swords clashed against each other in perfect synchronisation. Each soldier in this room bar Thurian had trained with each other for years, becoming one perfectly tuned unit but as of this very moment the battle lines had been drawn and their brotherhood had split, committing to their beliefs instead of their comradery.

Luke Morgan

Thurian battled against the two black blades with a flurry of his instinct and training as he tried to put a wedge between their combination of attacks as his opponents were using each other almost as an extra limb, as if they could read each others attack before they made it.

The Emperor cackled, "This is the most fun I have had in years!"

Thurian managed to parry one of the black blades and push it back with a swipe of his swords razored edge, interrupting the balance of one of his opponents where he then ducked the swipe of the second and forced his silver sword underneath the opening of their helmet, where the sword entered the bottom of their jaw and clanged the top of the inside of their helmet. The Prince then yanked the blade from the man he had killed and took his opponent's black blade where he wielded both weapons to release a flurry of strikes onto his other opponent to finally behead him with a cross of his two blades. Returning the Scaleguards first intent.

The Prince bolted between the line of the twenty Scaleguard and jumped forward, diving over the attacks of a few more black blades, then rolling and slicing sideways to cut the back of one of their knees, where the unlucky enemy was quickly stabbed by one of Thurian's Scaleguard.

Thurian climbed to his feet and pointed the black sword he held to his father, "Fight me, I will not kill an unarmed man," he called out to him, throwing the sword towards The Emperor with its obsidian blade embedding into the stone floor just an inch away from his foot. The Scaleguard continued to fight as The Emperor tilted his head and creased his smile further - he pushed himself from the Throne with some of his rotten flesh sticking to it, with wet strings of meat following him. The Emperor took the handle of the weapon with the rotten grasp of his larger hand, "You should have just executed me. I did not teach you to be weak."

The Emperor breathed in and out for a few short moments until a glow of purple began to seep from inside of him with his size growing a percentage larger, the purple in his skin radiated downwards towards the hilt of the sword where it ignited a violet fire across the dark sword in his hand.

"No man is weak, every single one of us has the power to defy - that is what you taught me!" Thurian spat back at the rotten man in front of him, "You were my father once, but you stopped being that man the moment you chose addiction over me."

"I don't care for your speeches," The Emperor grimaced as he hurried forward with his Arcane-Enabled body, crossing swords with his son.

Thurian had never believed that his life would come to this moment. His father raised him to be a good man and that's what he had always strived to be - his father had always wanted the best for him which is why he had Thurian and The Princess of Resnia aim to be married. Thurian had loved her all his life, since they were children, and when she was murdered right in front of him his father appeared from The Emperor and comforted him. Yet he could see that his father was barely in the man before him anymore. All that was left was the rotten monster who cared nothing for him. His father appearing yesterday was his last ditch effort of getting through to his son. Be aware of what lies below.

The Emperor met Thurian's blade with skill and position with his long rotten-growth arm, his reach and strength giving him the advantage against Thurian but The Prince knew he could turn this situation to favour him, all he had to do was stop The Emperor's connection with the Arcane, once that was done he would not have his buff of strength.

The Scaleguard slowly began to end their fight as The Prince and The Emperor did battle - the Elite Knights moved around the duellists creating a circle, the bodies of their fallen comrades lying scattered around them.

Thurian remembered the teachings of his mother, The Empress, that the best way to sever the connection of The Arcane was to find the thread a user had made and remove it any way that you can - where most Arcanists would create a tether by swiping their fingers from the source around them, some skilled users were capable of absorbing the tether into them, which Thurian knew his father was capable after his intense use and studying of the power.

"You were always a disappointment Thurian. I wish Dira was here now to rid me of you with ease," The Emperor goaded, "Your sister was always my greatest creation."

Thurian flipped to the side of The Emperor's diagonal slice towards him, landing cleanly on his feet to then take a chunk out from his opponent's rotten arm, revealing a glow of purple, "If Dira was here I am sure she would cheer my name."

"Thurian!" All of The Scaleguards chanted in unison. Their metallic voices echoing through their helmets with a thunderous roar. Thurian's name was repeated over and over amongst his men.

Thurian swiped downwards against the coming horizontal blade of The Emperor, parrying it with such force that the purple-glowing arcane sword split in half, releasing an explosion of power knocking the two duellists backwards a few feet but both remaining on their feet.

Arvuria: The Ethereal Children

"I will not let you kill me you insolent child!" The Emperor screamed as his Arcane Aura grew larger and brighter. Thurian flipped the sword in his hand so that he wielded it backwards, he knew what he had to do. The Emperor charged towards him with incredible speed and uppercutted Thurian's chest, sending him far into the air where Thurian battled through the pain that tried to drag him into unconsciousness and looked downwards to the Arcane glow in his fathers rotten arm - he pointed his silver sword downwards and aimed it towards his target as he fell. He only had one chance.

The Emperor raised his rotten arm with what Thurian assumed an intent to catch him and snap his neck but Thurian was a step ahead, he tilted his body just enough before his opponent caught him and stabbed downwards unto the arm splitting it in two - severing The Emperor's connection to The Arcane as his golden blade slid through the tether.

The Emperor screamed in agony but was quickly silenced when Thurian climbed back to his feet and beheaded his attacker, the same way that he had done to the failed assassin who had tried to end Emerie.

His father's head dropped to the floor, where the golden crown with its draconic imagery bounced off it, separating from his rotten skin. In that moment all noise was silenced apart from the roll of the crown as it headed back towards the throne.

The Scaleguard lined up again between the door and the throne, giving Thurian a pathway to the empty seat of The Theothen Empire. The Prince looked towards the chair as the simple white-gold throne stood imposing before the golden pathway that led towards it, with the golden crown continuing to correct itself as it twirled as a coin does when one is dropped to the floor. The specks of blood dripping from it splattered slowly against its surroundings. Thurian floated towards it all. He looked downwards to the crown and lifted it onto his head to then take his rightful place as The Emperor as he sat in his Father's rot... while the blood on the crown dripped down over his brow.

He leaned back into the uncomfortable throne knowing that everything was about to change. Knowing that he was about to change everything, no matter what he had to do. He was going to defeat Resnia, he was going to correct his country, and he was going to prepare for the Golden Girl that everyone seemed so afraid of. Thurian Theothen was going to bring His Empire to a second Golden Age.

Just as Emperor Theo was, he too would be The Golden Emperor.

Arvuria: The Ethereal Children

- Chapter 22 -
SHIN WATERMAN
The Shallow End.

STEAK, THAT WAS what was on the menu tonight. To The Blood Dragons, that only meant one thing: War.

"Our Princess sends us to fight once more! Drink the tankards down my brothers for we may not see another night like this!" Markus cheered among the small pocket of Dira's unit.

Shin walked from the row of chefs after collecting her meal of Steak, rice, and a random selection of vegetables the chefs had to offer. The Chefs were known to dollop food onto plates without care as to whether the meal particularly made sense. The smartest Blood Dragons always made sure to thank them for many a soldier had been killed for asking for other options.

Arvuria: The Ethereal Children

Underneath the grey showering sky were hundreds of Blood Dragons sitting in the Mess Hall which was just a series of benches and tables underneath multiple large tents to shelter them from the rain that began to trickle down over the War Camp. Surrounding the benches were heated lamps each made from a small Ressoran stone where the energy source was used to keep the troops warm amongst the cold Spring night.

Shin walked towards a portion of her unit and placed her tray at the edge of the bench where Markus had been cheering and gloating about the battle to come. All her brothers sat in their crimson under-armour of leather padding and wool, with most of their clothing covered in ale and food.

"She has seen what we are capable of first hand, I must ask Sergeant Brennan to volunteer us for the Vanguard!" Markus toasted his tankard once more with the brothers cheering in agreement.

"Markus you should be resting still, it has not been near a week since you were wounded," Shin spoke matter-of-factly.

The Blood Dragon turned to his left and looked down towards his healer, "You are eating with us tonight?"

"Yes," Shin smiled.

"Why? You are known to eat with The Menders."

Shin remembered why. As much as she liked a good ruckus and the fun that comes along with it, she usually enjoyed peace and quiet while eating much more. Meathead soldiers shouting weren't the best option for a quiet night - but they were certainly a fun one. She didn't want to tell them all the real reason why she was eating with them. She didn't want them all to know that she was enjoying what might be her last evening with the people whose lives are in her hands. She didn't want them to know the incredible doubt that she had in her heart about laying siege to her own city. If she were to find Mathane, alive or dead, she wondered how she would act. What would she do?

"The Menders don't have steak tonight. They have turkey. I don't like the turkey they cook, they always make it so dry," Shin scoffed as she cut up her steak into pieces ready for her to pick at with her fork.

"They have turkey?!" Frenk complained with his head tilted backwards, "I fucking love turkey."

Shin breathed a laugh as Jeffer slapped Frenk around the back of his head, "You love everything. All you do is eat."

Markus placed himself down onto his seat next to Shin and turned to her with a wry smile.

"You know, I haven't spent much time with you outside of our battles. I haven't realised how pretty you are," he grinned.

Shin battled her face's need to scrunch up in rejection.

"I haven't realised that you have a couple of grey hairs in that beard of yours. We are all learning something new tonight," Shin smiled happily in return.

"You got a man waiting for you back where you're from? You are always sending letters," Markus asked rather politely as he turned his body towards her.

'Here we go' Shin thought in irritation. She just wanted to eat her food and leave. So much for platonic bonding.

"No, I am sending to my brother," Shin replied as she scooped up some rice from her plate, "I have no man."

"Do you want one?" Markus smiled again.

"Markus," Shin smiled in return, "I am not looking for a suitor - If I were I would absolutely not be looking for one from those in this Warband. You lot are much too filthy," She finished with a louder voice and a raised tankard, to which her fellow Blood Dragons cheered in unison.

"To us filthy bastards!" Frenk cheered.

"To you filthy bastards!" Shin called out in response with her eyes remaining locked with Markus who looked at her inquiringly. She had unintentionally garnered his attention, and his thoughts. His distraction quickly ended when his eyes shot behind her - they widened in fear. Shin felt someone just behind her with a cold presence etching into her skin. All her brothers and sisters stood up from the bench while other soldiers around them watched with interest.

"Mender Waterman," Dira announced, "Filthy Bastards," she then acknowledged, which garnered a few fearful laughs.

Shin stood up and turned around slowly where an awkward smile followed suit. She looked upon the woman she had spent the previous evening with to find that The Princess was hiding a small smirk on her lips underneath her aura of authority. The Princess was, too, wearing her under-armour that was similar to the red of her troops except in colour, for hers was a black that was just a hint lighter than her short obsidian hair.

"Princess Dira," Shin saluted.

Dira nodded to Shin who placed her arm down to her sides after the acknowledgement. "You will join me tonight for we have much to discuss."

"By The Ethereals she is asking for Shin," Jeffer whispered.

"Quiet fool, The Princess is right there," Frenk replied.

Shin let slip a smile to Dira but the alarm bells in her head were ringing as if they were the war sign itself. This woman wanted to siege her home city, yet she felt excited to spend an evening with her - she did not know how to feel. She just felt awkward, and dirty about the hope she had.

"Finish dining with your brothers and sisters. Once you are done head to my tent. Do not make me wait for we have much to discuss," Dira ordered before turning around and walking away. Shin could almost swear she saw a hint of pink on The Princess' face.

Shin watched The Blood Dragon walk away from her with no guards and no armour - walking through the War Camp as if she was any other soldier. She was known to act as common as everyone else, she wanted to be respected out of her own display, not simply because of her title, and because of this the thousands of men and women in this camp followed her devoutly.

"How the fuck do you know The Princess?" Markus questioned as he yanked her back down to her seat with the pull of her wrist.

Shin pulled her arm away from her comrade and frowned at him, "I will not speak if you treat me in such a way."

Markus lifted his hands in apology but his faint scowl still covered his face, "We have been fighting for her for years yet she just sees us as soldiers. You are just a Mender yet she knows your name. You must tell us how."

Shin looked around the table to see the eager attention of all of her given family. She sighed. "One of her Claws needed medical attention and I was the Mender who was close enough to help. It is as simple as that. So maybe she wants to thank me?" Shin lied and finished with a shrug as she turned her attention back to her meal where she began to scoff it down as quickly as possible. She wanted to see Dira.

"The Blood Dragon doesn't thank anyone, I have never heard such a thing," Markus disregarded, "You've been up to something haven't you?"

"Markus be calm," Frenk spoke up, "Shin saved us all days ago, perhaps the notice she had gained with the Arcane dome has brought her to Dira's sights, and as such she was brought to help one of those Claws that guard her tent."

Shin was trying not to give the man next to her any sign of her lying. If she was to speak of her evening with Dira all hell would break loose - to become close to Dira is to become a target. In an army that respects strength above all else, you would be required to prove that you are able to stand beside Dira, to be able to protect her with all your might. Shin would not be capable of that, she knew that she wouldn't. She wasn't a killer like the rest of them. She didn't want to be.

The Mender ignored all of the bickering surrounding the table and the eyes that were fixated on her from all around the Mess Hall. She finished her meal and quickly hurried from the table towards the Northern part of the camp where all the highest ranking officials would spend their evenings planning, drinking, and sometimes both. It was the social hub for those who had earned their ranks but in this army, it was a surprise to know that the most bloody were the most civilised.

THE WALK TOWARDS Dira's tent was a tense one, she felt as though everyone was watching her. She felt the stress of her comrades' interest bearing down onto her. It had been a year since she was recruited into The Blood Dragons after her training, and for that amount of time she had been able to keep her head down but for some strange reason she knew that The Ethereals had a plan for her, it could be any of the thirteen but in her heart she prayed that it was Anelli who was guiding her path. She could see the tent underneath one of the ridges of the mountain cove their war camp was set up under.

"Shin!" Markus hurried up beside her, matching her pace down the final muddied road towards Dira's red and black tent. The Mender tried to ignore him for she did not want to be on the receiving end of his questioning again.

"I need you to do something for me. Please," he requested as he sped up and stood in front of her.

"What is it? If you are to ask me one more question I will not speak to you outside of the battlefield again," Shin threatened towards the scarred and gruff man before her.

Markus sniffed amongst the cold air and scratched his beard, "I need you to volunteer our Unit. Sergeant Brennan will not do such a thing, yet we all hunger for it. We hunger to be the Vanguard."

"You wish for me to sentence you to death?" Shin asked, "I save lives, I do not take them."

"We will not die, we are stronger than every Unit here. We have not once failed a battle which is something you know to be true!" Markus argued as he took a step towards her.

Shin shook her head and attempted to walk past Markus but he would not allow her, "I will not do this Markus."

"Why? Why not?! This is all we have! We have spent our lives serving under Dira, and we have spent most of it fighting at the edge. Brennan does not know how to lead us to our strengths. Help us prove our worth! We can do this without you if you find cowardice in your heart, we know your weakness."

"Do you want to know why we have always survived our battles?" Shin questioned with venom, "Do you want to know why you are here today?"

Markus scowled, "Tell me, Mender."

"You are all still alive because of me. Every battle I have healed you all and sewn up your wounds. More than half of the scars on your body are from my power, from my skill to fix your meat and bone with The Arcane - yet you and our brothers and sisters continue to treat me as if I am an outsider, as if I am lesser because I refuse to cause harm. Tell me Markus, if I am so weak, why is it always all of you who are crawling amongst the dirt to find me?"

Shin grimaced at the words she had spoken to the man who had grown silent in front of her as his confidence shrivelled back inside of him.

"Leave me," Shin said, "I will volunteer us. I will be one of the first through those walls with you and you will prove that you don't need me since you are a warrior of such talent."

The Mender walked past Markus and headed towards the tent. She wanted to apologise for her words but in her heart she knew they were true no matter how heartless they were. She swore to be a protector of life under Anelli's watchful eye - to mock their own care for their Wisps felt as though it was a sin. Her thoughts rattled around her mind as she walked into Dira's camp without being checked by The Claws, Dira's personal guard. They acknowledged her with no requirements from her - a true sign of respect.

Shin heard unintelligible Dira's voice coming from her dimly lit tent, but there was no reply for a second, it seemed to her that The Princess was talking to herself.

"Princess Dira," Shin's soft voice travelled through the almost open flap of the tent.

"Come, Waterman," Dira invited with the husk on her voice.

The Mender took a few breaths to calm herself and then walked into the shelter from the drizzling rain. Dira's tent was incredibly warm, almost too much so for Shin - The Princess had placed many heated lamps within the tent and was using their small glow of light to illuminate her home away from home in a calming way. The tent had a large bed in the middle placed against the mountain face that the tent was attached to, to the left was a dining area and to the right was a simple chair with a simple desk where The Princess of The Theothen Empire sat as if she was any other soldier writing home. She was scribbling on some parchment, and from what Shin could see, her handwriting was not as beautiful as she expected it to be - it was rugged, and messy.

"You summoned me," Shin said calmly, "And so I am here."

"Good," Dira answered.

An awkward silence filled the tent as Dira continued to write.

"My brother has killed my father to ascend the throne in my absence," Dira spoke aloud.

Shin's eyes widened. The Emperor was dead? The Prince had committed regicide? Why was Dira not turning their attention back to Arvur, why were they not marching south? None of it made any sense. Was she surely so intent on finding this golden-haired girl that it mattered more than the murder of her father?

"You have my deepest apologies," Shin quickly answered, "He was a great man. He always put our Empire first no matter what."

"My father was a sack of shit. He was evil, vile, disgusting, and used me to torment my little brother. I am glad he is dead. I am glad that Thurian was the one who killed him - he deserved to be the one to do it and I deserve to be the one to kill him to take back my crown. It is humorous, I can imagine the torment the runt feels over killing the man who hadn't cared for him in a decade. I bet he is trying to find some righteousness in what he has done... He is always so self-absorbed," Dira finished with a little chuckle. The Princess then looked over her shoulder to Shin who was standing nervously with her fingers fiddling with each other, "You may sit," Dira motioned towards the dining table, "I have other matters to speak of. Personal matters."

Shin looked towards the dining table where a bottle of wine and two glasses sat waiting for them. She walked towards one of the nearest chairs and took a seat as Dira finished writing on the parchment. She finished her signature with a loud scratch, almost tearing the bottom piece of the paper. The Mender watched as the damaged woman lifted herself from the desk and walked over towards her with her thoughts running along her face.

"You are from Beonyth's Laketown. I read your file from the Archivist. I would like to extend my apologies for the siege to come, I know it is not much, but I am willing to offer you a chance to get ahead of the army to find your loved ones and help them leave the city," Dira offered as she took the bottle of wine and began to pour it into their glasses.

"Why?" Shin asked, "For what reason would you offer me such a chance."

"I do not know," Dira answered, "You have been in my mind since you helped me last evening. You make me curious. Why would a woman from a state outside of my Empire train to be a Mender within our borders, and then accept the offer given to you to join my ranks instead of all the better, safer options. Not only this, you do not kill."

"You offer me the chance to help my family to satisfy your curiosity?" Shin asked.

Dira thought for a moment and caught herself a laugh as she thought about it, "Yes, it seems that way doesn't it?" She chuckled, "Though that isn't the only thing that interests me about you."

Shin took the glass of Wine that The Princess had poured and took a sip of it. She had to stop herself from drinking all of it in one as she discovered the incredible taste of the best Wine that had ever met her lips.

"What is the other?" Shin asked nervously as Dira turned one of the chairs towards her and dropped into the seat with her weight causing a thud. Shin took another sip of the wine as Dira downed hers and leaned in towards her.

"You are using the most dangerous kind of Arcane, and I do not believe you realise you are doing it," Dira smirked. "You are powerful."

Shin finished her glass of wine quickly, and motioned Dira to pour another which she eagerly did so.

"What is wrong with how I pull The Arcane? I do it as every other Mender does," Shin answered with her talent of lying but it was clear that the woman in front of her was no fool.

"Are you aware that you are draining the Wisps of my soldiers?" Dira questioned as she passed Shin her glass, now filled further up to the rim than last time.

To drain someone's Wisp? Shin knew that had to be impossible, only The Ethereals are capable of anything to do with humanity's life force. Shin had to find out more, no matter how dangerous the truth of her power was.

"I am aware that I am trading longevity for immediate health. I do not have the capability to touch someone's Wisp. My studies of the method have only hindered age progression, there have not been any other side effects," Shin answered matter-of-factly.

"How have you studied this?" Dira leaned back into her seat.

Shin's throat tightened.

"You haven't studied it at all have you? You are doing it until something goes wrong. Do you not see the foolishness in that?" The Princess questioned.

"Foolishness?" Shin sat offended, "If I am saving lives, what does it matter?"

Dira sighed and rubbed her face in stress, with her fingers rubbing into her eyes for a moment. "I do not mean to offend you Mender Waterman," Dira apologised, "I just wish to make you aware of what you are doing. You may be healing their mortal bodies, but you are destroying their chance to be selected by an Ethereal in The First Layer. I do not believe you should be touching such a power, it is not fair for you to play an Ethereal's game. It is not fair to those you heal."

Shin looked away from the woman giving her warning in front of her. Who was Shin to deny people a chance at an afterlife? What she was doing was wrong, and she knew that now but in the same vein if someone is bleeding out, if someone is dying while begging for help she has a duty to give them care - that is her duty as a Mender. Duty above all else that is what is drilled into their minds during training.

"I don't know what to say," Shin mumbled, "I just want to help people who need it. That is all I ever wanted to do. That is the reason why I became a Mender, I discovered that I could pull The Arcane when I almost drowned in Anelli's Tears - I thought it was a gift from The Ethereal of Life herself. I wanted to give that blessing to more people and I thought your army would be the best place to do it. Yet I find myself surrounded by men and women who find glory in ending lives, both innocent and guilty, defenders and invaders. Where do I stand? Someone sworn to help everyone having to choose sides - and now you force another onto me, you force me to choose my home or my mission. Do you know how unfair that is? Do you even care? You speak of fairness yet you are above everyone else."

Shin found herself standing up at the end of her rant with her face bearing down towards Dira who was watching her curiously with her arms folded.

"I care," Dira answered, "I have offered you a chance to save the ones you love."

"At the expense of my home all in search of one girl."

"One girl who can help me take the Throne. One girl who can help me take the entirety of Taundrad."

"What if she doesn't want to?" Shin questioned, "Are you like your father? Is all you seek power? What happened to you searching for your destiny to make all of the blood and destruction worth it? You are so set in your ways of war that you cannot imagine anything else, can you?"

Dira stood up from her chair and pulled the back of Shin's hair, forcing her to look up to the angered Warrior. "You know nothing of who I am. Nothing."

"I am trying to make my Empire a better place for all - I will be instructing my soldiers to capture blondes and to not kill anyone as long as they leave my soldiers be. I am doing this because of you."

"Why me?" Shin winced at the grip of Dira.

"Because…" Dira huffed as she released Shin from her grip, "I want to be better."

Arvuria: The Ethereal Children

"Then call off the siege, give Laketown a chance to give up the girl willingly," Shin begged as she ignored the relief of pain.

"They will not," Dira answered, "Their protector has a vicious hatred for me. He took my eye and he still wants more from me. The Glades and Laketown's forces will not heed my warnings, they will not surrender to me. You know the pride that your people have - you know the belief they have in The Green. If they wake him while we wait outside of the walls, he will kill us all."

"You cannot start the road of redemption with an act of violence, you simply cannot no matter your reasons. You can be a better person Dira," Shin reached a hand up from her side and placed it onto Dira's chest, "I know that you can be the person you wish for yourself to be - all you must do is take the first step. I will take it with you if you want this."

Shin felt Dira's warm hand caress the one she had placed onto her chest, "You have entered my abyss and made me doubt everything in but two days. Perhaps my destiny is coming to a crescendo quicker than I realise," Dira muttered.

Shin looked over the mighty warrior in front of her whose walls were crumbling, allowing some semblance of vulnerability towards her.

"You don't need destiny to know when to start anew," Shin whispered in return. Her heart was filled with pity and care. The woman in front of her was broken, her body scarred and damaged by foes she had cut down, her Wisp tormented by the actions she had deemed necessary. She could tell that The Princess sought forgiveness, or some form of redemption, but how do you help someone break from the way they have lived all their lives?

"Let me help you," Shin spoke, "You have to let someone in. Let me in."

"We are not friends, Shin Waterman. You are just a soldier under my command," Dira answered as she quickly removed Shin's hand from her chest and sat back down into the chair, "All you know of me is what I have allowed. You garnered my interest and that is all - but now you step too far from where you stand."

There it was, Shin knew it was coming, this was how everyone in this forsaken War Camp behaved. The moment any form of vulnerability is shown they stamp it down and hide it away.

"I am not a soldier," Shin answered as she began to walk towards the exit of the tent.

"Go on, leave me, all you have done is throw my generosity in my face," Dira spoke with a raised voice.

"Generosity?" Shin turned around, "Generosity?" She repeated as she stepped back towards The Princess.

"You will realise that your destiny is not what you expect it to be Princess. You will not become the Emperor if you walk the path you are on, and you will not be the hero to the people that you desire so dearly to be. I have admired you all my life from your stories and the legends you create, but now I see clearly that you are just like any other who wields a sword - you believe your power is above all because you are capable of taking a life. That isn't strength, that is weakness. If you want to be strong, you need to discover what it means to be merciful."

Shin stormed away from the most powerful woman in The Empire and left the tent to walk into the rain that had become torrential.

Arvuria: The Ethereal Children

- Chapter 23 -
OWAIN RODERICK
Code Red.

"ARVURIA," OWAIN whispered as he peeked his head into their shared dorm room. After what had happened at the beach earlier Owain had given his friends time to themselves. It was something he had realised after living with so many people at the farm, that sometimes life is just a little easier if you can sit in your own corner and let your mind wander through the thoughts that worry you. Whether they are good or bad, he always felt they needed to be put in order - or at least that's what he did, especially after what happened at Firvan's. He had realised life is much too short to be worrying about the journey to tomorrow when your feet are already running through today.

"What is it?" Arvuria mumbled underneath her bed sheets as she tried not to awaken Martell who slept in the middle bed of the room. Owain managed to silence his heavy footsteps to make his way to the bedside of his target. His master plan was about to begin.

The redhead stopped beside Arvuria's bed and dropped on top of her a blue all-in-one that he had found in one of the training rooms. He had cut from it the legs up until halfway up the thigh, and unthreaded the sleeves from it to make an impromptu outfit - and adding onto the pile he also added a black shawl thick enough to keep her warm amongst the spring air. He hoped that the two colours would sit well with the gold of her hair but he had no idea for fashion.

"Put this on and wait outside the tavern," Owain smiled to himself all too excitedly. He tried not to snicker as Arvuria forced herself to sit up in the bed and rubbed her eyes to look at the weight of clothing that was placed onto her.

"For what reason?" Arvuria question, "It has been a long day Owain, I do not wish to scurry around before we venture tomorrow."

"I hear you, I respect it, but trust me," Owain replied, "It's going to be a lot of fun," he added as he hurried out of the room.

"*Owain,*" Arvuria hissed in frustration.

"*Ten Minutes then go outside. You have no say in this,*" he mockingly hissed in reply before closing the door.

Luke Morgan

Arvuria: The Ethereal Children

- Chapter 24 -
SHIN WATERMAN
Home.

THE HEAVY POURING rain impacted her sight as she barged through the army that quickly began to prepare for war as the horns sounded moments after she had left Dira's tents. The battle hadn't even begun and she was covered in bruises caused by the bumping of armoured soldiers as she tried to make it to her Unit. She dipped to the right of a Giant-Kin as his large gauntlet swung over her head as he turned the corner, "Watch it!" Shin shouted as she hurried through the wet mud towards the station-point for her Unit. Shin had no time to make it to The Mender's Quarter to find her equipment, she was already drenched in her red leathers, all she could hope for was that one of her comrades was able to give her something else to wear.

Arvuria: The Ethereal Children

The drums of war sounded all throughout the camp, no matter where you stood you would hear the heavy beats of death, and alongside it the call and response of the musicians to soldiers began.

"Made of blood!" The Drummers called as they made their ways through the camp.

"They will bleed" The Soldiers shouted in response.

"Made of blood!" The Drummers called once more.

"They will bleed!" The Blood Dragons roared.

The chant of the battle hungry army filled the air, with the bass of the drums, the clash of metal, and the heavy footsteps beginning to play a tune like no other as they began to funnel their way towards the exit of the war camp in perfect rows and incredible coordination. They were marching to Shin's home, to Beonyth's Laketown. She was praying her entire journey towards Sergeant Brennan that her real brother would for some stupid reason be boating on the lake when The Blood Dragons would arrive.

She eventually saw her Unit lined up in rows as Sergeant Brennan's voice shouted towards them but she couldn't hear his words, only the anger and furiosity appearing across his face as he roared to his men. Shin was a few feet away from her squad when she tripped over a bow that had been hidden in the mud, causing her to fall face first into the dirt - ruining her clothing further.

"Damn it…" Shin croaked, tears appearing in her eyes at the stress of it all.

"Damn it all!" Shin screamed towards the mud as she began punching the ground in anger, an emotion she always tried to bury deep within her. Her home was going to be under siege, and all she could do was fall into the damn mud.

"Mender Waterman," Sergeant Brennan's voice spoke softly through the heavy songs of war.

Shin continued to punch the mud, splattering it around her.

"Shin."

Shin looked up to see the old grizzled Sergeant standing before her with an outstretched hand as his soldiers stood rank and file looking towards her. Not with anger, but compassion. Shin hesitantly took the Sergeants hand and in turn he pulled her up from the mud, and then began to wipe the dirt from her face with his gloves that almost felt like sandpaper.

"Our army is only searching for one person. If the authorities of your city give her over to us, no harm will come to it," The Sergeant spoke softly, "So let us pray they have the intelligence to give up one life to save everyone else."

Shin sniffled, trying to find some strength within herself - but the thought of innocents being harmed could not stop appearing inside her head.

"My family are behind those walls," Shin mumbled.

Shin felt Sergeant Brennan's grip around her hand remained after he had brought her to her feet, he brought their clenched fists to their chests and closed them together, "If your family is anything like you they will survive the worst. So steel yourself girl, we are going to war. If you don't get it together you put our lives on the line, as well as yours. You are a damned Blood Dragon, not some snivelling coward. Remember who you are"

Shin closed her eyes and thought about the memory of when she collected the sand from the bottom of the lake. Her little brother Mathane had been telling her the rumour that if you are able to swim to the bottom then Anelli will guide you with her own hand when it is time for you to be judged. She remembered how she took the boat out one night with a small vial of glass to store the sand in and made it her mission to collect some - a mission which almost caused her to drown when she reached the bottom but somehow she had made it back onto the boat where she awoke aboard the craft in the centre of the lake. Today was the day that she hoped Anelli, The Ethereal of Life would guide her. Shin's irritation towards Dira returned when she remembered she had gifted The Princess the White Sand from the bottom of the lake.

"I will do what I can to keep you all alive," Shin spoke, deciding on the strength she had within herself, "It is what I swore to Anelli. I will help those in need."

Brennan pressed his forehead against hers with a small painful bump and turned back around to the soldiers where Shin hurried to stand just in front of them as the Sergeant began his first words.

"I have been informed by those monsters above that Princess Dira has volunteered us to be in her Vanguard. Such a glorious honour we have been bestowed! Our Princess has ordered us to find a blonde girl who is a powerful Arcanist, and that is what we will do even if it means taking the city and bringing this war to another border. The politics do not matter to me, and I'm damn sure they do not matter to you," The Sergeant laughed, causing the men and women before him to follow suit as they cackled with tools of death in hand. Shin remained silent. What was to come was beyond her.

"I know what you want. But remind me, Dragons. What do you want?"

"Blood!" The Blood Dragons screamed.

"Where are you going to get it?!" Sergeant Brennan interrogated.

"The Weak!" The Blood Dragons shouted behind Shin, who managed to hide the jolt of her body as their viciously loud voices filled the air.

"Fly, my Dragons. To War!" Sergeant Brennan roared with all of his might. Repeating the last two words multiple times as he pushed his soldiers to join the march towards the exit to excite them for battle.

Shin stood in the middle of the four long rows of armoured men and felt the tether of The Arcane around her - she ripped her fingers through the air attaching an ever so faint strand of pink arcane to each soldier that only she could see. She could feel their Wisps, and she remembered the warning that Dira had given her.

She felt anger in her heart, towards all of the soldiers around her. She didn't want to be here anymore, she didn't want to be a Blood Dragon.

She attached her Arcane Tether's to the Wisps of her unit - she felt disgusted with herself as she did so.

Arvuria: The Ethereal Children

Luke Morgan

- Chapter 25 -
VANN ERENDON
While She Was Her.

VANN WAITED OUTSIDE the Melodies of Trees with the scrapped ball of the paper flyer in his hands. He huffed his breath into the night to see the mist of his breath appear in front of him. The Spring evenings would still be around for a few more weeks before the Northern summer would arrive to try to melt everyone. He kicked a rock in front of him which bounced along the cobbled street to hit one of the black lantern poles that rowed down the main street. His patience was never his strong suit.

The scrumped up ball of paper unravelled in his hands when his anxiety rose upon the idea of going somewhere new; he looked over the small article that Owain had stolen from the pork stand at the beach and read Griff 'n' Nex's Final Show at week's end - Castle Walls Show Hall.

Arvuria: The Ethereal Children

He didn't even know what they were going to sing and that was what worried him the most, what if he was going to disappoint Owain by not liking his type music. Vann had only ever really heard acoustics from travelling buskers or classic Tavern songs such as those from the evening before. Music of a wider variety is the luxury of a rich man, and those who live in the larger cities. A Ryther is much too expensive for common folk even if it was becoming much more common for music to be played without the singer there.

Vann heard footsteps that were much too light to be Owain's. He huffed in irritation because he knew exactly what his friend had done. The young adult turned around to see Arvuria stood in front of the tavern's door with it slowly closing behind her.

"By The Ethereals... you are beautiful," he spoke aloud before his mind could register what he had said. He had grown so used to her wearing his stained and torn tunics that to see her in something other than that almost took his breath away. To see her hair tied up into a bun was something he never expected to see.

Arvuria smiled at him - her sight then quickly turned to the cobbled ground beneath them.

Right. Yeah. I fucked up.

"Arvuria about earlier-"

"Do not say anything," Arvuria interrupted, "We should await Owain and do what he wanted to do."

"I don't think he will be coming," Vann exhaled a laugh, "I think he has set us up."

"Why would he do that?"

Vann straightened the article in his hands and passed it to her, "If I know my friend, he wants us to go and see this band. Just us."

"Are you sure?" Arvuria questioned as she looked over the torn paper, "He told me to wait outside for him."

"Trust me," Vann stepped forward and slowly opened a hand towards her to help her from the steps but she didn't take it.

You are not ready to hear the truth - nor do I want you to be part of it. To be around me is to die. That must not be your fate

He curled his fingers back into a fist and brought it to his side, "Arvuria, I-"

The blonde girl held onto the paper and began to walk down the hill of the path, "Come," she told him, "It may be that Owain is already headed there."

Vann stood for a moment in disbelief that for a second time she was trying to avoid him, to avoid talking about what she meant from earlier. Though at the very least, she hadn't walked back into The Melodies of Trees. That must be a good sign... right? His understanding of women always felt as though it was lacking.

THE TWO WALKED the short journey down the winding pathways of Beonyth's laketown until they came across the large hall attached to the inner walls of the city. If Vann hadn't known any better, he would have thought it was the home of a rich noble. It was built with smooth limestone and had a display of the Green Dragon with trees and vines surrounding it built onto the roof - it was almost as large as Avane's Keep. Escaping the rows of windows that ran vertically down the front he could see a large crowd inside with an array of colours flashing inside of it and at the far side of the crowd was a stage larger than he had ever seen with a group of performers dancing around the stage with their instruments.

Arvuria stopped before they reached the crossing in the road that led to the Show Hall. Vann could have sworn that she wanted to say something but no words escaped her.

"Now I look a fool," Vann shook his head, "Arvuria, look."

Standing on the other side of the road was Owain, Lyra, Martell, and Harnon who all dressed in their own styles. Owain stood with spiked hair and a leather jacket that he had clearly borrowed from Harnon, who himself had tied his usually messy hair back into a ponytail that sat on a tight brown shirt. Martell stood a woollen hat and a green rain jacket on as he held onto the hand of Lyra who was wearing loose Ideneorian robes with paint placed around her face and exposed arms.

Vann and Arvuria hurried to the other side of the road to meet the group who had noticed them as they stood at the back of the queue to enter the establishment.

"I knew you would be here Owain," Arvuria cheered as she ran towards the redhead to hug him, "Vann said that you must have set us up."

Harnon and Lyra snickered - they whispered something that only they could hear.

"Harnon was watching me enact my plan and caught me out," Owain smiled and shrugged, "I asked Harnon and Lyra if they would allow it, and since they were going anyway they offered to bring Martell and I along. I was at least half successful."

"You wouldn't have let us go?" Vann questioned the two Glades.

"Not without protection," Lyra quickly answered as she reached into a pocket hidden in her robes to pass Arvuria and Vann two stamped tickets for the show, "Though it was a good excuse for us to use the favour the band owed us for security. Though you must thank Harnon, he thought you all deserved a night of fun after all you have been through."

Vann accepted the two tickets and passed one to Arvuria as she continued to speak with Owain. The blonde girl took the small paper without looking at him.

The group waited in the queue for a few minutes where Vann stood in silence as everyone else chatted and laughed and danced along to the music that escaped the walls. He felt Harnon's hand place itself on his shoulder from behind. "Trouble in paradise?" He asked.

"You can tell?" Vann faked a laugh before taking a step back to stand beside the man who had been helping them all these past days.

"She is going through a lot, and there is a lot more to come. The best thing you can do is be there when she needs it, and when she doesn't, give her time to spread her wings," the grizzled warrior advised. "One of the worst things you can do to a woman is cage her with your expectations."

Vann inhaled the crisp evening air and then exhaled it to see his breath once more. "I realise that now, believe me. I just don't know how to apologise for how overbearing I have been."

Harnon tightened his grip on his shoulder and shook him for a second, "Are you a fool? My friend, you are both about to share a first experience in listening to music like this - let her be wild, let her be free, and let her be herself while she still can. She holds you and the boys dearly in her heart, you more so than anything else. This night will not last forever so dance with her and everything else will fall into place," Harnon smiled as if he was reminiscing in his own memories.

Arvuria: The Ethereal Children

"A romantic and a monster slayer? You can do it all Harnon," Vann teased, causing the gruff man to chuckle.

"I've had my fair share of both - sometimes at the same time. It happens when you're as old as I," Harnon laughed. Before Vann could question the age of his mentor he was pushed forward as the gap between them and the others in the queue had grown wider as the guardsman began to allow more people into the Show Hall. The group scattered once they entered the party where the flashes of colours beamed from the stage with the voices of Griff n' Hex belting out from the Ryther's - their music drowning out all worries and nerves that Vann felt. He could not feel the panic in the hearts for the beat of the music replaced it.

Vann smiled as he saw Harnon place a leather winter cap over the head of Martell where the fluffy flaps of it fell over his ears before he was lifted onto the man's shoulders with Lyra following closely behind. All the while Owain and Arvuria hurried between the crowd to make their way to the dance floor where Owain easily made a path for the both of them with his broad shoulders. They would have vanished if not for the redhead towering over most people.

Not yet. Vann thought to himself. She needs to spread her wings.

He walked over to the bar where Harnon, Lyra, and Martell stood waiting to be served. It wasn't as busy as Vann would have expected but it seemed that since they were late most people had already purchased their drinks, were drunk enough, or were happy for the spaces that they had claimed on the floor.

"What are you having Vann?" Lyra welcomed him with an arm around his shoulder. He still found almost a sense of shock in her change of demeanour from the night before - maybe this was how she was all the time and

Harnon had just pissed her off. They seemed to be okay now though, he was happy for his mentor.

"I have no coin, I'm just-"

"A whisky and some ale to wash it down with for the boy!" Harnon shouted over the loud music to the bartender who questioned the age of Vann. Vann wanted to explain to the barman that he was of age but Harnon demanded the drink nonetheless, which was of no surprise as nobody tells Harnon what he can or can't do.

"One sip of alcohol and he tries his hardest to feel drunk again after all these years," Lyra laughed into Vann's ear so that he could hear her.

"How old is he?" Vann asked in return.

"How many centuries is too many?" Lyra replied with a finger over her lips. There was absolutely no way Harnon was more than one hundred years old. That old bastard looked about forty.

"You okay up there Squire?!" Vann shouted towards Martell whose head was almost hitting the platform above the bar where the seats were on the higher floor for those who wished to watch the performances in a more refined way.

"Yeah!" Martell called down with excitement, "I like the booming, it feels funny! And there is lots of dancing!"

"There sure is, buddy!" Vann called back as Harnon passed him a glass of whisky and a tankard of Ale before grabbing his own.

"You ready little man?" Harnon challenged him.

"Oh the night begins," Lyra, the leader of The Glades, complained as she walked into the open spot at the bar where Harnon's belligerent self had been.

"I'm ready old man," Vann frowned in acceptance of the challenge. The two men clinked their glasses and chugged the small glass of whisky that had been filled to the brim and then chased it with Ale. Martell was holding on for dear life when Harnon was tilting his head back to gulp the whisky neatly.

Vann wanted to vomit.

"Keep it in!" Harnon pointed and cheered. "Keep it in! Keep it in!"

Vann didn't vomit. Harnon cheered and in turn caused a few patrons around them both to do the same.

"Why the hells did you make me do that," Vann complained.

"You needed it if you were going to dance. You're too stiff," Harnon straightened his posture to mock Vann, "You need to let loose otherwise those runts over there are going to be dancing with her first," he looked towards a group of men similar in age to Vann pointing towards Arvuria and pushing each other - all being goaded by one another to go and speak to her first.

"Go Vann!" Martell called down once more.

"I'll hinder the Grozmins and you can go and tell her how you feel," Harnon pushed Vann towards the dance floor as he made his way towards the three teenage boys. "What the fuck are you saying about my daughter?!" Vann heard Harnon's voice begin to muffle amongst the loud of the music.

Harnon, you are one hell of a mystery.

The young man stood between the bar and the dance floor and scanned the hair of everyone to try to find Owain. It took a moment to find him but luckily one beam of light managed to illuminate the orange just enough to catch his eye. The two friends he had travelled with were dancing with just enough space to spin each other around, and just enough space for them to make fools of themselves, if anyone had cared - but nobody did. He had never been anywhere like this. Everyone was here for one reason: The music. This wasn't like the taverns he had been to. This was something new. He loved it.

Amongst hundreds of souls, it was always easier to feel lost than to be in the woods alone.

His eyes could not be pried from how Arvuria moved amongst the dancers. She was graceful in every sense of the word - it was as if every move of hers was calculated yet she flowed so smoothly to the melodies and the beats that it seemed as though she was a part of the music. Her smile was wider than it had ever been before. She was beautiful. Utterly Ethereal.

Vann closed his eyes and felt the burning in his stomach that the alcohol had caused. He was feeling it, at least in his feet.

Nobody here cares. Let loose. Be yourself. Tell her how you feel.

A three step plan.

He bounced on his feet for a few moments to get his blood flowing before he began to feel the music the same way as everyone else did. He moved to it and let his body do what it wanted as he slid through the crowd that were having what fun they could at the last show. Some people were nice enough to step out of his way and others were enjoying themselves enough to not notice him, he was happy either way.

Owain's eyes lit up when he saw Vann - the redhead winked towards him and kept Arvuria's sight away until he was just coming up behind her. The redhead motioned with a tilt of his head for Arvuria to look behind her with. She turned to Vann.

Her face grew with worry. Guilt too.

Arvuria: The Ethereal Children

Owain danced away from the two of them and joined another group as Vann took hold of one of Arvuria's hands.

They began to dance.

Everyone around them vanished.

At that moment it was just the two of them.

Arvuria, and Vann.

They were surrounded by the array of colours and the music that had become tangible around them.

Arvuria danced towards him and placed her arms around his shoulders, and he put his hands on her waist. They were interlocked.

"I do not want to lose you Vann. I push you away for I am scared," Arvuria spoke into his chest. He could hear her clearly amongst the volume. "If I let you in then you are tied to me. I know the man that you are, and the hero you will become. I've seen it. Yet I fear that it is not a life that you wish for - I wish you a peaceful one, you will not have this with me."

"You won't lose me," Vann answered, "I will stand beside you no matter what may come."

Arvuria looked up. Her yellow eyes met his blue.

"You do not know what is coming. The world is on the precipice - one wrong decision from you or him and everything ends," Arvuria muttered.

"I know that you must have a grand destiny to fulfil," Vann frowned in thought, "but…"

"What is it?"

"Can't it wait until tomorrow? I want this night to be about us, whatever we may be."

Arvuria's eyes widened and her arms tightened around his shoulders. He felt her make the decision to choose him there and then. She gently moved her hands into his messy hair and pulled him down to kiss her. All Vann could focus on was her. There was no music anymore. There were ghosts around them. There was only her.

A WHISTLING APPEARED to grow louder and louder in the air. Vann refused the distraction from Arvuria.

Fire.

Ruin.

Death.

Vann and Arvuria, and everyone around them were drowned under the rubble of the building as rocks of fire began to rain down onto Beonyth's laketown.

The Blood Dragons had arrived.

They had come for Arvuria.

Arvuria: The Ethereal Children

- Chapter 26 -
VANN ERENDON
Battle of The Bloody Lake I

VANN'S EYES IRRITATED in dust. The Hall had crumbled around them. They were under siege. His hearing was muffled yet the screaming pierced his ears all the same. Standing above him was Arvuria who fired a beam of white light out into the open air towards another incoming fireball - shattering it into a million pieces.

"Vann! Get up damn it!" Arvuria looked over her shoulder as her hair burned in Arcane - but in distraction another fireball grew closer amongst the sky.

"This one is mine!" Harnon ran through the smoke of dust with a pull of green Arcane running along his fingers. He leaped into the air and slammed his fists into the ground where the earth in front of the hall lifted into a wall large enough to defend from the burning rock. It crashed against the defence with a shatter and a rumble.

Arvuria: The Ethereal Children

Vann lifted himself from the floor as his head rocked between consciousness - Everything hurt. His body was scarred and burned yet his Wisp forced him to his feet; today was not the day he would die.

"Martell," Vann croaked, "Where is he?!"

"Martell?!"

Arvuria took his arm and placed it over his shoulder, "This way," she encouraged as they stepped over the corpses of the people they had been dancing alongside. He did not know how long he had been on the floor but everything had changed in an instant. He prayed to all Thirteen Ethereals that his friends were okay.

"Harnon, get in here!" Owain called from a hatch in the corner that led to the cellar.

Thank Anelli you're still here. Vann fought back his tears.

The girl beside him handed him off to Owain who helped him down the steep stairs where unfamiliar faces were hiding from the assault of whoever was attacking them. At the back of the wide space filled with barrels of alcohol, tools, and broken furniture was Lyra who held Martell in her arms - the boy was okay but his little right leg had been wrapped in a splint.

"The civilians are to stay here until this all ends," Owain informed Vann where his worried eyes looked towards Lyra and Martell.

"What of Arvuria and Harnon?" Vann asked as he held onto Owain who leaned him against the wall so that he could catch his breath.

"They'll be fine. You saw that shit they were pulling off, right? Harnon is a fucking Arcanist!"

"He is much more than that," Lyra answered across the cellar. She had finished tightening the bandages around Martell's leg and hurried over to the two boys.

"The civilians will stay here, we will move rubble over the latch to keep them safe. You and I will make our way to The Inner Walls at the centre of the city where we will coordinate The Glades with Laketown's forces," she ordered Owain.

"I will not leave Martell here. He is under my care," Owain responded.

"He cannot walk."

"Then I will carry him."

"Owain," Vann muttered. He knew that his friend would not take no for an answer - he had felt just as responsible for the boy as Leon did at the farm. "He is safe here."

Vann saw the shame scatter across Owain's face - he pushed himself from the wall and hugged his redheaded friend, "None of this is your fault brother."

The men embraced together for a few moments. Owain kissed Vann's forehead before they let go of the other - both determined to do what they must.

The hatch to the basement opened once more where Harnon and Arvuria dropped down to their feet.

"Dira," Harnon spoke almost excitedly, "That vile witch has found us."

"The Princess of The Empire. A powerful user of The Arcane - she will kill us if we stand alone," Arvuria answered as her white glowing hair returned to it's golden blonde.

"Bullshit, I can kill her. I just need to get close to her. I still have her other eye to take," Harnon spat.

"Wait," Vann looked to Arvuria. He remembered the power she displayed against the Arachnex - he remembered what happened to her in the lake.

Arvuria: The Ethereal Children

We must return to the city. I should not have come here. It is too soon.

"We came here to find your uncle, he was going to help you with his power, was he not?" Vann queried.

"Yes, I believe so," Arvuria answered.

"What if I was to take you to someone else. Someone who could be of help to us right now? There was a woman at the lake, she appeared after you left me and vanished without a trace. She looked like an older you, Arvuria. She spoke as if she knew my future. I think it was Anelli. I think it was the Ethereal of Life herself. I mean, that is her lake isn't it? The one she created upon seeing Brigir's evil?"

Silence.

Arvuria's pale skin grew whiter.

Harnon immediately climbed the steep stairs again and lifted the hatch of the basement with Lyra quickly behind him. He had not even been in the basement for a minute before he returned to the destruction above.

"If Anelli has made herself known to us once again, she did it for a reason. The Ethereals do not come down from the First Layer unless they're meddling again," The Marauder spoke as he climbed into the mist of dust once more.

"Arvuria, Vann, I will get you to The Ethereal of Life. I will get you there and then we will hunt down Dira and finish that bitch for good," Harnon ordered.

"Lyra, Owain, you will to the Inner Walls and coordinate our forces with the Mayor and the Laketown Guard. Establish a defence in the inner city where the buildings are dense, their army will not know how to fight in urban terrain as we do. I am Harnon Kelmar, Chosen of The Green Dragon. I *will* defend this city until my dying breath."

That's who you are. Vann was in awe of the man standing on the platform above. That was the man he wanted to follow.

THE GROUP PREPARED themselves in a matter of minutes - yet Vann could see that Martell didn't understand why he was being left behind. He couldn't understand why it was safer for him to be here with these strangers than it was to be on the battlefield, to be on the streets that would be filled with blood soon enough.

"I want to go with you," Martell cried as he tried to lift himself from the ground.

"We will save the city, and then we will be back for you," Owain choked up.

"Put your faith in us, one more time?"

Vann tapped his cheek in the same mocking manner as Martell had done so on the farm - the inside joke of Owain's mannerism when he thinks. "And we can even go dancing once more. How about that?"

"No!" Martell snapped, "You cannot leave me with these strangers! I lost my friends already! You cannot leave me!"

Vann kneeled in front of Martell and placed a hand onto his shoulder, "Squire, there is death and destruction up those stairs - we are not abandoning you, we are keeping you safe."

"But," Martell climbed to his feet with all his little might ignoring his wounds, "I don't want to be here, I want to be with you both... I do not want to die here..." he began to cry.

"Fuck this," Owain huffed, "You are in my care, I will keep you safe. You hold onto to me, and you hold on *tight* no matter what, and you keep your eyes closed. Leon would not leave you here and I will be damned if I went against what he would do."

Vann closed his eyes in fear and hesitation of Owain's choice in taking Martell to the battle outside but he knew that his friend would do anything to protect the little Squire - and any one of them.

"Are you sure?" Vann looked up to Owain as he lifted Martell into his arms.

Owain nodded sternly. "We do not leave each other behind. That has been our promise since Firvan's Farm."

Once the boys were ready they followed the others closely behind - they climbed up the almost vertical stairs and returned to the Show Hall. The death and destruction was clearer now and the smell of blood was much more potent.

"Try not to look at them," Lyra spoke as she handed to them a sword each that she had taken from some of the few guardsmen who had been given the task to defend this place, "If you do, remember their faces. For they are counting on you to protect their families."

The rubble around their feet shifted as a green glow emanated from the steps of Harnon's feet - the stone around them rumbled past them as they covered over the hatch towards the basement. "They'll have time enough to breathe," Harnon muttered as a green aura hovered around him.

Vann, for once, kept his mouth shut and his questions to himself. Now was not the time to quiz Harnon. They had work to do. They had to stop Dira's Army.

The group of five walked out of the broken walls and in front of the uprooted Earth that The Chosen of The Green Dragon had used as defence. Vann rubbed the dirt smoke from his eyes and coughed it from his lungs, and upon raising his sight from the ground the city no longer looked as peaceful and beautiful as it had done the last days. The warm yellow colours of the limestone had turned red and orange as fire rained from the sky - there was no calm sound of the still lake or the birds chirping as they flew above, there was only screams and clashes of steel. The thick walls of the city had been breached before them, and flowing into the city were soldiers in black steel armour with a promise of blood.

"Which way is the quickest to the lake?" Vann asked as they all huddled against Harnon's wall.

"Through them," Lyra answered as she walked in front of the group, "You think you can do this again?" She requested Harnon as she tapped the wall.

The green aura around the Chosen deepened.

"Stay close." Harnon's voice echoed.

The Chosen bolted forward, almost gliding across the ground as the stone beneath his feet helped him propel forward as though he was skating on the cobbled streets.

"Go!" Lyra shouted to Arvuria and the two teenagers who held onto their weapons as they sprinted forward in hopes of catching up to Harnon.

"Don't stop Vann, keep your feet moving!" Owain shouted from behind him as they ran. Ahead of them Harnon had jumped into the pouring army that flowed through the walls. He swirled the cobblestone path around their feet causing the invaders to collapse on the unstable ground where he then moved the stones over their bodies and sealed them, trapping the Blood Dragons - then he leaped towards the breach and pulled the two sides of the walls shut creating a shorter, but sealed, barricade to hinder Dira's army.

Vann looked towards Harnon who stood on top of the barricade firing from his clenched fists beams of Green Arcane while Laughing.

Arvuria: The Ethereal Children

"Remember me?!" he cackled from the ramparts.

Lyra looked over her shoulder to Vann and the others, "Let him have his fun, he'll catch up with us before we split!"

I am the Defender of The Green; I am he who stopped the Kings March. I am one who fought The Pale Dragon. I am he who will usher in The Gold!

Harnon's voice had become deafeningly loud as he projected his voice to the invading forces. The shock of the volume jolted Vann's body and he almost lost his footing as he ran over the imprisoned soldiers in the streets. For a moment the chanting from the other side of the wall was silenced but the most peculiar feeling was the shift in tension where he could feel an aura of confidence emanate from Beonyth's Laketown. He looked up the hilled streets above him to see the colours of blue begin to flow down the streets - the Laketown Guards were hurrying towards the walls to fight Dira's onslaught.

"Next right, we split! Keep running towards the lake, Owain we will take the main street to the centre! Ready your steel for they will strike you down if given the chance!" Lyra shouted from ahead of them.

The group met the next turn where Lyra led Owain to the right and

Vann hurried Arvuria forward. Vann looked over his shoulder and shared a brief moment with Owain - a little smile shared between the both of them before they were separated. The little smile between them promised the other they would see each other again. It promised that they would both make it out alive.

"Stay alive Vann! Arvuria, keep him alive!" Owain shouted as Vann's sight of him turned away as the building began to separate between them.

I'll get her to the lake. I'll help her save us all.

The duo hurried towards the arch to the lake where they were much earlier in the day. The gate had been shut with a few Laketown Guards standing firm behind it and atop the walls.

"Let us pass! We must make it to the lake!" Vann shouted as his feet began to slow to a stop.

A Guardsman brushed him off, "Go back to your homes, find somewhere safe until this is all over kid, the gates open for *nobody*."

"You don't understand, this girl is powerful. We must get her to Anelli's Tears!" Vann pleaded.

"Go home! This is no time to play!" The Guard dismissed once more as he attempted to push Vann back.

Vann flicked his sword to his side, "Let us pass. I will fight you if I must."

The Guardsman tilted his head and placed his hand onto the hilt of his own sword.

"Let them through!" Harnon's voice ordered as he landed down onto the road where the stone beneath him indented to soften his landing. "If you want to live until tomorrow we only do so by getting this girl to the waters. Open the *fucking* gate."

"Open the gate!" The Guardsman turned around and beckoned to his comrades. "The Chosen and his friends must make it to Anelli's Tears!"

The gate slowly creaked open enough to fit the width of a single person through.

"Do not wait for us, we will take a detour," Vann ordered the grizzled soldiers as he led Arvuria and Harnon through the steel defence. Their feet sped them up once more as they hurried to the Sapphire Lake ahead of them that twinkled underneath the light of the two moons. Despite the destruction and death behind them, the creation of an Ethereal still slept peacefully.

Arvuria: The Ethereal Children

"A detour?" Harnon asked.

"If we can get you and Arvuria to their leader, I know the two of you can defeat them," Vann believed, "All we need is their uniform and to circle towards their army."

"It won't be as simple as that. Dira is always directly in the centre, I can only launch myself so far I will not be able to get to her." Harnon answered.

Arvuria sped up past the two men and hurried further ahead, "We should wait to see what happens to me first. Everything else will come afterwards."

Vann wanted to tell her to wait, that they should all go together but he knew now that Arvuria was so much more than he could possibly ever have understood. "Go!" He shouted. He believed in her.

She sped ahead at twice the speed Vann was capable of, he watched her get ahead of them farther and farther until her feet met the silk sand once more where the footprints left behind began to glow a luminescent white. When his feet met the sand alongside Harnon the white of her footprints grew brighter and stronger.

"I hope you are as ready as she is Vann. This isn't just about her anymore," Harnon spoke.

"I will do anything I need to. Innocents will die if this doesn't work - Owain and Martell are behind us, I will not lose them as I have the others."

"Then she has made the right decision."

Vann's questions refused to escape him once again. His curiosity in what was to happen to him had dwindled with each day of the journey he had been on. He had come to know that everything that has or was going to happen to him was always something he didn't expect. All he could do is trust that he could do the right thing when the impossible came to him. All he wanted for himself was to stay the man he was trying to be: A good man.

Arvuria's slightly lit silhouette stopped as she stepped into the shallow blanket of the lake where before her a woman was rising from the still tide. It was the woman he had met earlier, it was Anelli, The Ethereal of Life. She rose from the lake dry as a bone, with no effect on the world around her. No footprints in the wet sand and no ripples within the water.

Arvuria and Anelli turned to look at Vann as he came to a slow stop, finishing his journey towards them with slow steps as Harnon remained further behind with his black sword drawn with his eyes keen towards any threats.

"It is good to see you again dear protector," Anelli's voice calmly swam amongst the air.

"Vann, you were right," Arvuria smiled with happy tears in her eyes, "This is Anelli, The Ethereal of Life. This is my Grandmother."

"Your grandmother?" Vann breathed, "That is impossible… isn't it?"

"No," Arvuria answered, "I remember now. Parts of my past that still remain blurred - yet I never forgot the face of the woman who raised me. I was unable to recall her name yet now that I see her again I know I am of her blood."

"That would mean you are an Ethereal," Vann replied, he looked to Anelli to see if she would confirm the statement with her voice yet all she did was close her eyes and slowly tilt her head.

"Arvuria is so much more than I could ever be," Anelli answered, "My people can only touch this world through the Arcane. Arvuria is a creation beyond this Layer and The First- As are the other four of her kind. They can walk amongst all worlds, as can their Chosen."

Arvuria: The Ethereal Children

Vann stood beside Arvuria and looked over at her. There was something different about her. An aura of pure confidence.

"What is to happen?" Vann questioned, "Will you restore her memories?"

"I will restore what I can, the rest will be up to her Uncle for he has the sands required from the centre of the lake and the stone needed," Anelli smiled and turned to Arvuria, "To unlock your true power you will no longer be who you are. As of right now, you are a Human. That is the difference between you and your father. Arvur, your father, wanted you to understand the lives you are tasked with protecting against the dark that lies below. For The Pale is stirring once more - it is why you are here. If you are ready to become so much more, give me your hands," The Ethereal finished by turning her open palms towards Vann and Arvuria.

Arvuria placed her left hand on her grandmother's and looked back to Vann to encourage him to follow.

"I am but a human, I can only swing a sword," Vann spoke hesitantly.

"You are what I need you to be," Arvuria spoke softly to him, "I choose you Vann Erendon - you will carry my Wisp. I trust you to be my anchor to this world."

"Come," Anelli spoke, "You are to be The Warden of Gold."

Vann had no idea what the women were alluding to in front of him, but he trusted his friend enough to take one more step forward, one more step to take the hands of her and The Ethereal in front of him.

"Put your faith in me, one more time," Vann whispered to himself as he remembered all of his friends. He took a deep breath and closed his eyes for a few moments until a blinding white light shattered the dark shelter his eyelids had given him once again. His body felt as though it burned and melted. He wanted to scream in pain - the agony that swelled inside of him almost turned him mad. He could not cope with it for a second longer than he thought he could bear but as it almost became too much he awoke in an infinite puddle that sat along dark grey stone beneath him. He lifted his face from the shallow water and looked ahead of him. The stone floor surrounded him to no end and above him was a higher roof made of the same dark stone.

Vann lifted himself from the puddle where his clothes remained wet - he then looked over his shoulder to see Arvuria behind him. He turned the rest of his body to see his friend wearing golden plate armour adorned with symbols of dragons imprinted into the metal with white sash running down her chest-plate and flowing down to her knees.

"Are you okay?" Vann asked with worry.

"I am," Arvuria replied, "She was right. I am so much more. I feel such incredible power swell inside of me. Do you feel it? Do you feel the Wisp of mine that you carry? Do you feel my life-force that you protect?"

Vann looked to his hands to see faint golden patterns flowing around his skin - he had to lift the sleeves of his coat to see how much further the art went to find that it continued to run up his arms and most likely around the rest of his body.

"What has happened to me? What has happened to us?"

"I Chose you Vann Erendon. You are now my anchor to this Layer - you are the reason that I can be what I was truly born to be. I am The Golden Dragon, and you are my Chosen."

Arvuria: The Ethereal Children

Vann's heart almost gave out. Not once could he possibly have dreamed this would be his fate. There had only ever been one Chosen of The Golden Dragon and that was King Theo and Arvur The Gold - the two beings who created The Theothen Empire. To be standing before the woman clad in gold in front of him, to be told that he was as a mythical hero had been. It was almost too much.

"This is what you promised me, isn't it? This is how you are going to help me save my friends."

"Vann. This is how you save everyone."

He looked away as the weight of the world fell onto his shoulders. He had avoided responsibility all his life - this was not what he wanted. Yet he knew that he had to be the one to do it. He returned his gaze to Arvuria and his face lit a fire of belief. Belief in who he was, and belief in who he will become.

"I have spent these days with you that have felt as though a lifetime has passed. So much has happened and in turn so much has changed. I have wondered what would have happened if Harnon had found you, or if the Soldiers did instead. I do not believe it would have been a better fate for either of us - I am glad it was me who found you. I will not waste the gift you have blessed me with."

"You are holding my Soul, my Wisp. It is not a gift, it is a task. One I have deemed you capable of," Arvuria walked forward where she took the hands of her friend.

"That's not what I meant," Vann replied, "You have given me the chance to make a difference. You have given me belief that I can become something. Someone. That is the gift you have given me."

Arvuria smiled, "What better way to become more, than to do it beside someone that you love."

Rot and ruin. That is what you will become.

The vicious voice scraped through the infinite room and Vann's eyes opened once more to see Arvuria beside the lake who also jolted as she awoke amongst the real world once more.

"What was that?" Vann beckoned as the fear the voice instilled escaped his body. He looked to Arvuria to see her rubbing her eyes and shivering her body as if she was removing some ilk feeling.

"You heard him too?" Harnon spoke from the distance as he dragged over a third body of a Blood Dragon, placing it lined up beside the others. "Here are the uniforms you wanted. Thought I'd get ahead of the plan when I spotted these scouts."

"The voice, who is it?" Vann quickly asked.

"He is an echo of the past - Brigir The Pale Dragon. Bound by Arvur to forever be stuck between Layers, unable to hinder your world or mine," Anelli answered, "He is an issue for another time, for now you must save this city for it will become your bastion in the wars to come."

"We will not fail, grandmother," Arvuria promised.

"You cannot. It is your task to protect this land, for too many others have fallen."

"I will not be able to help you in this Layer anymore, my power is all but spent for now. The one to guide you next is Beonyth, seek him after this battle," within not even a blink, Anelli The Ethereal of Life vanished.

Vann looked down to his hands once more to see the faint golden patterns around his skin were no longer there but he still felt the swell in his chest. A warm radiant feeling. Confidence and power. Arvuria was not the only one who had become so much more. He was now her

Warden. Her protector. Yet above all, he was still her friend.

"You survived the first part of tonight. Now all we have to do is kill the most dangerous woman in the Empire," Harnon huffed as he began to remove the uniforms from the corpses on the floor, "This should get us into the rank and file at least."

"One step at a time," Arvuria said with authority, "You and I will keep the soldiers away from Vann while he stops Dira."

"Me?" Vann interjected, "I only know how to fight from my father. I am not a master swordsman."

"You don't need to be," Arvuria answered, "You are The Warden of my power, what I have is yours to wield. You are stronger than her. It is better you focus on her instead of the army around her. Harnon and I are much more suited to fighting the mass of steel and blood. Trust in your own strength and your body will wield it as needed. Feel the Arcane around you - feel it inside of you - and use it to your will. You will not fail."

Harnon tossed a bundle of clothes and armour to Vann, "Are you sure Arvuria? I have had Dira dead to rights before, I can do it once more."

"It has to be him," The Golden Dragon answered, "He must be the one to announce who he is, and to announce to the world that I have arrived. The true war begins tonight - Dira will see the destiny she craves so much. Valen has guided her thus far."

Vann looked at the helmet that sat on top of the bundle in his arms. Steel with the painted art of a bloody dragon's face running down half the side of it. A man had worn this, a man who had died all because he needed his clothes.

Such is war that you spoke of, father.

Luke Morgan

Arvuria: The Ethereal Children

Luke Morgan

- Chapter 27 -
SHIN WATERMAN
Battle of The Bloody Lake II

ALL SHIN COULD hear were the screams of help. All she could see were the corpses of the innocent. Corpses of her people. To what end was Dira going to go to find this one blonde girl in a sea of people? A stupid question for Shin to ask herself, she could see it before her: Death and destruction to be traded for a throne. A seat that was made by a stonemason and a goldsmith a few hundred years ago. Was it truly worth all of this?

Shin watched as her squad split apart, her tethers of Arcane vanishing the further they moved away from her as they charged towards the civilians breaking rank, with every young blonde woman being grabbed and taken to the nearest open space to be checked over by Sensors while the siege raged on. Shin followed ten of her comrades, sectioning off from Sergeant Brennan who was mounted on top of a wagon with a series of coloured flags attached to horns to give instructions. The Blood Dragons hurried through her old neighbourhood, almost as if The Ethereals had some twisted sense of humour in sending her down this path.

She remembered her old street as she slowly walked down it as the spray of bodies littered the streets. She looked at every face she walked over in morbid curiosity, wondering if she knew any of them - each face she saw she was thankful it was that of a stranger's.

"Shin, make haste!" Markus called out to her as a fireball impacted just ahead of them as he cut down a Guardsman of Beonyth's Laketown with ease.

"Collect every blonde girl you see!" Markus shouted amongst his men, "Kill everyone else!"

Shin watched as Markus and two other comrades hurried forward behind another who had begun to chase a woman from her house. A house that Shin recognised all too well. Her careful walk slowly began to pick up speed as she fixated on the fireball that had landed in front of her old home. He had to be alive in there, especially if that stranger had just left. Mathane had to be in there, her little brother was okay, nothing bad could happen now that she was here. Her legs charged her forward in a pace that she never knew she was capable of, in this moment nothing hindered her speed - she stepped on whatever was in front of her with disregard, no matter what it was.

"Mathane!" Shin shouted in worry before tripping over a corpse. She rolled a few times before coming to stop, turning to look at who she had tripped over to see an older woman, 'Aunt Harriet' who used to swing by with dessert in an attempt to flirt with her uncle before his passing. Shin mourned within just a second and stood back up to her feet, running the final length to her home. She stood before it seeing her old door shattered with the large remnants of it flung into her living room beside the crumbling dining table. Shin cautiously walked into her home as the fire burned outside, "Mathane?" she called out nervously.

There was no answer. She noticed the plates of food amongst the splinters and the broken table. She pressed a finger amongst the pasta to feel it lukewarm, just a hint of heat remaining in it. Her little brother must have left the home as the horns of the city sounded. "Matty…" Shin croaked with the sliver of hope that he was still alive, a small hint of a smile appearing on her face amongst the ruin of her city.

She ran across the living room to take hold of a frame, removing the small portrait sketch of her, Mathane, and her Uncle - folding it and sliding it into one of her pouches.

"By Anelli I pray for the safety of you" Shin muttered to herself before leaving her home, giving it one last look as she stood in the doorway.

She hurried through the streets in hope of catching up to Markus and the few others who had hurried ahead, looking straight forward in an attempt to ignore the innocent people and the soldiers of both sides lying dead amongst the streets.

"Grab her and take her to the rest!" Markus ordered as the three men surrounded the girl who had fled Shin's home.

"Mathane!" A feminine shriek pierced through the roar of battle.

"Mathane!"

Shin bolted from her home and forced her feet to remain connected to the cobbled streets as she focused on the group of four ahead of her - Three Blood Dragons standing around a pregnant blonde woman begging for her life.

"Markus! Leave her!" Shin ordered. She had heard her brother's name, she would not let anything happen to this woman.

The grizzled soldier looked over his shoulder with his bloodshot eyes and specks of blood on his face, "We have our orders. Blondes or kill them!"

One of The Blood Dragons placed his swords against the throat of the blonde woman and the other held his blade in his hand as he watched Shin arrive to Markus while he scanned the area around them. The woman was beaten and bloodied as Shin closed the final distance

"Leave her!" Shin shouted once more as she ran into Markus and tackled him to the ground. She tried to wrestle with the man but he was much too strong for her - yet her Arcane tether to him remained faint.

"The fuck are you doing Shin?" Markus gritted as he rolled her over and pinned her to the ground, he ripped his dagger from his sheathe on his thigh and held it to her throat, "You attacked me? A brother?"

"Who are you, how do you know Mathane? Mathane Waterman? Is that who you are calling?" Shin rambled to the captured woman.

"My partner... He is my love," The woman croaked as the blade against her neck caused blood to trickle down her throat. Shin's anger subsided for just a moment - her little brother had never been able to send a reply to her letters, she had missed so much these last few years, and before her now was his partner, and his unborn child.

"Please don't kill us," Mathane's partner cried amongst the fire and smoke of the city, "Please! I am with child!"

Shin watched as Markus looked to the crying woman and then back to her. He took a deep breath and stabbed the dagger into the ground beside her face before raising his fist once more, "I knew you were never one of us, it is a shame it took until our conversation to realise it truly. You should have forsaken your family when you became one of us. Now you forsake us," he seethed before crashing his armoured gauntlet into the face of shin.

"Your blood was never in our cause! Was it?!" The Blood Dragon screamed as he continued to pummel her face.

"Leave her!" The Blonde screamed before the knife was removed from his throat to have her hands tied behind her.

Shin took the strikes with barely any fight - her face cut and swelled after each strike of the steel knuckles. She couldn't fight back. It wasn't her nature. She didn't believe in it. She was a healer, not a killer. The feint tether of Arcane she had attached to the three men surrounding her grew stronger, just strong enough for her to pull on it.

"I am not..." Blood splattered from her mouth as Markus' fist retracted once more, "I am not a murderer," she tried to convince herself as her eyes lit a pale blue as the Arcane Tethers became visible. She shrieked as piercingly loud as a Banshee and the three soldiers who were once her brother's became stiff - their bodies refused to move. She had reversed her ability to heal. She had saved lives by using the Arcane to to exchange peoples longevity for the health of their bodies - now she took one part out of the equation. Now she was simply using their Wisps - their source of Arcane - as a battery to heal herself. She ignored the warnings from Dira. With their Wisps dwindling their bodies husked and shrivelled slowly while the wounds Markus had inflicted on her began to disappear.

She was killing them.

She wanted to kill them.

Arvuria: The Ethereal Children

Shin closed her eyes and listened to the silent pain of her comrades as their final breaths escaped them. She had spent so long trying to make a difference in her country as a Mender - helping her comrades recover from their injuries and healing the innocents they would come across. She thought she was better than the killers she surrounded herself with. She was better. That's what got her through each day, that's what got her through all the death and destruction she had seen. Now, she was no better than the men she was killing.

It felt good. They deserved it.

The healer looked into the eyes of the man whose Wisp she was taking - her face grimaced in disgust. She was done with it. She was done with being surrounded by such monstrous people. She lifted her arms from the ground and wrapped her hands around the Arcane Tether and roared with all her might as she pulled on it. The final thread to kill the man who had to die.

Markus' grey husk collapsed onto her. The weight of his corpse forced the air from her lungs as she laid there in defeat.

The Mender looked upwards towards the kneeling woman who sat there in fear of what she had seen where beside her stood the two men who had captured her standing between life and death. They were husks, they were still breathing, but their Wisps were destroyed. Shin rolled Markus from her torso and forced herself to her feet while pulling the dagger from the stone ground - she walked to her comrades and stabbed their hearts while wishing them a prayer to find The Ethereals they worshipped in the afterlife. If they were even still able to make it to the afterlife.

"Who are you?" The woman cried and quivered as Shin cut the ropes around her wrists.

"Mathane's Sister. Shin" The Mender answered coldly, "Are you able to walk?"

The Woman nodded and stood up from the cold ground with the help of Shin. "I am Kinne," the woman mumbled.

"Where is he? Where is Mathane?"

"I don't know. We were split by fire, we were headed to the second wall but… I don't know."

Arvuria: The Ethereal Children

Luke Morgan

- Chapter 28 -
OWAIN RODERICK
Battle of The Bloody Lake III

OWAIN HURRIED WITHIN the middle of the group with Martell in his arms, pushing through the crowds as their attempt to escort the group hurried them away from the walls to go deeper and higher into the city. Martell was quiet in his arms, burying his face into Owain's neck under the red-heads orders to trust him to get them both to safety. Lyra was ahead of them, leading them all towards the second and last bastion of safety in the centre ring of the city - the same place where people would be able to head towards Beonyth's Green, the mountain forest that surrounded the city and Anelli's Tears.

Rain of arrows and the fire of catapults soared through the sky, landing amongst the people and the condensed limestone buildings. There was no safety as far as the fire could reach them - the only luck they had was the stone of the buildings and the condensed alleyways to keep them sheltered from a portion of the death.

"Owain, I'm scared," he heard Martell mumble beside his ears, and in turn Owain grasped the back of Martell's head and held him tighter.

"We'll be okay little Squire," Owain promised before he felt the glow of a fireball above him causing him to look behind into the sky to see it barrelling down towards them all.

"Everyone scatter!" Owain roared to those around him as he leaped with all the strength in his legs towards a door to his right, with the burning impact of the fireball causing him to burst through the heavy wood door where he landed amongst the splinters. The fireball that impacted heavily into the stone ground outside with a monstrous thud scattered into the local area igniting what flammable objects were around. Martell screamed in pain amongst the shattered wood, every other sound in the world was muffled, all except for his ward in need.

Owain lifted himself from the ground and pulled the small pieces of wood from his body to see a large fragment of the door embedded into the right side of Martell's abdomen - the boy held onto it gently with panicked breaths.

"O-Owain," Martell croaked, "It hurts…"

"You're okay," Owain quickly promised as he scurried across the destruction to look over the boy. He couldn't remove it from Martell, it was too deep. Owain bounced his gaze around the room that they had landed in amongst the siege. He ran towards the table of the family who owned this house and pulled the table cloth from it, spilling the unfinished dinner that sat on top of it around the room. He ripped the tablecloth into pieces and held it in his hands to then snap the piece of wood that was embedded into Martell into a smaller piece where he followed quickly by tightening the cloth around the boy's stomach as Martell screamed in pain.

"Stop! It hurts!" Martell pleaded in tears. Owain continued through his broken heart - he tightened the bad attempt of a tourniquet around the boy's stomach further.

"This will help you I promise," Owain apologised and hoped through the tears in his eyes. Martell sobbed as he weakly put a hand to Owain's face, placing a print of blood onto the teenagers pale face before he passed out in shock. The Redhead's heart grew sorrowful and the fear that was always buried deep within him bubbled to the surface - he would not allow another person that he cared for to perish under his care. Losing his family in Resnia was enough, he would not let Martell fall to the likes of these bastards that dared attack him.

"They are inside the walls! They have breached the walls!" Calls from The Guardsmen sounded alongside horns of alarm, "Retreat to the centre! Towards Beonyth's Green!"

The redhead kicked one of the legs off the table in anger and began to hold it in his left hand, his grip wrapped around it with such strength that the wood almost began to splinter. He had a blade in its sheath, but the club was what he needed. He then returned to Martell to pick him up with his right arm, holding him as delicately as he could so as not to injure him further.

He looked to his ward and kissed his forehead, "Put your faith into me, just one more time," he asked Martell as he stepped out of the burning building into the fire outside to see the armoured invaders just at the bottom of the street cutting down civilians as they made their way deeper into the city.

They were murdering everyone that they came across, only the blonde women seemed to stand a chance at survival.

"Lyra!" Owain called out, "Lyra!"

Owain stood amongst the fire on the street to see the civilians they had been escorted scattered around the streets, some corpses, some injured, and others clambering to their feet.

"To the centre!" He heard the voice of The Glade, he looked through the fire in between them to see the guild leader pushing civilians towards the final street where an archway in the second walls stood. It was well-defended, and it wasn't far.

"We are almost there Squire," Owain secured Martell in his arm and ran through the blaze between them and Lyra, he and others around them hurried towards the main street, he could see her not far now as he stepped over the bodies amongst the cobblestone paths.

"By The Ethereals," Lyra's bright eyes widened amongst the painted black soot on her face. She saw the dirt, filth, blood, and injuries on Owain's body. She saw the little boy dying in his arms.

"We must hurry," Owain met her amidst the fire and destruction where abandoned goods and wagons were left scattered, "I can't lose him."

Lyra's eyes looked to the sky in worry as an orange glow covered the night sky, she pushed Owain and Martell to the floor where they all rolled underneath a wagon. A shower of fire and arrows landed amongst the streets setting ablaze the inside of homes, the trees inside the city, and wagons as such that they hid under.

Owain looked towards his leg as a burning sensation and a sharp pain began to grow. An arrow had impaled into his calf - he scowled, snapped the arrow in half, and ripped the fabric from below his knee to throw the fire from himself. He saw then in the distance a group of twenty or so Blood Dragons heading towards the bottom of the main street - the last run towards the only chance of safety.

Lyra and Owain crawled out from underneath the wagon where Owain struggled to stand without the strength of his right leg, "Take him," he handed Martell to Lyra, "Let nothing happen to him, I cannot outrun them," he nodded towards the invaders. He picked up the table leg in his left hand and held the sword that Lyra had given to him in his right, "I will hold this street. None shall pass me."

"You cannot be serious!" Lyra shouted to him as she took Martell into her arms before beginning to step away from him.

"Made of blood."

"They will bleed."

"Go!" Owain shouted, "Save him!."

The Young Warrior turned around and hobbled a few steps back where there was a small choke point between the burning wagon and the end of the street. A few more civilians hurried past him while they could. None stopped to help him.

Owain closed his eyes. The image of his Uncle appeared in his mind. The Orange Knight. A man turned from shame to legend. He always wanted to be like him, to be someone who stuck to his principles no matter what. To be someone who can stand up for his own ideals.

The Blood Dragons slowed their advance as they saw Owain standing between the wagon and the stone building. One of them stepped forward and removed his helmet, he was bald and looked as strong and burly as Owain did, "Dying for nothing eh?"

Another laughed, "Frenk kill this Copper headed fuck."

Frenk looked towards Owain who was scowling in reply. The redhead took deep breaths and began to bounce his body in an attempt to limber up.

"He's just a kid," Frenk pointed and laughed, "A kid playing at being a hero-"

Owain bolted forward and cracked Frenk across the side of the head with the table leg causing the thick piece of wood to splinter slightly. The soldier's limp body fell towards the floor and his neck cracked onto the curb of the street.

There was a silence amongst the burning buildings, the crackles of embers - amongst The Orange Knight and The Blood Dragons.

This time, the invaders hurried towards Owain who hobbled back a few steps as the arrow that had wounded him remained embedded into his calf, he played the choke point - he swung his sword side to side to cause the Blood Dragons to hesitate an approach and parried their attempts to disarm him.

Owain blocked an overhead swing from another soldier with the thick piece of wood and then stabbed his borrowed sword into the throat of the man before him, he then kicked the body forward towards the group trying to scurry between the point - He followed by prodding his sword forward multiple times where he caught a few pieces of flesh with the edge of his blade.

"Is this all you bastards have?" Owain shouted, "You fight in numbers for you have no strength of your own!"

The Blood Dragons collected themselves and attempted another rush on Owain, they pushed through the choke point causing the red head to hobble a few more steps back. He readied his weapons as they stood before him in three rows of five each with their weapons ready to kill him. One of the soldiers stopped in between the makeshift ranks - his helmet dropped to the floor where anger sat on his face and venom dripped from his eyes, "You killed my friend."

"How sorrowful it is for you to meet someone defending themselves. Fucking cowards," Owain retaliated.

The singular Blood Dragon stepped ahead of the ranks and readied his sword - a challenge.

Owain took a deep breath and made a decision, he dropped his blade onto the ground and held onto the thick table leg with his right hand and left the other free to use.

"Two would be unfair," Owain smiled through the pain.

The Soldier stepped forward and swiped towards Owain who parried with the wood in an intent to lock the blade into it. A plan that went perfectly. The redhead yanked the joint weapons towards him and disarmed The Blood Dragon - he let the weapons drop behind him before swinging forward his right arm to lamp the soldier before him square in the jaw with his meaty fists. He then picked up his sword from the ground and slashed across the guts of the soldier, spilling his red onto the floor.

Behind the ranked soldiers began a rumble of footsteps - behind them Owain witnessed a militia of men running towards them all.

"Ranks!" One of The Blood Dragons ordered amongst his men. They shifted their attention behind them with only a few keeping their eyes on Owain. The Redhead began swinging his blade toward those that remained focused on him as the invaders huddled within the choke point to defend against The Militia.

The two groups slammed against one another and the screams of pain and splatters of blood crashed near the burning wagon beside them all. With the distraction of Owain behind them, and the greater number of The Militia, The Blood Dragons were cut down. The redhead battled the last one who attempted to flee, the weapons of the two duellists met each other with each strike but the fight ended as a sword cut down Owain's opponent behind him.

Behind the collapsing body stood a man in a white sailors tunic with red blood splattered across the fabric, his hair was shaved and his face was tired.

"Give me your arm," The Sailor motioned Owain who hobbled over and placed his arm over the man who had helped him, as did another member of The Militia.

"Thanks," Owain said, "I didn't think I'd get so far there."

The two walked amongst the group of men and women who wielded old swords and other tools that could be used to kill.

"You trained?" The Sailor asked.

"Yeah," Owain answered, "Not trained for this though."

"None of us are."

The Militia and Owain made their way up the incline of the final street, the final walk to a second chance of safety behind the thick walls of the city centre. Guardsmen dressed in blue hurried to open the large thick stone doors for them as they pulled levers on the other side and cranked the gears to open the defence. Owain looked around to see all the people of laketown in despair as their city was destroyed and their families killed. He didn't understand it. Was The Princess really capable of doing all this just to find Arvuria? Were his three friend going to come out alive in the middle of the army they were going to find themselves in.

"Owain!" Lyra called out to him from a distance. His mind came back to him and his sight scoured around the people to try and find the Guild leader.

"By the tree!" The Glade shouted again.

Owain's attention and that of the sailor turned to the woman shouting towards them. Lyra was kneeling beside Martell who was led on a stone bench while a woman dressed in pink bloodied robes channelled Arcane into Martell's wounds, and beside Lyra sat another woman who looked towards the man beside him with tears of happiness beginning to roll down her cheeks.

"By The Ethereals," The Sailor croaked as he hurried Owain and himself towards the group. Seeing the desperation of the man who had helped him, Owain pushed the man ahead to let him run to the women that he must know. It seemed to Owain that more paths were to cross tonight.

The Sailor ran towards Kinne and kneeled towards her, he place their foreheads together and kissed one another. Lyra lifted herself to her feet and hurried over to Owain and helped him limp towards the bedside of the young Martell whose wounds had grown smaller - the splint around his leg removed and the chunk of flesh that had been gouged out had begun to grow back.

"Will he be okay?" Owain asked The Mender.

Shin looked up to the injured redhead and gave an eager nod, "He is strong, he will be okay once I am done. Is he your brother?"

Owain lips quivered and he beat back the croak in his throat, "He is."

"Shin?" The Sailor spoke nervously behind The Mender. Owain watched as Shin turned over her shoulder and a look of disbelief and shame washed over her as she saw the man.

"Mathane... You're alive," Shin's face scrunched as she tried to hold back her tears but they came flooding down. Her face red and the emotion flowing out of her as she tried to focus on healing.

Owain stood with Lyra as they watched the reunion, with Mathane hugging Shin from the side and kissing her forehead.

"Thank you, to the both of you," Owain bowed his head after they had their moment, "You saved me, and you will save Martell. I owe you two lives."

"You owe me nothing," Shin answered, "Just make sure this boy focuses on his recovery when he awakens. Owain lifted his head and smiled to her, acknowledging her words and taking a step back to allow her focus to shift back towards her task. However, he noticed Lyra's attention shift towards the view below their hill that gave them a small glimpse towards the battlefield.

"Owain, look," Lyra pushed lightly on his shoulder to turn towards the view of the battlefield outside of the walls below. Amongst the river of fire there were flashes of other colours. Green. Red. Gold.

They had made it, and they were fighting for all of them.

"I am with you Vann. You have my faith."

Luke Morgan

Arvuria: The Ethereal Children

Chapter 29:
VANN ERENDON
Battle of The Bloody Lake IV

THE SIEGE AHEAD looked as though a river of fire was flowing towards Laketown as thousands of invaders walked amongst the blaze of their torches. Vann stood on an outcropped rock after he hurried for a better view of the army as it flowed into the entrances of the broken walls - Vann turned to Harnon, peering through the helmet he had taken from the dead scout. Vann's skin was pale in fear as he saw the banners of black and red sway forth in the fire, "They are going to tear through the city, we cannot delay any longer."

Harnon walked beside Vann, his black cape dropped to the floor before meeting him to reveal his own stolen Blood Dragon armour with the black sword on his back remaining wrapped in its leathers.

Arvuria: The Ethereal Children

"There she is," Harnon pointed to one of the many platformed stone hills that were scattered before the city. Dira was mounted on her armoured horse with bannermen and red armoured soldiers around here

"Do you think we can do this?" Vann doubted himself for but a moment, he gripped his father's sword - he finally understood what it meant to be given it.

"We must do this" Arvuria steeled underneath the red hood she wore with her hair tied up to hide its colour, "We will follow your plan, Vann. Harnon, when we are close enough you must launch us towards The Blood Dragon.

Harnon turned to The Golden Dragon who stood behind them both, "Dira is as strong as you and I, her mastery and genius in The Arcane has made her an incredible force - let alone her martial prowess. Vann, are you sure of yourself?"

Vann's panic and fear steadily increased as he considered the idea of being in the middle of a war. To be in the middle of an army trying to kill him. The confidence of his new power dashed away in fear of taking yet another life, but if it came to it - if he had to defend a loved one by taking someone else's… he would do it again. He steeled himself, he feared loss, but it would not come if he found courage once more in himself. Owain and Martell were in that city somewhere, and Vann would be damned if he was going to let anything happen to them. He looked over his shoulder slowly, peering his gaze towards Arvuria who had now closed her eyes, taking deep breaths.

"I will stop her," Vann announced as he held onto the hilt of his Father's sword with determination.

"I will not let our friends come to harm," Arvuria determined as she stepped onto the outcropped pointed rock beside him.

"You two have come a long way in little time," Harnon smiled to the Golden Dragon and her Chosen.

"I have waited hundreds of years to unleash Beonyth's power once more," Harnon cheered with thumps to his chest with his fists as he dropped ahead of Vann and Arvuria from the rock, "Stay close to me."

Vann followed his mentor closely as they scurried towards the army in an attempt to join the ranks. The Blood Dragon's on the edge of the tide looked to them with evil intentions until Harnon lifted an insignia from the belt of the Scout's uniform, instructing the Soldiers of their position, "Make way!"

An opening formed for them to enter and the three hurried into it.

The sound of steel and heavy footsteps drilled into Vann's body, the vibrations catching him almost off guard alongside the chants of war that The Blood Dragons sang. There was no going back now. What was to happen from here on out was up to the three of them - if the city was to survive, if their friends were to survive they needed to take the head of the army. They needed to kill Dira.

Vann focused his sight on Arvuria who led ahead of him after Arvuria, he followed her footsteps and her path, he trusted her and she trusted him. She had given him her Wisp to carry, she had entrusted her life unto him. He would not fail her. He would not show her failure.

Their route towards Dira moved them in between the soldiers for as far as they could get until they were halted by another man in the same uniform as them that held more heraldry upon it.

"Halt," The Chief Scout ordered loudly through the noise of war, "Give the word of your station."

The word of our station? Vann thought to himself.

"They are barricading all entrances, they are keeping the civilians in their homes," Harnon shouted.

"The word of your station!" The Chief Scout ordered, "Give me your code! Identify yourself or be slain."

The Blood Dragons nearby halted and formed a watchful warning as their swords unsheathed. They had been caught if Harnon couldn't say the correct thing for once, Vann lessened his nervous grip around the sword at his waist and readied to pull it with his other hand.

Vann watched as Harnon looked over his shoulder with a raise of his eyebrow, "Bend your legs and tap into her Arcane before you land."

The Chosen of The Golden Dragon took a deep breath and did as instructed. He looked towards Dira and aimed his body towards her as The Blood Dragon's around them took a step forward towards them.

"Arvuria, are you ready?" Harnon asked.

The Golden Dragon pulled the hood from her hair and unleashed her golden hair to cascade down onto her body. The torrential rain began to steam around her as it lit up in the white fire that caused her harm before.

"Now!" Arvuria ordered.

Harnon lifted his sword from his back and the leathers around it unravelled as he brought the blade to slash the man before them, while his sword swung upwards it glowed a verdant green as he brought it down back into the ground where the earth beneath them shifted a few feet into the ground. After a few seconds the circle of indented earth beneath them shifted upwards at an angle and launched them to the stone platform where Dira stood.

They soared above the army of blood and fire. Vann clenched his fist and focused on the swirling power inside of him - he was searching for it the key to it, the way for him to unleash it. He remembered his father and mother who were so intent on keeping him safe that they sent him away from the war at their borders. He remembered his times at the farm filled with worry each day, but the laughter and friendship with the others always helped him through. He remembered Tristan and Emerie who were always true to him. He remembered finding Arvuria amidst the smoke of the crater.

Vann's eyes lit up gold as Arvuria's, he felt the warm spark in the centre of his chest and ignited it into a roaring blaze - a golden aura surrounded him as he felt the power of The Golden Dragon. He soared through the air and managed to give himself strength enough to survive his impact against the armoured men he landed upon once he had finally descended closer towards The Blood Dragon's platform. The Golden Dragon's Chosen stood up from the ground and circled his father's sword around himself on instinct with the power of Arvuria flowing through the blade, extending its reach by a few feet, slicing men around him in half, cauterising their bodies as it went through them. His father's voice rang through his ears a final time, the same words he would hear each time he held the old blade. He wanted to regret unsheathing it, but it was him or them, he understood it now, what his father was trying to teach him. That he must know what he was fighting for, and Vann knew it now. He was fighting for those he loved.

The army of soldiers that stood around the halved bodies barely hesitated before charging towards him with their weapons drawn. In turn Vann stabbed the sword into the ground to release a pulse of energy knocking them backwards into the line behind them.

"Princess Dira!" Vann shouted with all his might as he looked towards her ascended position. He pointed his father's sword towards the mounted warrior whose collective watched Arvuria soar across the ranks of armour, flying above them with a stronger aura of Arcane that covered Vann.

The soldiers around Vann stood watching him as they waited for an order from their Princess - whose head slowly turned towards Vann as she looked at him in annoyance.

"Kill him quickly," Princess Dira disregarded his challenge, "Focus on the girl!" She beckoned, pointing towards Arvuria who floated amongst The Blood Dragons as she fired her beams of white fire towards them from the air.

The Blood Dragons began to run towards Vann once more but were quickly dispatched by beams of Arvuria's light - she was giving him an opportunity.

"Take her down Vann! I will get you there!" Arvuria vowed as her aerial assault continued.

Vann ran forward towards Princess Dira who now had begun to dismount her horse readying herself for a fight. If she was as strong as Harnon said she was, this was going to be one hell of a fight, and for a man whose training consisted only of morning sparring with his father and Tristan, Vann didn't favour his odds. Nonetheless, he had strength within him to fight and that was enough for him. Vann was done running away from danger. There comes a time in every person's life where they need to stand for themselves, to look at the world before them and decide that they can have an impact, no matter how great or small. Every choice matters. Every voice matters. Every person matters. And in this moment, Vann knew that him being here... it mattered.

Vines appeared from the ground from Harnon's creation, forming a series of steps towards the large mound that Dira resided on as he fought against his own pocket of infinite soldiers. "Fight! Fight for all those behind the walls!" Harnon's voice roared. "Fight!"

Vann climbed the vine steps and began to flicker a golden hue with each part of his ascent with each moment of doubt in himself. On the final step he leaped the last few feet in distance as he held his sword over his head with the aim to bring it down onto Dira.

Vann sailed downwards towards his opponent who stood in awe, just barely collecting herself to parry his blade with her two axes that began to drip a blood red of Arcane as she pulled from her own Arcane Tethers. Their weapons impacted each other, their eyes met - Vann saw in hers an anger and fury that would frighten even the strongest warrior. It frightened him. Her lips turned into a smirk before she booted Vann in the chest forcing him a few paces backwards across their stone arena.

Dira clicked her neck and looked towards her leaders and guardsmen, "Join the siege. It seems I have met my destiny," she ordered the ordained who began to climb down from the platform to the army below.

"Stop this senseless battle," Vann himself ordered to The Princess of The Theothen Empire. "If you value the lives of your army, and your own damn life, surrender. Now."

The Princess smiled before bolting towards him with inhuman speed. Without the power of The Golden Dragon Vann would have been dead in almost an instant, but his body reacted in the nick of time as he parried every strike from her as she swung her axes with every slash a move to kill. Vann had a reprieve when Dira moved back to her original position after failing her attempt to behead him.

"Who are you?" Dira questioned. Her sight pierced right into his soul and a feeling of uncomfortableness appeared within Vann, as if some kind of demon was looking at him.

"I'm just a peasant. Someone like you wouldn't care," Vann frowned towards her, the grip of both his hands tightening around his sword. Around the two of them Dira's army was ever so slowly being dismantled by Arvuria and Harnon as their element of surprise stopped the soldiers from rallying. Harnon's use of controlling the crowds with his vines and stone proved incredibly effective as he created sections and walls within the army - sewing confusion and frustration amongst the soldiers. The forest rumbled at the use of Harnon's power.

"I wouldn't care that you are just a peasant?" Dira asked with a laugh, "Look around me. I have an army of them. An army of men and women that I have brought to legend. The small-folk are the ones who make the story of my Empire. These people are family, not soldiers."

Vann sped forward as Dira did, their weapons exchanging blows again but once more neither of their attacks landed onto the other's person.

"Your family is a blight on this land!" Vann shouted to Dira as his blade interlocked with her two axes once more, "You cause death and destruction everywhere you go! How many of these peoples' homes have been destroyed by you?"

Vann was pushed away by Dira with her own human strength against his amped up power. "I bring order! I bring strength! I fight for my people's future! What do you bring? What have you ever done for this country?" Dira shouted as she began to swipe her axes against the air, ripping red arcane from the sky to fire it towards Vann in scythes of power. Vann dodged and ducked underneath The Arcane and rolled into the dirt of the mound, sliding sideways as he curved back onto his feet. The aura of gold that covered Vann began to seep back into him causing his hair to ignite a paler glow of gold with his eyes becoming the same - all the while the golden patterns his skin wore during his time in The Planescape began to softly appear once more.

Vann stood up back to his feet, accents of his stolen armour turned an incredible gold, his hair began to flow as a fire and the hue of his iris turned as yellow as the sun, glowing brighter than even the star itself.

"I haven't done anything for this country, but we must all start somewhere," Vann spoke simply, "I think stopping you is a fine beginning."

Vann threw his blade into the dirt below, the handle pronging upwards with the blue leathers of its handle standing amongst the sea of red and black.

Dira seethed at the disrespect.

She returned Vann's display by angrily slashing the air with both axes, creating two large blood-red arcane tears that hovered beside her. She dropped her weapons just as Vann did and reached her arms into the Arcane scars, pulling them out again to reveal Arcane Armour that ran down her arms towards her gauntlets which now resembled five blood red sharp claws of a dragon on each hand ready to be used to cut Vann apart.

The two warriors sprinted towards each other once more and combated each other with their fists. It was brutal, and it was bloody. Both Vann and Dira brawled and battled amongst the ongoing tide of the soldiers around them running to battle Harnon and Arvuria, while those ahead of them continued to siege the city. With each strike that Dira landed onto him, Vann felt the claws slowly chip away at his now blessed armour - he thought about how Owain would fight with his fists, his larger friend was always best when he could brawl without technique - when his opponents didn't know what Owain was going to do, that's when he was at his best. Vann took inspiration, he waited for the perfect moment when Dira would pull both of her hands back and when she did he grabbed hold of her wrists to then tilt his head back - he landed headbutt her square in the nose. A crack sounded and her bridge bent. Dira ignored the pain and spat the blood that poured down towards her mouth into Vann's face, hindering his sight for a moment as the blood burned against his skin, it was enough time for Dira to wrap her large claws around his throat.

"It's a pity to kill such a powerful Chosen," Dira grimaced with excitement as Vann felt the pressure of her grip slowly tighten around his neck - she was trying to savour the kill on him. He could feel himself slowly dwindle away. What strength was given to him was faltering and what strength he had in himself was all but spent.

Vann hands searched across her arms for a way to break her hold of him but the Arcane Claws she wielded gave him no leverage to find his freedom, so he reached for her neck where his fingertips barely scraped her body as he tried to pull at a piece of her armour, a piece that felt like rope. He looped a finger into it and yanked it, pulling it away from her with a faint snap. Vann witnessed Dira's gaze look downwards as he pulled a small vial of white sand from her neck which began to exhume such an incredible white light outwards as Arvuria's power beamed through its glass into the almost pure sand. The white light quickly exploded and spread across the entire army, knocking them to the ground - when it hit Arvuria she came barrelling downwards from the sky to land between Vann and Dira. She rolled far and her golden aura dimmed with each impact, her armour dirtied and sullied as she took the damage of her fall.

All who had been involved in this siege on both sides of the walls were impacted by the blast but those closest took an incredible hit.

Vann's eyes were heavy as he shook the weariness from the blast away from him to see Dira climbing to her feet, her Arcane power had vanished but still she wielded a dagger in her hand as she slowly stumbled towards the girl with murderous intent.

"You," Dira seethed a few feet away from Arvuria who was rolling and grimacing in pain from the blast. Her aura was glowing immensely and vanished in intervals.

"Vann…" Arvuria murmured to herself, "…The beach."

Vann rolled to his feet with great pain but stumbled back to the ground in weakness from his blunt force wounds. In desperation he crawled forward as quickly as he could amongst the seared dirt underneath him, "I'm coming!" he called out to Arvuria as he tried to find the strength in his now-weak body. He had brought her here from the very beginning of his journey, he would not let it all end here… but the pulsating of her power grew faster and brighter, and much more unstable.

"Get away," Arvuria reached out towards Dira as The Princess staggered towards her, "You'll die," She warned. The Princess stopped in her tracks upon the words of Arvuria, her face grew sombre and worried at the sight of Arvuria showing her compassion.

"I am no longer a wanderer of my path. I have had enough of the continuous bloodshed. I grow impatient! Show me my destiny, Valen!" Dira roared as she dropped towards Arvuria with her dagger in hand causing a second blast of immense power that rocketed towards the sky in an incredible pillar of light.

Arvuria: The Ethereal Children

The pillar of light encircled the area around them. Vann watched the silhouette of Dira grab hold of a branch that stood out from the dirt beneath them as the power that unleashed from Arvuria attempted to pull them both up into the sky, and with nothing for Vann to grab hold of bar his sword that slipped from the ground as he grasped it he was pulled into the tornado of light - he was flung into the sky amongst the heavy winds of Arvuria's Arcane.

He had no idea how far into the air he was, all he knew was that he continued to go higher and higher with the ground looking like a distant memory.

He grimaced in pain as his body rag-dolled upwards until he was able to steady himself with the short burst of Arcane that he had left in him from his fight with Dira. He looked downwards to see a grand silhouette heading towards him, growing larger and larger as each second passed... until an incredible beast flew past him, Vann barely caught a glimpse of it as it sped past - all he saw was gold.

Within a second later the beast circled underneath him in the pillar of light and carried him further upwards. His body crashed against the golden metallic beast whose force of ascent kept him attached to the body. The bright metallic gold hue of the scales was an incredible sight as its armour unravelled across his new mount almost smooth in feel, its wings as long as a galleon as they slowly and beautifully warped the sky with its beats. Vann gripped one of his hands into the scales and held tightly onto his sword still, fearing the idea of how high he was but fearing more losing his only tie to his father.

"Fear not Vann, you are safe with me," Arvuria's voice spoke warmly as her ascent halted - the upwards draft of the pillar of light ended where it had now slowly began to turn into a heavy mist. She corrected herself as they hovered so that Vann could collect himself, for as much as possible in this moment.

"Arvuria?!" Vann spoke in shock as he lifted his head up from the scales to see Arvuria's horned dragon head looking over her shoulder. Vann began to laugh in disbelief, "I don't know how, but you still look like you!"

The Golden Dragon's head shook, releasing a series of huffs as it attempted to laugh before shaking its head and batting its wings to stay afloat in the air. She was sleek yet armoured with the light of the two moons glistening against her through the mist, the horns on her head curved downwards with a fin running from the back of her head towards Vann, finishing just where he sat mounted.

"Our battle is not yet over," Arvuria announced with a heavy tone.

"I know," Vann answered, "We cannot fail now, this is the moment we have been waiting for."

Arvuria lifted the both of them higher into the air before arching her body forwards as she began to dive back towards the ground. Vann immediately regretted his request. His stomach churned as they dropped, he fought the urge to vomit by releasing a fearful yet courageous shout as the wind battered his face again. A shout filled with so much adrenaline that he was sure all who lived underneath the shadow of Arvuria's wings would hear him before they were to see them.

Vann's mass fixated downwards onto Arvuria's scales as she turned her body back upwards, levelling through the heavy mist of arcane that she had created in an awesome show of force as she announced her return with her draconic roar across the army below who had stood recovering from the blasts. Vann looked downwards, fighting the disorientation of seeing people so small, but he couldn't help but cheer in excitement as he soared above them - with all eyes on him and his dear friend.

They flew over Beonyth's Laketown to see the front quarter of the city burning still but the fighting had stopped as The Golden Dragon announced her arrival with the beating of her wings. She took Vann past the city to hear the cheering of both civilians of Beonyth's Laketown, and The Blood Dragons below. The second coming of The Golden Dragon was a sight for all to witness.

Arvuria flew finally over the Lake of Anelli's tears, the birthplace of her father, and then circled back around to the mound where she landed in front of Dira who watched them with awe. With a thud of impact Vann's ears almost deafened as Arvuria screeched above Dira who stood in admiration of what she saw.

"Stop your siege, and surrender," Vann shouted towards her with his sword pointed towards the air in sign of peace atop the Dragon, "The Golden Dragon has returned to Taundrad, and I am her Chosen. Surrender. Now."

There was silence around the three of them. A heavy silence. Vann's eyes fixated on Dira, trusting that Arvuria could keep him safe from any cheap arrow or sling of Arcane.

Dira kneeled before Arvuria and Vann.

Dira's army kneeled before Arvuria and Vann.

The Horns of Surrender sounded from their vicinity, carrying across the army until it reached the city where it continued through the streets.

The siege had ended.

Arvuria moved a wing forward towards Dira to allow Vann to slide down to meet The Princess.

"Do you yield?" Vann asked Dira, lifting her chin with his blade to see The Princess shedding a tear from her blind eye.

"I yield."

The Chosen looked back to Arvuria who nodded the head of her new form in agreement. She lifted her large wings and forced herself from the ground to begin to fly above the kneeling Blood Dragons below, gifting to them a close look at her might while Vann sheathed his blade and extended a hand towards Dira who refused to take it.

"I am offering peace," Vann spoke bluntly as Dira's wet eyes remained fixated unto him.

"You are the Chosen of The Golden Dragon. You are the destiny I have been searching for for so long. Valen's path has led me to this forked road, and I have made my decision," Dira muttered in front of her silent kneeling army.

Dira climbed to her feet and walked past Vann towards the largest section of her army.

"What are you doing?" Vann asked her, attempting to grab her wrist but she moved it too quickly for him to stop her.

"Blood Dragons!" Dira commanded attention, " We came here in hunt of a girl who was rumoured to have incredible power. Power that I wanted for myself. As I stand here, as you all stand here - it is clear to us that we are on the wrong side of this war. We have lost our way. I lost my way. I have spent my life chasing destiny – walking Valen's path. I have led a path of blood and destruction but I see clearly now," she continued as she bent down to pick up half of the glass vial that Shin had gifted her, the one containing the sand from the bottom of Anelli's Tears. "Destiny can be discovered in the smallest places. It can even be gifted to you by those you least expect,"

Dira spoke softly as she gripped her glove around the glass vial before shattering what pieces remained, "We will spend our lives making amends for our folly here, and to atone for our intent to harm those who steered away from war."

Dira turned to Vann and kneeled once more, "I ask for your forgiveness. And if you would have it, my loyalty."

The Warden of Gold stood before the army - the strongest Legion in Theothen. Each soldier bowed to him. Arvuria returned and landed behind Vann, standing just above him - giving his nervousness shelter. Vann looked at his blade in his hand and remembered Arvuria's words: "Vann. This is how you save everyone."

Vann raised his sword high to hear the clanks of metal of helmets and armour as the soldiers before him lifted their heads to see the man of legend - what then followed was a thunderous bash of steel at the sight of Vann standing tall beside Dira, as The Golden Dragon stood above him.

The Golden Dragon and its Chosen had returned to the land of Taundrad.

Luke Morgan

Arvuria: The Ethereal Children

Luke Morgan

- Chapter 30 -
THURIAN THEO
Beware The Dark Below.

THE WIND HOWLED against the large stained-glass window behind his bed. It stirred him from his slumber. It stirred him from the one dream he had had in months. He was atop the very same battlement he had been standing on when he witnessed the golden meteor land - back when nothing mattered to him anymore. In the dream he was the one who found this mysterious blonde girl that started all of this, and in doing so he led a rebellion against the crown in the manner of how a hero would, how it should have been done from the start - not the way that he had done it. No hero would murder their father and threaten their people.

Thurian stared at the white marble ceiling far above as Emerie laid on his chest - she was the only feeling of warmth he had in his new room that was stationed at the top of the fifth spire.

He turned his sight towards the colourful window surrounded by the dark black stone of the walls, where rain had peculiarly begun to fall. An extremely rare occasion in the city of Arvur, something so rare that some would say it was a blessing, while others would say it was a dark omen. Thurian looked at the art, it angled upside down as he laid still in his bed - the mosaic art of The Golden Dragon standing behind King Theo while he raised a sword high over his head as an army surrounded him in defence. Thurian looked towards the face of the dragon, its eyes staring into his as the rain ran down its cheek.

"An omen," Thurian whispered delicately so as not to awaken Emerie. He pondered. Pondered as to what he was to do now that he had the world under his boot. His father had spent too much time playing political games within the court, The Nobles had become lax, lazy, and they had become all too fond of the freedom he had unintentionally given them outside the walls of the Five Spires; The Empress' influence on his decisions could only go so far even with his most drastic of decisions. Thurian had already begun to remedy the mistake of his fathers false reign. He had begun creating an iron grip around the most problematic nobles by sending one of his own Scaleguard to watch over them personally - an Incredible threat, and an incredible promise of death should they sway too far from Thurian's ideals. Never before have the Scaleguard stepped out from the city of Arvur - forever they had been tied to the walls of the city, never being able to see the lands they had once roamed as Knights.

Even with all of the problems associated with his crown, he couldn't help but worry about how he had become so focused on fixing the court, and the country, that he hadn't spent enough time with Emerie since uprooting her life to use her as a political piece. That's all she ever was from the start, a political piece to use in the next few weeks to settle the uproar of his regicide with the common folk - to subdue their worries with the promise that he loves them as he loves his peasant-born Queen. She was only ever a part of his and Markarth's plan yet somehow with the time he had spent with her he had begun to see something within her, a spark of something he hadn't felt since Princess Ryenn first looked upon him.

Emerie stirred for a moment as she slept, her head moved into what Thurian assumed was a more comfortable position for her - Thurian lifted one of his hands to stroke her hair that she had braided before sleeping, telling him that if she didn't do so her hair would not be able to be tamed in the morning. He smiled at her as she slept, a small hum coming from her as she almost snored.

Lightning clapped past the window of The Golden Dragon and before Thurian, across the distance from the bed to the door, he could have sworn a shadow of a beast appeared. He remained still, holding Emerie with a scowl towards the other side of the room. Whatever it was, he was ready to face it. Dhulo or Riteus he cared not, for this time he would protect the woman he loved.

The rain grew heavier, and it grew louder.

The shadow appeared again, more obvious was its silhouette. It was the shape of a dragon's head, large and monstrous. Thurian was going to pass it as an effect of the mosaic window above him but he noticed the silhouette of this dragon had no horns, and it's head shape was sleeker than the armoured and plated Arvur placed in the glass.

Arvuria: The Ethereal Children

"Theo" The Shadow beckoned in a vile and cunning voice as it slowly dissipated towards the doorway, slithering underneath.

Thurian very carefully removed Emerie from his body, and placed a kiss onto her forehead as he sneaked out of the bed.

"Thurian..." She murmured in her sleep, almost begging for him to stay. The Emperor took a moment to take in the sight of her sleeping peacefully before walking slowly towards the exit of the room. The naked steps of his feet pattered across the black tiling as the lighting and the howling of the wind outside became muffled, as if something was blocking the noise from his room.

As he walked closer towards the metal door he began to notice white mist peering through from the other side of the iron. A dream, this had to be. He reached out towards the handle of the door and slowly pulled it, where the room shifted past him - Thurian stood now with his feet in an infinite puddle of water, with a dark expanse surrounding him. Scattered around the area was debris, and boulders of archaic stone with a language that moved etched into the rocks, and art that he couldn't comprehend. The infinite expanse seemed to be damaged with holes in the roof and floor, beams of sunlight peering through the holes above and the water running down into the open tunnels below. Thurian walked toward one of the damages near him and peered over it to see the water that surrounded his feet constantly falling downwards, where below was the world of Taundrad - an ever expanse of the world's green, and the cities, and the mountains and the forests. He stood above the clouds that drifted under his death, periodically removing the beautiful landscape from his view.

"Theo..." The Horrific Voice sounded all around him. Thurian looked upwards to try to see ahead in the dark infinite expanse before him, and in that darkness a shadow grew closer, the same shadow as before.

"Who are you?!" Thurian shouted into the void, his voice travelling far away from him but never ending.

"You know me, boy," The Voice answered The Emperor from behind him. Thurian spun around to see The Shadow growing larger again.

"I am in no mood to play games, shadow. Show your true self, or I will force it upon you," Thurian threatened.

The Shadow snickered.

Thurian turned around again to see an incredible sickly white dragon appear through the shadowy mist as it slowly stalked forward. Its wings attached to its front legs which delicately and tactically slithered its body forward. The beast's long neck moved its head just above the water that sat on the floor, moving the forever still liquid. The dragon's body was smooth, no armour or heavy scales were placed onto its body, it was snake-like, naked except its jagged teeth that sat on its face with no cover of skin - almost as a smile that would never fade. Its claws carried some of the only colour on his body that wasn't white - they had a hint of pink near the meat of his skin.

The Dragon's neck reached its head upwards and forwards where it then looked down upon Thurian just a few feet away.

Emperor Thurian froze.

"Brigir…" The Emperor muttered, "The Pale Dragon."

"Thurian. The Emperor of Theothen. Descendant of My Jailer. Bringer of My Freedom," Brigir spoke.

There was no doubt about it to Thurian Theo. Before him stood Brigir, The Pale Dragon. The child born of Dhulo and Riteus. He was The Bringer of Order, and the Executioner of The Guilty. There was no greater power in the known world of Taundrad than Brigir - Thurian knew that he had to choose his words here very carefully.

"I have been watching you, in the halls of my brother's home. You have proven… entertaining," Brigir decided.

"You have been watching me?" Thurian asked with his chest, attempting to push back the fear and speak with bravery.

"Yes," Brigir answered, "The walls have been my eyes, your mother my voice"

"What do you know of my mother?!" Thurian quickly questioned, regretting the raise of his voice. Brigir's jaw carried forward at the disrespect Thurian had just shown. "I have witnessed all that has occurred in this castle for several hundred and sixty one years. I have seen every betrayal, every scheme, every kill, and every sin that has occurred in the golden city of my 'honourable' brother. Yet, I find myself interested in you - one of the few who have garnered my true attention,"

Thurian took a step back from the mouthing jaws of Brigir, splashing a few drops of water across his linen trousers as he did so. "What am I to do with your attention?" he asked, his voice wavering with his small retreat.

"What are you to do?" Brigir repeated, a huff of air escaped his slitted nostrils. "Child, you have earned my gaze. Eyes that have seen the history of humanity, an ever present being who has seen all, and will continue to see all. From the arrival of your people, to the end of it. Yet I find myself wanting. I killed my brother, and in his last final act he sealed my form in golden chains and cast my Wisp towards The First Layer. I am the dark below. I am the shadow that creates the night. I am the abyss that sits in every man's heart. I want the light. I want freedom. You will give it to me."

"Freedom? That is all you ask?" Thurian questioned, tilting his head as he somehow attempted to judge Brigir's intentions. "You are the Dragon of Ill-Will, and you request, to me, your freedom? Since when does the boot beg the ant for a favour?"

Brigir stood silent amongst the mist and smoke, his body a statue, except for his sickly pink eyes that focused ever so slowly on the man before him.

"You speak as though you are not in dire need of my help. I have seen you before. In one of your most opportunistic grand-sires. An Emperor who alienated himself from the court, only to find the most violent of acids in his supper. Your court already plots to murder you - there are hooded individuals dead in your room as of this moment. They had their knives pressed to your throats, similar in fashion to how Princess Ryenn died, is it not?"

"Is Emerie safe?!" Thurian shouted, fear for her ran through his blood even though the monster that Brigir was remained fixated on him.

"Your companion is none the wiser," Brigir answered. "Free me, Thurian Theo. Free me and I will owe you a favour. Free me and together we will create 'True peace', an ideal that The Golden Dragon Arvur denied to me. We will create a world where every human lives the life that they have always dreamed of - there will be no war, no strife, and no hurt in our world. Every life will be important. All will matter."

Everything that Thurian wanted was promised to him, he knew that Brigir was playing on his ideals yet... the dragon was speaking earnestly. The history of Arvur and Brigir goes back hundreds of years. Could he really believe that Arvur was such a righteous Dragon if he had decided that the world shouldn't have peace? Thurian was a Theo... If anyone knew how much history was written by the victor, it would be him.

"How would I free you? I do not believe that I know how to shatter the bindings of The Golden Dragon. I do not use The Arcane, I refuse to," Thurian questioned, curious as to what the plan would be.

Brigir moved, he slithered his body around the area of Thurian, "You are to speak to The Mother Empress, she has been a loyal servant of mine since her birth. She will bring you to the very foundations of my downfall, and there you will find me - there you will become my Chosen."

Thurian blinked and before him was the metal door of the bedroom, in his hands was his sword, bloodied red, and in its reflection - his eyes, pale and white. The hue of his iris diminished, with just a hint of its green colour remaining. He looked over his shoulder to see the bloody bodies of three men, each of their arms cut off from the shoulders, and in her bed still in a deep slumber was Emerie.

Thurian walked through the red liquid towards Emerie's side of the bed where he stood as a statue, taking in the peaceful sight of the woman who had slowly earned his heart. He wondered if she would side with him again in freeing the Pale Dragon. He wanted to wake her and ask for her help once more but he knew deep down that she was not as desperate as he was - she wanted to change the world slowly, by going the honourable route. What honour would there be in working with Brigir? He did not care for the answer.

Luke Morgan

Arvuria: The Ethereal Children

- Chapter 31 -
Vann Erendon
Uncle Borrenthus.

ATOP THE WALLS they hurried under last night, Vann and Harnon looked towards Anelli's Tears once more. This time without the fear of death coming their way. Underneath them, trailing from inside the city towards the white sands of the lake were crowds of people all carefully lining in excitement to meet The Golden Dragon. Arvuria stood on her hind legs in the shallow entrance of the sapphire waters where her wings extended to all allowing them to touch her - to feel the grace and warmth that emanated for her.

"Do you think she is okay?" Harnon asked Vann as he leaned onto the walls, "Maybe this is too much before we head to Borrenthus."

Arvuria: The Ethereal Children

Vann leaned beside his mentor and chuckled, "I thought we learned that we have to let her do what she believes is right."

"That's all any of us can do," Harnon released with a sigh, "I still think we should have killed her."

"Dira?" Vann asked.

"Yes," Harnon answered, "I am waiting to see if your mercy made you a fool. Yet I know that you will need to have an army to serve you in the war to come. With Brigir's voice carrying farther we must be ready for his eventual return. Even a whisper from him can lead to the end of our world. It cannot happen again, we need Arvuria to do what she was made for. "

Vann pushed his body from the walled ledge and huffed away his stress at the thought of everything that was to happen, "If we are going to get answers about Arvuria's part to play in all of this, we are going to have to reach Borrenthus, aren't we? That is the next step. Everything truly begins with him."

Harnon laughed at him, "I still can't believe you don't realise who he is."

"He is her Uncle, is he not?" Vann questioned, "Some old man in the mountains."

Harnon laughed again and patted him on the shoulder, "More surprises come your way Vann. You must really start opening your eyes to the obvious. How one can gain such power and still be oblivious to the simple things is beyond me."

"I am who I am," Vann chuckled.

Vann looked back to Arvuria and watched as a young girl walked towards her leaving small prints of her sandals in the white sands. The crowd stopped to allow the girl to have a moment and in return Arvuria slowly bowed her draconic neck downwards and invited the girl to touch her head. The girl hesitated for a moment before a fatherly voice from the crowd cheered her on - after she plucked up the courage she patted Arvuria who smiled in return - bearing her sharp teeth that were hidden underneath the huffing out of golden smoke from her nose which created beautiful patterns of gold mist around the girl.

"How are the boys?" Harnon spoke up once more, "I haven't had the chance to find them amongst trying to keep the crowds settled and stopping the nobles from creating more political bullshit."

"I can see why you left the city with the responsibility you have. Must be hard being a protector of such a place as this," Vann confided, his own worries riding his tone. "But Owain is okay, Shin - I think her name is - has healed his leg and she continues to look after Martell. She's a strange one, she offered to be with Dira when she meets with us upon our return."

"There's too much to keep on top of," Harnon rolled his eyes, "Too many people for my taste. I think I'll slink off to the woods once again after this has all blown over."

"You are much too involved now Harnon," Vann shook his head with a smile. Vann was happy that Harnon was treating him as an equal now, he didn't know how he had proved his worth to the older man but he was glad that the respect was there from the both of them. The Teen placed one of his hands onto the ledge of the wall once more and cupped his left left onto the hilt of his sword, the one that his father had gifted to him - he looked back towards Arvuria whose attention slowly shifted towards him, she lifted her head from the art she had created for the child and moved her eyes towards him. Following her intentions, the crowd of Laketown all turned their heads and bodies in unison as The Chosen of The Golden Dragon stood above them all in his Glades

Arvuria: The Ethereal Children

Armour and deep yellow cape that had been given to him by the Mayor of the city, a signature of Vann new station as a protector.

"Are you going to keep them waiting?" Harnon patted his shoulder, "They aren't just here for her you know."

Vann felt as though he should have been nervous, terrified even of the public's awe of him. He was just a young man who was in the wrong place at the right time, and now here he stood with the world's fate on his shoulders. Yet somehow, he felt confidence within himself - whether that was because of Arvuria's Wisp that he carried alongside his own, or the belief he had gained after defeating Dira, but in the end it doesn't truly matter. He had his friends, he had Arvuria, and he had everyone behind him cheering for him. He was The Warden, The Chosen of The Golden Dragon, he was who he had become.

"Will you follow closely? I am not used to this," Vann asked Harnon with a smile. His Mentor nodded and motioned for him to move towards the stairs. Vann turned from the ledge and walked towards the spiralling limestone staircase that carried them down towards the inner walls where the crowd cheered and clapped for him and Harnon, they cheered for the heroes who had saved their city. Within the first row of the crowd beside the gate he saw Owain and Lyra whose voices all grew louder as he moved closer towards the archway. Vann walked towards Owain and the two dear men embraced in a hug that almost squashed Vann's chest - The Warden pulled away from his redheaded friend who ruffled his hair and pulled him back towards him so that he could kiss his forehead.

Vann laughed and shook his head, "Are you sure you can't come with us?"

Owain looked towards Lyra who declined with a knowing look, "You should not even be out here."

"Afraid not then Vann, Boss-lady's orders," Owain laughed, "But do greet Arvuria's Uncle for me, and if you could, could you ask him about The Roderick Tree?"

"The Roderick Tree?" Vann questioned loudly through the roar of the crowd.

Vann noticed Harnon tilt his head at the words Owain spoke before lightly pushing him forwards to move along, "I'll ask," Vann answered - as he moved away from the three he clasped the hands of Lyra to thank her for escorting Owain here, and for protecting Martell in his absence.

The Two Heroes continued through the archway and past the crowds that opened a pathway for them out of respect, their names continuing to sound through the air - within a few more moments Vann stood before Arvuria who nuzzled her snout against him as the Dragon and It's Chosen embraced how they could.

"The nose mist was adorable," Vann teased with a whisper, "Do you do that when you sneeze also?"

Arvuria lightly nudged Vann away from her and huffed from her nose once more, creating steam as a sassy answer before tilting her body forwards to give both Vann and Harnon an easy path onto her back.

"It is time that we head to Beonyth's Green, do try to hold on tight," Arvuria spoke with excitement riding her voice.

Once Vann and Harnon had climbed onto Arvuria's back and secured themselves to the makeshift straps that bound around The Golden Dragon, she lifted herself from the shallow waters where the liquid gleamed from her glorious scales and rebounded the sun's glare. As The Golden Dragon turned its body to take off towards the mountains, Vann lifted his body from her armoured scales and raised a fist.

"People of Laketown, we go now to secure the future! Keep hope in your heart for us, for we feel it in ours. With The Golden Dragon, and Harnon of The Green, I will not stop until we have brought peace to the lands of Taundrad!"

Arvuria's wings battered against the ground creating a tornado of sand and water around them as she bolted into the sky. Vann held tightly onto the straps as the wind harassed his face as the incredible speed of Arvuria continued faster and faster as she became one with the wind.

"Are you secure?" Arvuria's voice echoed through the wind, "That was a good speech Vann, I apologise for not giving you a moment to see if they cheered."

Vann's grip white-knuckled as the adrenaline he felt coursed through his veins, "I'm secure! I do not believe I will let go!"

Vann heard Harnon's happiness escape him in the form of a heavy laugh and a cheer - in that moment The Warden saw his dragon turn her head a few inches towards him to see both his and Harnon's excitement of being in the air, to which Vann knew that she was going to take that as an invitation to increase her speed.

Vann almost let go as the wind grew stronger.

AFTER A FEW hours Arvuria's pace slowed and she curved towards a wide platform on the mountain that sat off the edge of the middle of it. It was created of the same stone as Laketown's buildings and was wide enough to hold the scale of Arvuria and strong enough to hold her as she landed heavily onto the structure.

"I will never tire of that feeling," Arvuria spoke in tired breaths as she lowered her body for the riders to slide off.

Harnon touched the ground and collected some dirt in his hands, "That's the good stuff."

Vann's boots landed onto the stone and he looked towards the mountain face that sat wrinkled and rounded. Before them all was a pedestal which was the starting point of indents in the ground that all led towards the strange rock face. "Is this what we were looking for? The entrance of whatever this is is sealed off."

Harnon lifted himself from the ground and pulled from one of his pouches the green gem that Lyra had given to them when they first entered The Melodies of Trees Inn, he flicked it into the air before shooting a green Arcane Tether from his fingers where he began to glow a luminescent emerald and hover into the air. The Gem cracked and revealed a scale much like Arvuria's, only it was a deep green.

"No more questions Vann, just watch," Harnon instructed with a pointed finger. The Old Warrior took hold of the scale in his beaten gloves and moved it into the oval within the pedestal where the green glow of The Arcane surrounded it began to funnel into the indents of the ground leading towards the mountain face where artistic floral patterns appeared before the stone began to crack and fall.

Vann steeled himself for whatever was to come their way but he heard Arvuria's slow steps move closer, with her head pointing towards the Mountain in excitement. The rock face continued to shatter and crumble for a few more moments, until the dust almost created a new barrier.

Harnon motioned a hand towards the dust and then sharply moved it to the right, causing the new barrier to vanish in the wind, and what was hidden behind the dust and behind the mountain walls that had crumbled was something in a shade of green that Vann had never seen.

Arvuria: The Ethereal Children

A draconic eye as large as Arvuria, one that stared directly towards him.

The Eye of Beonyth, The Green.

End of Book One.

Thank you.

Arvuria: The Ethereal Children

Dear Reader,

I want to thank you for taking the time to read through my story to get to this page - and if you skipped to the last page to sneak a view at the ending… tut tut.

I started writing this story after leaving a job I hated. Genuinely hated. I was looking for a world to escape to as I was so tired of living in mine. The world of Taundrad was originally a tabletop setting I wanted to play with my friends, which then turned into half a story three years ago, which has now been rewritten to this one: Arvuria: The Ethereal Children. Only Thurian and Dira made the true jump to this rewrite, two characters that I am very fond of. The Dragons made the jump too but their personalities changed so I won't count them. I'm so glad I brought Thurian with me because he has become my favourite character in my own story. He's a man so intent on helping people that he is taking the most drastic options to do so, and I have to tell you, it is so fun to write him. He is going to be such a joy in the next book.

Then there is Vann. My girlfriend hated Vann. She joked that every decision he made just put him in a worse situation, and to be honest, that's the point. He's not the smartest of people - he wasn't supposed to be. I wanted to try to write a character who has to overcome his weaknesses and find confidence in himself before he gets the power to save the day. A good old fashioned hero's journey. I am so excited for you to see Vann evolve in the future - he has found his confidence, and unfortunately for him he has found responsibility. Let's see how he is going to deal with that.

Luke Morgan

I also want to talk about Arvuria, a character who has grown very dear to my heart. I wanted her to be this beacon of love and light amongst this dark world Taundrad is sinking into, and I really hope I have managed that so far and I hope that her happiness and eagerness to love touched you somewhat. Not to say that Arvuria doesn't have a temper, which we have seen hints of - she is a Dragon after all. She does however want me to remind you that it takes no time out of your day to smile at someone, and I think Arvuria would scold you for not doing so.

Although Vann and Thurian, I believe, are the two pillars of this story - the heart of it, through my eyes, is those that support them both. Arvuria, Emerie, Tristan, Harnon, Martell and Owain. I am lucky to have a great support network in my life, with my girlfriend, my parents, and my close friends; but through writing this story it made me realise that maybe I haven't been giving back to them as much as I should, and that maybe I hadn't been making enough effort with everyone I love.

Appreciating people who care for you is the driving point of this story for me. This book was a somewhat sentimental letter to all the people that care about me - and I want you to know that people also care about you.

If I could ask you to take one thing from this story, it would be this: A hero is made when someone asks for help, but it takes more of a hero to ask for it.

You can be someone's hero, and you can be your own. All you need to do is take one step to ask for help, as hard as that may be you will always have the strength to do it.

Arvuria: The Ethereal Children

This book has been a great learning experience, and this might be the number one thing I am proud of in my life. If you have loved this story, if you have liked it, if you have hated it or disliked it, I would like to wholeheartedly thank you from the bottom of my heart for putting your eyes to the first part of the story I want to tell. I try to use my social media pages to post updates on my writing where I can so if you wish to follow along in my journey you can find me in various places online. I will try to be active but book two will more than likely take a lot of my attention. In the meantime my dear friend Tay, who was the illustrator of the book cover is on the up with his art and is open for you to contact him for book covers, or art, or anything else for your book. He's an absolute gem of a man.

There is much more to come in the next book in the series, hopefully releasing in later this year (Don't take that as gospel) with hopefully a lot more drama. Oh also, you will absolutely find out where Leon has gone and what he is up to. You do remember Leon, right? I am so excited.

Thank you so very much,
Luke

Support us further:

Luke Morgan
Instagram: www.instagram.com/lukemorganauthor/
Patreon: www.patreon.com/c/LMorgan

Jack Taylor
Instagram: www.instagram.com/tay_illustrate/

Map made with the tools of: The Map Effects Fantasy Map Builder - mapeffects.co

Arvuria: The Ethereal Children

Luke Morgan

Arvuria: The Ethereal Children

Luke Morgan

Printed in Great Britain
by Amazon